A BLEAK PROSPECT

A SAM JENKINS MYSTERY

WAYNE ZURL

First Printing: 2017

ISBN: 978-1-68046-633-1

Melange Books, LLC
White Bear Lake, MN 55110

www.melange-books.com

Published in the United States of America.

Cover Design by Lynsee Lauritsen

For Bazzie

Don't try to compute the hourly wage I get to write these books. When it's all said and done, we should have enough for a meal at the Chinese buffet once a month.

ACKNOWLEDGMENTS

I'd like to thank several people who assisted me in taking this from a working idea to a story good enough to be published. This is not an account of a true crime or composite story of actual crimes. It is, however, inspired by documented events that I have embellished and fictionalized. A BLEAK PROSPECT is a figment of my imagination for which I take all responsibility.

To my old friend, M. Albert Mendez, who spent his valuable time kicking around my theories, adding his own ideas and helping me muster up the enthusiasm to write this novel.

To my former partner, retired Suffolk County (NY) Police Detective Paul B. Thomas, who sent me numerous accounts of things that happened long after I retired. I used two of these actual events as vignettes to enhance this story and add authenticity to it.

And to a few other people who, for not so obvious reasons, should remain anonymous, but nonetheless contributed priceless information for me to make this piece of fiction look better than a true crime drama.

To a few people who have lent their names to characters I used in this book: My long-time friend Alfred W. Hahn Jr. whose name I've used for a recurring character.

To retired Nassau County (NY) Police Captain Michael J. Butler, my friend, former interdepartmental counterpart, former FBI counter-terrorism operations specialist and author of the popular Nick Brennan thrillers, for providing me with a name for a young FBI agent.

And, lastly, to my former high school classmate retired Officer John Hanshe, Nassau County (NY) Police Department, who allowed me to use his dad's name for a character important to the story and Sam Jenkins' flamboyant arrest procedure.

Thank you all.

CHAPTER ONE

Police officers who work in the foothills of the Great Smoky Mountains occasionally require equipment not often needed by cops in cities or semi-urban neighborhoods.

Crime scene investigator Jackie Shuman and I were standing waist deep in the briskly moving waters of Crystal Creek wearing our police issue rubber waders.

Deputy Medical Examiner Morris Rappaport, his assistant, Earl W. Ogle, four other police officers, and a partially controlled crowd of tourists stood on the bank as Jackie and I approached the fallen tree that snagged a very dead body as it floated downstream, adjacent to the Creekside RV Park in Prospect, Tennessee.

"Go easy when you remove her from those branches, Sam," Morris said. "If she's been underwater for a few days, you might get surprised."

From the color of the corpse, it seemed like Morris was giving us sound advice. The once light-skinned female, now only partially clothed, looked roughly the color of a blue Italian plum.

"Jackie, block the moving water with your body," I said. "It's forcing her into the tangle. I'll see if I can free her arm from this branch."

"Times like these, I ask m'self why I didn't volunteer fer the traffic division."

I understood his complaint but ignored it. "Okay, go slow, and pull the branch down while I lift the arm."

"Oh, Lord have mercy."

It took us almost ten minutes of finessing the body out of the gnarled branches of the dead sweet gum before we could float her to a spot clear of debris. Jackie's partner, David Sparks, met us on dry land with an aluminum-framed rescue litter. Once we maneuvered the body and secured it onto the litter, we pushed, while Sergeant Stan Rose and Officer Junior Huskey pulled her onto the grassy shore.

Several spectators appeared to be getting more curious and began inching their way closer to the action, craning their necks for a better look.

"Junior," I said, "Help Johnny keep the gawkers back."

"Glad to, boss."

Stanley covered the body with a yellow disposable blanket as the doctor set up his workspace.

To Shuman and Sparks, I said, "Get your stakes out, and cordon off the area." To Stan Rose, "I think you three can move that herd back toward the parking area. Let's give Mo and Earl a little privacy."

"Piece o' cake," Stanley said.

All three went about their business.

I stood over the body as Morris and Earl attempted to gain a little preliminary information and prepare her for a trip to the morgue and her post-mortem examination.

"Jesus Christ," I said, "I count twenty-three stab wounds to the torso alone."

"Look at the bruises across the carotid arteries," Mo said. "Strangled. That either killed her or rendered her unconscious. I'm only guessing about these wounds, but I think the killer wanted to get air out of the stomach and lungs, so she'd sink."

"Cold and crafty bastard. Only it didn't work. This is a pretty shallow body of water to think she'd make it down to Davy Jones' locker."

Morris nodded. "After the autopsy I should know if there was any forcible sex."

"That leather miniskirt and one remaining knee-high boot might indicate she worked in the sex trade." I shrugged. "Or she just liked to look the part."

"I'll let you know what I find, Samilah. But offhand, I'll bet you've just joined the lucky investigators looking for the Riverside Strangler."

I shook my head and blew out a large volume of air. "Just what we need in beautiful downtown Prospect."

Earl zipped up the black vinyl body bag.

Morris looked up at me but spoke to the corpse. "Welcome to the peaceful side of the Smokies, young lady."

———

For almost two years, detectives from the Blount County Sheriff's Office have been looking for a serial killer the media tagged The Riverside Strangler. So far, seven bodies were found in publicly accessed rivers and streams—all in county patrolled areas, but off the beaten path. These victims were young prostitutes, two male and five female, who posted their services with an on-line classified advertising site. Each had been sexually violated and murdered. Some were strangled manually, as it appeared with our current victim and others with a ligature. All were stabbed multiple times, usually, but not always, post-mortem. On four occasions, cheap, but sharp kitchen knives were recovered somewhere near the spot where investigators determined the body was dumped into the water.

All the knives could be easily purchased in most of the discount stores in most of the communities of the state. So far, no fingerprints were found, and no other trace evidence of the killer had been discovered. In essence, the killer sanitized the crime scenes and the victims before disappearing.

Our murdered woman, found in Crystal Creek by a vacationing RV owner taking his son fishing, bore all outward appearances of victim number eight. The last previous body showed up a hundred yards east of a boat-launching ramp along Topside Road in the town of Louisville, only eighteen miles from Prospect.

With luck, we'd get a fingerprint match and identify our victim. From there, we'd backtrack and conduct a complete background investigation on her. My operations aide, honorary Detective John Gallagher, excelled at this type of job.

———

J ane Doe number 118, the name Morris Rappaport gave the murdered girl, began her journey to the morgue to patiently await her autopsy. I stripped off my waders and used a cleverly conceived wire device to hang them upside down to dry from the raised tailgate of Jackie Shuman's Ford Explorer.

I walked over to where Stan and Junior were assisting PO Johnny Rutledge contain a crowd of almost thirty onlookers who preferred to gape at the scene than go about their business as some of the nine million tourists who visit the Great Smoky Mountains annually should do.

"Stanley," I said, "have you got your large scale map handy?"

"In the car, bwana." He pointed to the crowd. "What do you want to do with the huddled masses here?"

"I'll call the county duty officer and get a couple of deputies to hang around and keep them back while the ETs do their thing. As soon as they get here, I'll need people to find every spot where someone could have easily accessed the creek and dumped the body."

"Might be a lot of work," he suggested.

"Soon as we check the map, we'll know how much."

"I'll call Bettye and see how many 9-1-1 calls we're getting. You might have to pull in a couple of off-duty guys and send Junior and Johnny back on patrol."

"Okay, call her while I touch base with the D.O. I'll ask him to round up a bunch of auxiliaries, too. We'll send one of our guys out to supervise each group of them and start checking the spots along the creek. If we can't turn up something, I'll call Sevier County to check their end of Crystal Creek."

"We need a bigger department."

"Back in New York, the squad dick would call in an eight-man homicide team and a sergeant to do the dirty work."

"Yeah, but we're not in the big departments anymore."

Stanley had worked for LAPD before following his homesick wife back to Tennessee and landing a job with Prospect PD.

He called Sergeant Bettye Lambert, while I spoke to the Sheriff's duty officer, Lieutenant Ollie McClurg.

———

A ssuming our killer wouldn't tote a dead victim on his back through a thicket or take a scantily dressed hooker for a hike through the brambles looking for a secluded spot to get romantic, our wisest move was to search out a piece of shoreline accessible by vehicle.

An hour after Stan and I made our phone calls, I had four Prospect cops dressed for woods work and a dozen auxiliary deputies willing to tag along and perhaps get their boots dirty.

I sent out four four-man teams to eleven access points used by fishermen and kayakers.

I left the evidence technicians to finish processing the scene and returned to the PD to wait for their reports, photos and diagrams, the autopsy results and any clues the search teams might turn up—or not.

My big priority was identifying the victim. If her fingerprints were in the system, our job would be easy. If not, I'd need a forensics artist to sketch a facial likeness to post in the newspapers and on TV news broadcasts.

CHAPTER TWO

Days later, I walked from my office to the lobby of Prospect PD and tossed the folders holding the crime scene reports and photos and the autopsy results on John Gallagher's desk.

"Not a damn thing in these of any help."

John put aside a stack of field interrogation cards and looked up. "Nothing?"

"Nothing. No one found the spot where she was dumped into the water. No knife. No tire tracks. No footprints. No nothing. And who the hell knows if she had a car? Morris says she was strangled manually, and there were bruises representing the killer's hands. Immediately after the girl passed out, but still wasn't dead, the killer—he or she—started the knife work. The killer even skinned off her fingertips. There's something there, but nothing that can be used to find her in AFIS. The best he could guess is that she's between eighteen and twenty-three years old and had relatively lousy teeth.

Bettye Lambert dropped a pair of reading glasses onto her desktop and gave me her undivided attention.

"He cut off her finger pads? That's horrible," Bettye said.

I nodded. "But from a killer's viewpoint, smart."

"Stone cold," John said. "This guy either studied how to screw up a crime scene, or he's—"

I stopped him shorter than a pigmy who began smoking at an early age. "Don't say it, John. I've been thinking that all morning." I shook my head, considering the potential. "I know it's a possibility. A cop. And not just any cop, but someone well-schooled in criminal investigations. Someone who could keep us from finding the basics that would allow us to start a decent investigation."

"You gonna tap into the sheriff's task force and get any of the particulars they learned from the previous murders?" John asked.

"I have no choice. I hate to get involved with those people, especially since Ryan Leary is running the show."

Bettye saw a lull in the conversation and jumped in. "I'll call the UT forensics lab and get an appointment with their artist. I suppose I can just email him the pictures of the body to get him started."

"Good. I'll call the papers and TV stations and get their commitments to print or show the sketch."

"Whaddaya want me to do, Boss?" John asked.

"Accompany me to the sheriff's office. There are only a few people over there I can deal with. If my head explodes while I'm talking with one of his management types, I want you to bring my body back to Prospect."

"You're asking a lot, Boss. I'm only getting clerk-typist pay."

"John, stop bitchin' about how much money you make."

"Hard to forget how much I earned as a detective back in New York."

"If you don't stop reminding me about our New York salaries, I'm gonna grab your checkbook and chop it into little pieces."

"Careful, Boss. Your ears are turning red. I think your blood pressure is on the rise."

"When I retired, almost twenty years ago, you Irish weasel, I was making as much as I get today. So, John, I feel your pain."

"Sammy, I've seen your paycheck," Bettye said. "Just how much is your pension?"

"You'll have to marry me to find out."

"I'll bet it's more than my salary." She showed me a smile that could have lit up a coal mine. "Would it put me into a higher bracket if we filed jointly?"

"Can it, Goldilocks. You're getting as bad as this loony Irishman."

"Be nice to us, Sam Jenkins. We're your closest allies."

"Pfui."

———

The artist who worked at the world famous University of Tennessee Forensics Laboratory, home of the fabled 'Body Farm', prepared an excellent rendering of what he thought our Jane Doe might have looked like in life. The sketch gave readers of the local newspapers and viewers of the Knoxville TV stations something more socially acceptable to look at. The death photos taken by Jackie Shuman would have revolted them.

A day after I submitted the drawing to the media, John Gallagher walked into my office and tossed a copy of the Knoxville News-Sentinel onto my desk.

"You see this, Boss?"

"No, not yet." I snatched up the paper and unfolded it.

"Look at page one. That cowboy, Lew Schmecke, gets all the ink, and our sketch of the murder victim is only in a single column on page three."

"What the hell is Schmecke doing in Tennessee?"

"Read it, but before you do, I'll tell you. The sheriff hired him to assist with the Riverside Strangler task force."

"Oh, for chrissakes."

"Yeah. What makes him so special?"

"Special? He's a carnival act. I'm glad we never worked with him."

John and I had gotten louder than necessary in our conversation. Bettye stepped into my doorway to see why we were cutting up.

"Are you gentlemen having another argument, or are you just acting crazier than normal for a good reason?"

I shrugged and blew out a puff of air in frustration. "We're talking about the famous Lew Schmecke, private eye."

"And this Lew Schmecke makes you angry?"

"He's a loser, Sarge," John said. "We remember him from back in New York."

Bettye tilted her head to the right and gave me the eye. That meant she wanted an explanation. When I didn't respond immediately, she swung her hips to the left and rested a hand just below her gun belt. Bettye conveys a message with body language better than most.

"Sit down," I suggested.

She planted her lovely backside in one of my tan leather guest chairs.

"Former Detective Lew Schmecke used to work for NYPD. He was coming up as John and I were finishing our careers. We first noticed him when he was assigned to a robbery task force at Manhattan South. We, of course, worked out on the Island.

"Don't get me wrong. There were some good cops working there, but Schmecke wasn't necessarily one of them."

"More like some politician's pet gopher," John added.

Bettye did the head tilt thing again. Her shoulder-length blonde hair swayed slightly. She raised her eyebrows and blinked her hazel eyes—her way of saying, 'Keep talkin'.

"Schemcke was a relatively new detective," I said, "and what we didn't like about him, we learned from cops who were there, trustworthy guys who we knew had no reason to lie. When other people did something newsworthy, little Lew grabbed the notoriety by jumping in front of a TV camera as often as possible. He was only another cog in the PD's wheel, but he made it look like he was chief cook and bottle washer at the task force."

"And now the sheriff's hired him," John said, sounding exasperated.

Bettye wrinkled her forehead. I needed to elaborate.

"I haven't read the entire article yet, but it seems that chubby little Lew is here to assist in finding the Riverside Strangler."

"Oh, my."

"Exactly," I said.

John added more fuel to the fire. "This guy didn't even do twenty years at NYPD before he put in his papers to retire, Sarge. Then he started his own detective agency using all kinds of computers and electronic gadgets. He's just a showman. A phony."

"How could he retire with less than twenty years?" Bettye asked.

"The city system allowed for someone with fifteen years service to declare a vested interest in their pension and retire. On their twentieth anniversary, they would start collecting checks. That's what Schmecke did. And then he started peeping into keyholes."

"Haven't you seen him doing commercials for that potato chip company, Sarge?" John asked, his exasperation not even close to subsiding. 'Our chips have that *real* barbeque taste.' They call him the legendary detective."

It looked like a light went off behind Bettye's eyes. "Ah, that stubby little guy who always needs a shave?"

I nodded. "That's him. A legend in his own mind."

"Darlin' I'm thinkin' you two are not lookin' forward to working with this Lew Schmecke."

"You think, Betts?"

CHAPTER THREE

The day after our plea for assistance showed up in the papers and on the four networks, we received a phone call from a Mrs. Iris Wakefield who said she saw the facial drawing in the Maryville Daily Times. Bettye forwarded her call to me.

"I cain't be sure," she said, "but the pitcher in the paper looks like my Rosanna."

"Rosanna is your daughter?"

"Yes, sir."

Her voice sounded strained, as if her throat had constricted, afraid to ask and terrified to hear my response.

"When did you see Rosanna last, Mrs. Wakefield?"

"She hasn't been home for a few days now. Is she really—?" She couldn't make the word *dead* come out.

"I'm sorry you had to read that story and see the sketch. There's just no easy way to say it, ma'am, but the girl we found was murdered."

There was a protracted period of silence. "Mrs. Wakefield?"

"Oh, Lord have mercy. Are you sure it's her?"

"No, ma'am, I'm not certain of anything. The girl we found had no identification on her person."

"Oh, Lord. How can I be sure?"

"How old was your daughter?"

"Twenty-one, last February."

"About how tall was she, and how much did she weigh?"

"I think about five-foot-four. She weighed more'n me. Maybe a hundred and fifteen, twenny."

That sounded close enough for me. "Can you look at the girl, Mrs. Wakefield? It's the only way you can be sure." I carefully avoided using the words *dead, body* or *victim*.

She sniffed a couple times and finally answered. "I guess. How would I do that?"

───────

I arranged to pick up Iris Wakefield and take her to the morgue later that day. Without a Mr. Wakefield or anyone else to accompany her, I asked Bettye to tag along. She's great at offering sympathy and moral support.

Next to a shootout against overwhelming forces, there is nothing more miserable for a cop to do than make death notifications or accompany family members when they identify their dead loved ones.

This was an especially tough job. Iris Wakefield was a pathetic creature. The Department of Safety driver's license files showed her as thirty-nine years old—she could have passed for sixty. Iris was of medium height, but painfully thin, pale and unhealthy-looking. She told us that she worked on the assembly line at the Rubbermaid plant in the southern part of the county. Her fine medium brown hair lacked luster and body, and her skin had the color of a cancer patient. Her clothes made me think that she shopped more often at Goodwill than Dillard's.

We walked in through the main entrance of Blount Memorial Hospital and escorted Iris to the lower level and a viewing room next to the morgue where Earl Ogle brought our victim's body.

A small fifteen-watt red bulb popped on over the wide window telling me that Earl was ready for us to begin the identification. I pushed a button, and a screen lifted for us to see Earl standing behind a stainless steel gurney holding the unmistakable shape of a corpse covered with a sage green hospital sheet.

I tapped the glass twice, and Earl folded the sheet down to Jane Doe's shoulders.

"Oh, sweet Jesus have mercy," came out of Iris Wakefield as her knees gave way, and she began to crumble. Standing to her right, I wrapped my left arm around Iris as Bettye grabbed for her arm. Together we righted her and led Mrs. Wakefield to the upholstered bench placed along the side wall of the viewing room for just such situations.

"Can I get you something, Iris," Bettye said. "Water, maybe?"

Once her eyes snapped back to their normal position, Iris gingerly shook her head. "No, ma'am. I couldn't keep nuthin' down."

Tears began trickling out of the inner corners of both eyes. "Poor Rosanna. My poor, silly, little girl. She never shoulda done that."

It took Iris Wakefield a few minutes to regain her composure and the strength to walk.

"I think I can manage now," she said.

"We'll be right beside you," I offered. "Take it at your own pace."

"Yes, sir, I'll be fine."

"Are you able to talk to us about Rosanna?"

She didn't answer immediately.

"We'll need your help to find the person who did this to her."

"I unnerstand."

Iris wasn't overly talkative. I looked at Bettye who raised her left eyebrow half an inch. I've always wondered how she could move them independently. Mine only operate in tandem.

"Would now be all right, Iris?" she asked.

"Yes, ma'am, we could do that."

"The café looked pretty quiet when we passed," I suggested. "That might be a good spot to sit and talk."

"Yes, sir, that'll be fine."

We found the Atrium Café a few feet from the elevators when we landed on the ground floor.

Before we entered, I asked, "Can I get you anything, Iris? A drink or something to eat?"

"Just some sweet tea, please. I'm not hungry."

I nodded and looked at Bettye. "Coffee?"

She nodded back. "Iris and I will find a table."

The women retreated toward the back of the room, while I stepped up to the counter and ordered our drinks.

———

I placed two mugs of coffee and a glass of tea on the table. The big tumbler looked like it held enough liquid to fill the radiator of a Kenworth Class 8 trailer truck. The tea looked like it had enough sugar in it to give the entire UT defensive line enough energy to sack a quarterback ten times during the final quarter. I hoped Iris wouldn't slip into a diabetic coma.

I sat and tried the coffee. It was extremely hot, but fairly weak.

"Sam," Bettye said, "Iris was just telling me that she last heard from Rosanna the day before you found her."

"On the telephone?"

"Yes, sir."

"When did you actually see her last?"

"Day b'fore that."

"She lives with you?"

"Yes, sir."

"Did she often stay away from home for days at a time?"

"Sometimes."

"Where did she go when she wasn't at home or at work?"

"With friends."

Iris was a woman of few words. The only one with less to say might have been Marcel Marceau.

"What did you talk about on the phone?"

"She told me she'd be late if she got home at all."

I needed stronger coffee to fortify my patience.

Bettye must have sensed my frustration and took a shot.

"Iris, what did Rosanna do?"

"For a livin'?"

Bettye nodded. "Uh-huh."

"Used to work for someone, but now works for herse'f."

I gave my head a slight shake. "Doing what?"

Iris held the big glass in place on the table with both hands and moved her head and entire body to the straw and took a very long sip. Then, she shifted her eyes from me to Bettye and back to me. But she didn't answer for another long moment. "Um, she would go to parties and functions and such with people."

I began to get an idea what Rosanna did to occupy her waking hours.

"Who were these people?" Bettye asked.

"She called 'em clients."

I didn't want to create more heartache for Iris Wakefield by getting overly blunt about her daughter's activities, but I also didn't want the conversation to last forty-eight hours. "Iris, I know some things may be difficult to discuss, but to help us find the person who did this terrible thing to Rosanna, we'll need as much information as possible."

A tear rolled downward from the corner of her right eye. She wiped it with the back of her hand and sniffed away the congestion sorrow creates in the head. "Won't nuthin' ever bring Rosanna back though, will it?"

I shook my head. "Of course not. But just maybe the three of us can do something to keep the same thing from happening to someone else's daughter."

Iris nodded slowly but didn't speak. She again bent over the glass of tea and sucked on the straw, her eyes now focused on the tabletop.

"Was Rosanna in the escort business?" Bettye asked.

After a long pause, Iris answered. "Yes, ma'am."

"Rosanna was twenty-one," I said. "But in the recent photos you showed us, she looked much younger. She was a very pretty girl. Did she dress up when she went to meet clients?"

She nodded. "Yes, sir." And again attacked the straw and glass of tea.

"Will you show Sergeant Lambert where Rosanna kept her clothes?"

"Yes, sir."

"I assume Rosanna drove a car in her business, but we haven't found one yet."

"Yes, sir, she did. Little silver one."

"What kind of car?"

"Ford, I think. I'd have ta look."

I tried another sip of the scalding coffee and wondered why I bothered. "Finding her car will help us. Was it registered in her name or yours?"

"Mine. The in-surance was cheaper that way."

"You have an extra key?"

"Not on me, but I know where it is."

"Okay, good. You said Rosanna now worked for herself. How did she meet clients?"

"One of those computer lists."

"You mean classified advertisements, not a dating site?"

"Yes, sir. Charlie's List."

"Did she take phone calls or make arrangements on-line?"

"Both."

I still needed a pry bar to get the information from Iris.

"Is Rosanna's computer at your house?"

She nodded. "In her room."

"Did she use a home phone?"

"No, sir, her cell phone."

"Have you seen the bills from her phone company?"

"I seen them in the mail, but don't read them."

"We'll need a recent one."

"We can look in her room."

———

The conversation went on like this for another twenty minutes. Although it was difficult to extract information from Iris

Wakefield, she did provide us with helpful facts and one very interesting item.

"During your last phone call," I said, "did Rosanna tell you anything specific about where she might be going?"

Iris again drank from the bottomless vat of sweet tea.

"She said she didn't want to work that night, but claimed she had ta."

"Because she needed the money?" Bettye asked.

Iris closed her eyes tightly, but not tight enough to prevent several tears from escaping. Her mouth quivered, but she finally answered. "Last thing she said ta me was, if I don't show up on time, they'll kill me."

Bettye and I exchanged looks again.

"Iris," I said, "do you think that meant there was more than one person?"

She sniffed, and her lips quivered again. "I don't know."

CHAPTER FOUR

W e returned Iris Wakefield to her home on Tree Top Lane in Prospect, picked up a small laptop, the spare key for Rosanna's missing 2009 Ford Focus and documentation on her phone carrier, auto insurance, bank and credit card accounts, a recent visit to a walk-in clinic, school history and even bills from where she had her car serviced. From this and the public records we could access, we'd conduct a complete background investigation on our victim that even the CIA couldn't beat.

On our way back to the PD, I asked Bettye a big question. "You know what bothered me most?"

She answered as if she'd like me to think she could read my mind. "Certainly do, darlin'. What do you think about that?"

"Who knows? It might have been a common enough grammatical error. Or not. Maybe Rosanna had problems with her use of pronouns, or *they* meant more than one client."

She raised that eyebrow again. "Multiple jobs or two at once?"

"Good question. Maybe the computer will hold all kinds of information, and we'll see if she scheduled several johns back to back or an elaborate ménage a trios."

"I tried to look at her documents quickly in her room but got stopped.

It's password protected. Who do you plan on gettin' to crack open the computer?"

"I thought you could do that."

"I still ask Little Donnie when I've got computer questions."

"I guess we can't have a thirteen-year-old investigating the memoirs of a sex worker, can we?"

"No, Samuel, you may not use my son to read the life story of an online prostitute."

———

The next day, after a Mexican lunch at El Jibarito, a classy cantina only a quarter mile down the road from the Justice Center, John and I showed up for the combination press conference and Riverside Strangler task force meeting.

The sheriff's department houses two conference rooms. Both, like his personal office, are on the third floor of the Justice Center. A receptionist pointed us toward the larger of the two rooms.

More like a mini-auditorium, the room held an oval table about the size and shape of a broad-beamed, ocean going, double-ended cat boat. I lost count of the number of black leatherette swivel chairs that surrounded it. Behind the table were rows of posh easy chairs for onlookers not directly participating in the dog and pony show.

John and I found our place cards and took seats close to the end where the podium stood—like the wheelhouse on this ship of state.

In the ten-foot space behind the spectator's seats, several TV cameramen and newspaper still photographers stood prepared to record the event for posterity. I immediately recognized WNXX TV's cinematographer, John Leckmanski. When I caught his eye, he shot me a gunman's salute. I winked and assumed he'd like to see me after the festivities concluded.

———

At 1:35, only scant moments stylishly late for the meeting he had called, Chief Deputy Ryan Leary stepped behind the podium and tapped the microphone. After a muffled squeal caused by being too close to the amplifier and the three amplified bumps his taping created, he addressed the crowd.

"Thank you all for attending this meeting. I plan to bring everyone up to date on the progress the task force has been making and then introduce Chief Sam Jenkins of Prospect PD to tell you about the recent homicide in his jurisdiction that has all the earmarks of the person we've called the Riverside Strangler. And finally, I'll tell you about a new measure I've taken that should help us move further in our joint investigations."

He delivered his preamble and transitioned seamlessly into a recap of the progress (or lack thereof) made by the task force without a hint of regional accent. Previously, I learned that Leary had lived all his life in Blount County, but had inherited his speaking voice from his parents who were originally from northern Ohio.

I had never liked nor trusted Leary. He was the dangerous combination of a competent, but grandstanding cop and ruthless politician. And he looked the part. A couple inches shorter than me, I guessed him to be five-ten, a little stocky, but not fat—more like a power lifter than a ball player. Everything about Leary was conservative looking, from his salt and pepper hair parted on the left and always neatly combed to the matching mustache on a ruggedly handsome face scarred by adolescent acne. But looks can be deceiving. If I had to choose two words to describe Ryan Leary, they wouldn't be businesslike and conservative; they'd be potentially dangerous.

"But now," Leary said, "I'll turn the discussion over to someone you all know, someone whose law enforcement experience goes back decades and spans the entire eastern half of the United States—the chief of the Prospect Police Department."

I stood up and tried to appear modest. That was some intro. I half expected Clint Eastwood to take a spot at the podium before me. I thought modest, but not humble. I was only one of the jugglers in Leary's minstrel show, but I didn't want anyone to forget that these once-in-a-lifetime serial murder cases happened all too often where I used to work.

An old public speaker's maxim: Never miss an opportunity to get a laugh, so I attempted to capitalize on Leary's words.

"I guess the man that Chief Leary described couldn't make it, so you'll have to be satisfied with me."

That got a few snickers, but not the chorus of belly laughs I expected.

I began again, "Good morning." My presentation consisted of a description of fishing the body out of the babbling waters of Crystal Creek to learning the identity of the victim.

"At this stage, we're conducting a complete background investigation on Ms. Rosanna Wakefield and have a computer expert examining her laptop which has more password protection than a CIA cyber dead-drop."

Those snickers turned to hearty chuckles from the media people who wanted their colleagues to think they knew what a dead-drop was.

"As soon as we know more, I'll inform you and the task force members of our progress. Thanks for listening, and now I'll turn the party back to our master of ceremonies, Ryan Leary."

Leary took over by giving me a look someone might reserve for an older brother who drank too much and often made a fool of himself at family dinners.

"Thank you, Chief. Now that you're part of this task force, the Riverside Strangler has one more formidable adversary."

The words weren't quite out of Leary's mouth when Lew Schmecke pushed his chair from the table in preparation of making a grand appearance.

"Next," Leary said, "I'd like to introduce someone who I've brought on board to assist in our investigation of these heinous murders. Some of you will recognize him from all the national exposure he's gotten."

The term 'brought on board' meant hired for much more than he's worth. The national exposure meant prime time potato chip commercials.

"Please welcome former New York detective and now prominent private investigator, Lew Schmecke."

Please welcome? For chrissakes, was this a press conference or a segment of the Tonight Show?

As Schmecke blabbed about the expertise he'd bring to the investigation, I grew tired of his self-serving rhetoric and tuned him out to mull over what I knew about Ryan Leary, our *Leader of the Pack.*

He was fifty-three years old and had twenty-eight years with the Blount County Sheriff's Office. Like everyone else on that job, he began his career in the patrol division. From what I had heard, Ryan took an early interest in being more of an investigator than the average cop on the beat. He racked up more arrests and gained a reputation as a hard charger. From there, he was promoted to detective, but didn't stay with the sheriff's CID very long. Long-serving District Attorney Calvin Pitts requested that Leary be assigned to his office as an investigator—I assumed at the behest of some heavy-duty political benefactor. After a few years, Leary was promoted to sergeant and remained at the DA's office as a senior investigator. After a few more years, he was promoted to the rank of lieutenant. The DA chose to keep him on board and in an unprecedented move, filled the recently vacated position of chief DA's investigator with a sheriff's deputy—newly promoted Lieutenant Ryan Leary.

That lasted a while, and Leary enhanced his reputation for flamboyant police work. One member of the Sheriff's department for whom I have respect, told me that whenever Leary and his boys showed up, you smelled two things: his cigar and a rat. Leary always brought trouble along with him, from dodgy searches to knuckled-up prisoners.

When Sheriff Joe Don Hartung's predecessor was voted out of office, DA Calvin Pitts insured that he'd have a secure stranglehold on county law enforcement. Prior to Joe Don getting sworn in, Pitts went to the county mayor and requested that his man Ryan Leary be appointed to chief deputy. When the county's chief executive considered that the newly elected sheriff had absolutely zero law enforcement experience, he considered the DA's move as altruistic and logical and installed Leary as the top uniformed cop before his boss ever arrived. In essence, Joe Don would be the elected figurehead, but Ryan Leary would run the department.

I felt John Gallagher poke me in the ribs, and I snapped out of my daydream.

"Fatso just finished, Boss. This thing will be breaking up in a minute."

John was just about on target. Schmecke stepped away from the podium, and Leary made his closing remarks. For a few moments, the media personnel scattered, leaving the rear of the room still cluttered with sheriff's department brass and task force investigators.

Gallagher and I stood up, and John Leckmanski caught my eye. He made a motion with his head, pointing toward the exit—something I took for him wanting a word. I nodded, and he disappeared.

As many of the task force members enthusiastically flocked around Schmecke, the legendary detective, I decided to take a powder before the great meeting of minds kicked off at three o'clock.

"What do you say, Tonto?" I asked John. "Want to get some air before we have to listen to more bullshit?"

"Right behind you, Kemosabe."

We were only half way out of the room when Ryan Leary called.

"Sam, can you hang on a minute? I want you to meet Lew."

Gallagher snorted. We both turned. Leary stood only a few feet away.

"We were just heading to the men's room," I said.

"I understand. This will just take a minute. Let me get Lew over here."

When Leary turned to fetch the legendary one, I told Gallagher to run an errand.

"I think Leckmanski wants us. Find him outside and tell him I'll only be a minute."

"Will do, Boss."

I faced the podium and watched the sea of humanity part as the county's top cop presented his new hired hand to me.

"Sam, have you ever met Lew Schmecke?"

"No, I haven't," I said, with all the enthusiasm of a salmon who just finished spawning.

"Well, you heard his bio when I introduced him. Lew, this is Sam Jenkins, chief of Prospect PD."

"How are you?" I asked, maintaining my level of excitement.

He extended a hand that I reluctantly shook.

"I understand you were on the job in Nu Yawk." Schmecke spoke, wearing a grin as perpetual as the stubble on his chin. "Whereabouts?"

I was sure he already knew, but I indulged him. "On the Island."

The grin turned into a smirk. "Oh, yeah? I worked Manhattan South Detectives."

It was a common enough occurrence. Many cops who worked in Manhattan looked down on the rest of us slobs who covered the remainder of the metro area. They generally didn't see much reason for cops to work on Long Island, but they thought more of us than those assigned to Staten Island.

"Uh-huh." I tried to sound as unimpressed as humanly possible.

Schmecke smelled of pungent aftershave and dishonesty. It took me all of three seconds to decide that I wouldn't trust him any further than I could throw a pregnant hippopotamus.

He was short enough to make me think he joined the PD after they relaxed the height requirement. He was on the pudgy side, but not obese, with just enough paunch to add jowls and a double chin to the face he hid with an everlasting four day stubble.

His fawn-colored suit—one with a pale purple pinstripe—camouflaged his chubby body well. I assumed that the high-tech PI business was good because those threads might have ventured into the five-figure bracket. It gets like that when you use the higher echelons of wool, something buttery to the touch and quite silky. Lovely to look at and delightful to wear, but so delicate that it wouldn't last beyond the turn of the next fashion season.

"You could probably use some help with this new homicide you got," he said.

It wasn't a question and more of an assessment than an offer.

"We might. I'll see what I can connect between our vic and the previous killings. I'll let Ryan know what we learn. If we hit a stone wall, I'll raise my hand and yell for help."

Schmecke half snorted and nodded, at what I wasn't sure. "Don't the county investigate felonies for your little departments?"

I thought he put too much emphasis on *little*, but that may have just been me.

"We do our own in Prospect."

"Oh, yeah? Have much luck?"

Leary jumped in, perhaps sensing that a guy with whom he had to live might use his new hired monkey as a fence post.

"Sam's got quite a clearance rate, Lew. He's done exemplary work in the... How many years have you worked here, Sam?"

"Almost five." I wondered if Schmecke knew what *exemplary* meant, but I didn't explain.

"That's good," Schmecke said. "Nu Yawk street smarts versus down home skells, no?"

I nodded and cracked an obligatory smile. "You'll have to excuse me. I've got to visit the boy's room before the task force tango hits high gear."

I found John Gallagher standing next to the WNXX News van alongside John Leckmanski and an attractive blonde.

"Hi, guys," I said.

"How ya doin', Sam?" Leckmanski said and extended a hand. I shook it. "You know Karen Walters, don't you?"

"Sure, we've met." To Karen, I said, "How are you?"

She nodded and offered me a hand. "Good, thanks. Nice to see you."

At about thirty-five, Karen was one of the old-timers at WNXX.

Looking again at John, I said, "I smelled a little intrigue in there, Polish boy. What's up?"

"We figured you'd know the real story about why the sheriff hired this guy Schmecke."

I shook my head. "I don't, but I'll make two guesses. Leary probably did the hiring and not for reasons of efficiency, but because Schmecke is a famous face. I'm not convinced he's dreadfully competent, but thanks to TV commercials, he's a familiar personality in households across the country—for this year, at least."

"Private investigator and snack salesman," Karen said sarcastically.

I nodded once. "And while Schmecke may not see the possibility yet, if those murders go unsolved, Leary will fire his pudgy little ass and toss him to the wolves. Leary can use Schmecke to create a win-win situation. If Schmecke helps find the Strangler, Leary will bask in the public knowledge that he chose a winner. If Schmecke flops, Leary will take himself off the hook by saying that the *legendary detective* claimed his brilliance would find the killer. As chief deputy, Leary reassigned his task force guys back to regular duty to focus on new cases which were getting backlogged. After that, he can reevaluate the Strangler business—either resurrect a task force, let it go cold or, as a last resort, ask the Feds for help."

"Schmecke's a blowhard," Gallagher added. "He always liked to take credit for other cops' work."

I shrugged. "He's probably not useless, but based on our inside information, he's highly overrated—thanks to himself."

"If Leary were responsible for solving the Riverside Strangler murders, he could stick a big feather in his cap," Karen said.

"You bet," I said. "And he'd capitalize on it. For years, Joe Don Hartung has hinted that he'd like to run for some other office—either something in the state house or the US Congress. Leary knows that and may want to be sheriff. If he pulls off a coup here, he may have the horsepower to nudge Joe Don out and run for the top spot."

"He runs the department now, doesn't he?" Leckmanski asked.

"Sure he does. But the chief deputy just collects a salary. He doesn't get the opportunity to *redirect* excess campaign contributions to furnish and subsidize his home office. You ever see Hartung's house?"

Leckmanski laughed. Karen shook her head.

"Do you have any good leads on the Prospect killer you didn't mention in there?" Karen asked.

"While I'd love to smirk and tell you something you'd have to keep under your hat for a while, no. I'm clueless at this moment. But I've got a computer from our vic. She was an enterprising *working girl* running her own show. Maybe she kept secret but detailed records."

Big mouth Gallagher added, "Yeah, but we don't know how to bypass her passwords. We gotta find a computer expert for help."

"Can't your IT guy help you?" Karen asked.

"Prospect's IT man is a pretty good technician, but he's not a forensic hacker. I need a real cyber weasel to make the most of what we've got."

Leckmanski grinned like a snake with a fat mouse in his sights. "Have I got a guy for you." It wasn't a question.

"Someone from the station?" I asked.

"No, he's on his own. He's very good, but you might call him a little shady."

I grinned a little, too. "I can live with a shady super hero as long as he uses his magical powers for the greater good."

"Then Lonnie Ray is your man. You asked for a weasel. In the computer world, he's a wolverine."

"Lonnie Ray is his name?"

"Lonnie Ray Wilson. I don't have his number with me, but you can find him in the Yellow Pages. Calls himself Ether Technologies and Investigations. Tell him I sent you."

———

I heard my new computer expert before I saw him. The morning after John Leckmanski gave me the tip, Lonnie Ray Wilson showed up in the lobby of Prospect PD and introduced himself to Bettye.

"You have an Officer Jenkins here?" he asked.

I envisioned her dropping a pair of granny glasses onto her desktop, putting her blonde locks in motion to exhibit a little haughtiness and to look more alluring, and saying, "We have a Chief Jenkins."

She didn't disappoint me.

"Must be the one," Wilson said.

"And who shall I say is calling?"

"Mr. Lonnie Ray Wilson. Ether Technologies *and* Investigations. He called me."

"One moment, please," the good sergeant said. "I'll see if he's in."

From the sound of Lonnie Ray's voice, I surmised that he was African-American, but I heard no touch of Ebonics or the jive one might expect from a human wolverine. He sounded intelligent and professional.

The intercom on my phone buzzed.

"Chief, there's a Mr. Wilson to see you."

"I heard you out there. You sounded like the personal assistant of the US Attorney General. I'm so impressed I could just plotz."

"Yes, sir, shall I send him in?"

"You shall have our resident leprechaun escort him. That'll look ultra-cool."

"As you wish, sir."

"Oh, gads, that was good. I think I love you."

"Thank you, sir. Right away."

Fifteen seconds later, John Gallagher popped through my doorway.

"Boss, Mr. Wilson is here about the computer."

I stood. "Thanks, John."

Lonnie Ray Wilson was just on the shy side of forty. About the right age for a computer whiz. He had short hair and an equally close-cropped Van Dyke. At about six-one and maybe 210 solid pounds in a black leather jacket and jeans, he looked more like a hired thug than a computer geek.

He stopped six inches in front of my desk and stuck out a beefy hand. "Lonnie Ray Wilson. How can I help you?"

"Hi. Sam Jenkins. Thanks for coming."

His grip was firm, but not exaggerated. I thought I could get to like Lonnie Ray.

"I need you to get into the computer I mentioned on the phone."

"Crack a password?

"I guess. I know how to send emails and buy fishing tackle on eBay, but more than that and I'm computer useless."

He grinned. "No problem. Whatcha got?"

"Come around and use my chair." I opened the lid of Rosanna Wakefield's laptop. "Here's the problem child."

Lonnie Ray sat in my oversized swivel chair and gave the laptop a look.

"Toshiba Satellite L305. Three gigs of ram and 250 gigs of hard drive."

"If you say so."

"I do. It's nothing new, but still a pretty good machine."

"The whole shebang is password protected. I'd like to see her documents and emails and whatever."

"Understood. Can you fill me in on what you'd like to find?"

I gave him a basic rundown on Rosanna's murder, the Riverside Strangler's history and how I'd love to find a name and address and photo ID for the client she met who might have killed her.

"Hell," he said, "that ain't much."

"I love confidence."

"Give me a few minutes, and I'll see what I can do."

"Okay. You going out to your car to get a tool chest or something?"

"Tool chest?" He started laughing and almost split a gut. "This is the only tool I need."

He came out of his jacket pocket with a ring of a dozen keys and a single portable flash drive.

"Hmmm. I stand corrected. Take off your jacket. Make yourself comfortable. Want coffee?"

"Is it fresh?"

I frowned. "Of course."

"Okay. Light and sweet. Got any doughnuts?"

"This is a police station. You think you're dealing with amateurs?"

"Not me, boss." A little Willie Best crept into his voice. "Wouldn't mind havin' me a doughnut."

"You got it."

I stuck my head out of the office door. "John! Bring in today's selection of pastries."

"Comin' up, Boss."

I fixed a cup of coffee for Lonnie Ray, and John showed up carrying a box with three doughnuts left.

Lonnie Ray looked at the proffered snacks. "Oh, man. Looks like Richie Creamie stuff. I love jelly doughnuts."

————

I didn't get to watch Lonnie Ray crack the case of the troublesome password. My cyber investigator was only half way through his first doughnut when John Gallagher interrupted.

"Hey, Boss, Lenny Alcock called in on the phone. Says a couple o' kids flagged him down and showed him a body laying in one of the branches of the Little River—place they call Crooked Creek."

CHAPTER FIVE

L onnie Ray stopped hacking and looked up at me. "A body? I guess you're taking off."

"Yeah. Keep working. If you need something or find anything, tell Sergeant Lambert. I don't know how long I'll be."

"Okay. This girl was no Bill Gates, but she was clever. I'll be a while before I get in here. But don't worry. I'll have something for you soon."

I let out a deep breath. "I'll be back."

———

J ohn and I found Lenny Alcock sitting in his police car on a gravel road not far from the Prospect Air Park. He led us down a short dirt path surrounded by woods, to the banks of Crooked Creek. The shallow water was flowing rapidly over a rocky creek bed. Within sight of the gravel, the body of a young man lay half in the rivulet, almost fifty yards downstream from a series of three-foot tall steps forming a cataract where the clear water fell off the rocks and created strips of white foam which disappeared within a dozen feet.

"Lenny, have you looked around?"

"Not much, boss. I didn't want to contaminate the scene. But since the two kids who found the body walked in here, I figgered one more set of footprints wouldn't matter none. Did find somethin' interestin' though. I'm guessin' whoever dropped the body used a branch o' leaves ta try'n cover their tracks."

"You find the branch?" John asked.

"Yep. Jest off the path, 'bout ten, twelve feet from where the dirt meets the gravel."

"Where are the kids now?" I asked.

"One lives only a half mile away. I called his mother. She picked up the pair, and says she'll keep 'em handy. Here's their names and addresses."

He tore a page from his memo book and handed it to me.

"John and I have waders in the car. We'll look at the body. Use your phone to call for crime scene and the ME. Call direct and bypass the county duty officer. Let's limit the *need to know* here. Stay off the radio as much as possible."

"Gotcha, boss."

I didn't want anyone from the media, or the task force for that matter, interrupting our investigation. After we donned our fishermen's disguises and entered the stream, John checked the man's pockets. The corpse looked as if it might have been dropped twelve hours ago. It was still in rigor, and the lividity suggested that soon after death, it had been pulled down the path and turned face down into the water.

"Still got his wallet, Boss."

"Check it later. Let's flip him over."

John helped turn the body.

"Holy shit, Boss. This one is shot."

A long gray unlined raincoat was unbuttoned and showed a white silky shirt. Three holes were scattered around the torso.

"Lousy group," I said. "Not much of a shooter."

John nodded. "Even I could do better than that."

"He looks pretty young."

"Yeah, and look at his haircut."

"Not exactly mainstream."

Both sides of the young man's head were buzz cut—what we in the Army of the 1960s called whitewalls. But there was a pelt of long hair on top, and he wore a diamond-like stud in his right ear.

"Doesn't an earring on the right side mean he's gay?" John asked.

"Used to, but I'm not sure anymore. Lotsa guys wear earrings now."

"How about this weird haircut? What does that mean?"

"It means I'm not going anywhere near his barber. You think gay men like this style?"

"Beats me."

"We'll find out."

John pushed up the sleeves of the raincoat to check his wrists. "Still got a watch and bracelet. How often do you find a stiff with all his property?"

"Just a wild guess, but let's rule out robbery."

"Funny, Boss."

"Yeah, I'm a barrel of monkeys."

———

Thirty-five minutes later, Morris Rappaport and Earl Ogle drove up in the morgue wagon. They made a few preliminary checks, and we adjourned to the shore to wait for a team of evidence technicians.

"Looks like he was dragged on his back for a short distance on the dirt road and into the creek," I said.

"I'm guessing that the shot to his heart was the first," Morris said. "The motor stopped, and not much blood pumped out. The other two shots bother me. I'll have to check when I have him on the table, but I'll bet they were made from different angles."

"That's odd."

"Maybe more than one shooter. It would seem strange for one person to circle a dead body and shoot into it."

"Maybe more than one gun," John added.

We all nodded.

"The holes are clean and look like about a third of an inch. What do you figure, .38 wadcutters?" I asked.

"Good guess," Mo said. "But wait until I retrieve them. There are no exit wounds."

"Considering John's theory that this kid may be gay and considering the possible ammo used... Maybe target shooters? But why? A hate crime?"

"The young man looks a little flamboyant. Are you thinking male prostitute?" Morris asked.

"Possibly. And that might suggest the victim of choice for the Riverside Strangler. But he's not strangled or stabbed. You'd think a serial killer would have the decency to keep his crimes in character."

"Did he have any ID on him?" Morris asked.

"Had everything, Doc," John said. "Driver's license says he's Toby Lee Bowman with an east Knoxville address."

"Nothing says a serial killer plays by a set of rules. Except for the method of death, everything else fits the pattern."

"No one said we were put on earth to handle simple murders," I added.

———

Three hours later, John and I walked back into Prospect PD with disgusted looks on our faces and wrinkled lunch bags in our hands.

We found Lonnie Ray sitting at Bettye's desk working on her computer. She stood behind him, looking over his shoulder.

"What did you find, gentlemen?" Bettye asked.

"One rather dead young man," I said. "And unless the Riverside Strangler has graduated to using a handgun, it may be a half-assed copycat."

"The kid is dressed up like he could be a hooker," John said. "Might be a homosexual."

I felt a need to indoctrinate our new IT man. "Lonnie, you're hearing a lot of cop talk that can't leave this room. Agreed?"

"Don't worry about me. I learn more secrets about people by rummaging around in their hard drives. Keeping my mouth shut goes with the job."

"Was he strangled?" Bettye asked.

"Doesn't look like it, but Morris will check for internal damage. No visible knife wounds."

The thought of probing a corpse must not have appealed to Lonnie Ray who wrinkled up his nose and shook his head.

"You look like you just stepped on a dead skunk, Lonnie. Want to tag along when we watch the autopsy?"

"Me? Not on your life. I look into sick computers, not dead bodies."

"Just checking."

"You find *any* leads?" Bettye asked.

"Not much. Jackie and David just got there and will probably be a few more hours. It looks like he might have been shot on the dirt path and dragged down to the water. Lenny thinks he found a branch used to cover up evidence on the dirt. That looks probable. The water's too shallow to float a body. Like I said, the victim fits the profile of the others, but the method of killing doesn't. Who knows?"

"How'd he get there?" Bettye asked.

"Beats me. No car around, if he used one."

"The kids who found the body didn't see anything," John said. "They just went down to the creek to screw around and found our DOA."

Changing the subject, Bettye said, "Well, we've been pretty lucky. Lonnie Ray broke into Rosanna Wakefield's computer files. I'll let him show you what he found. And when he finished that, he helped me with a few questions I had."

"Good," I said. "When you bill us, forget to mention helping the sergeant. Our mayor gets all flustered when there's a murder in his city and tends to spend more to help me clear the case."

"At $75.00 an hour, I'll write it up anyway you want."

Lonnie Ray's hourly wage threw John Gallagher for a loop.

"Boss, you don't even pay me seventy-five bucks a day. I should start up a computer business."

"You're exaggerating, John. And maybe you should learn more about computers than just how to turn them on and Windex the monitor."

"Boss, that hurt. I do pretty good with a computer."

"Sure, John. You're compatible with a computer because you both speak machine language instead of English."

"Two *dispatchatory* remarks in one day. If we had a union, I'd complain to my delegate."

Lonnie's eyes darted back and forth between John and me, probably wondering if we were serious. Bettye just smiled.

"Before you get involved with Rosanna's laptop, Sammy, you might want to see the mayor. He called down wondering what the new murder is all about."

"It looks like you've got things to keep Lonnie busy. Should I eat first or see the mayor? If he aggravates me, I might lose my appetite."

"I doubt that would ever happen, darlin'. He sounded pretty anxious."

"Okay, but John's idea of a union is sounding pretty good. If I miss my meal period, I'd have someone to complain to."

———

I left John with instructions to start his background investigation on Toby Bowman and for Bettye to check Charlie's List for any advertisements that looked like something Toby could have posted. If anything linked Bowman and Rosanna to similar clients, it might be an obscure lead that we could back trace to people who answered their ads.

———

I sat in one of the Mayor's green leather, button-back guest chairs and brought him up to date on the Wakefield murder and what new information I had on the latest victim.

"I hate to say this, Sam, but I really wish this Riverside Strangler would have stayed in the county's patrol area."

"So do I, but…" There was no need for me to elaborate. "As soon as I put together a couple of case packages, I'll give all our information to Ryan Leary for his task force."

"You gonna be working with this expert detective they hired?"

"Schmecke?"

He nodded and adjusted the knot of his two-tone purple silk tie that, along with a pearl gray suit, made him look like an overdressed televangelist.

"I'd prefer not. I know something about him, and I'm not impressed." I shrugged and pushed my hands out to my sides. "If he can use the information I provide the task force and come up with something useful —and he doesn't try to steal the collar himself—I'll deal with him and give due credit."

"Long as you keep an open mind."

I could have smacked him for that.

"I've got our own expert downstairs right now. While Gallagher and I were out with the new victim, he cracked into the Wakefield girl's computer. As soon as I get back downstairs, he'll show me her business records, and we can begin the phone and field work."

He nodded again. "Then I won't keep ya much longer. I jest want ta let ya know that the council *finally* voted ta fill that PO's slot left vacant when Dallas Finchum passed away. They'd like ya to fill the vacancy by the next pay period. That way the new person could come on board and be ready for the next academy class they got scheduled for the end of Joo-lie."

"The next pay period?" I sounded shocked to myself. "That's in what, two weeks?"

"Twelve days, actually."

"How am I going to pick and process a new recruit in only twelve days?"

I wished I had been carrying a mirror to check if steam was escaping from my ears.

"Well, ya could hire someone contingent on them passin' all the exams."

"Does that make any sense? The council dicks around for months and finally, when they collectively get their heads out of their asses, they want a competent new cop lickety-split. That's asinine. Suppose we hire this individual and he or she fails the medical or psychological? Then we start from square one. These people aren't legislators, they're numbskulls."

"Sorry, Sam, but that works out best for us."

And they get to stick it to Sam as he has, in the past, stuck it to one or more of their political cronies. Sounded like bullshit to me. It was one of those times when I wanted to walk up behind Mayor Shields and mess up his lacquered hairdo.

CHAPTER SIX

I stormed into the PD lobby wishing I held something I could have thrown.

"You don't look happy," Bettye said. "Bad news?"

"Not exactly bad, but monumentally stupid."

"Uh-oh, Boss," John said. "What's up?"

"John, you'll make out like a bandit over this one. Get ready for some serious OT. His Royal Highness, Prince Nitwit the First, told me the morons on the city council finally decided to free up the salary to hire a replacement PO."

"That sounds good," Bettye said. "But that got you angry?"

"You're half right. It will be good to get another body on the road. The bad part is we have to hire this lucky person in only twelve days."

"That's stupid, Boss," John said. "How can we get the county to schedule the tests, give the candidates a fair warning and us time to complete the background?"

"He wants the new person hired before they take the tests."

"Stupid," John repeated.

"At least he didn't give me a name of some political hack's kid who wants to be a cop or would be just as happy as a ticket taker at the Cineplex."

"Yet," Bettye said.

I wiggled my finger at her. "You have no reason to discourage me, young lady."

She fluttered her eyelashes. "Sorry, sugar. Jest rememberin' past history."

"And don't pull your Daisy Mae act on me at times of extreme stress."

Bettye smiled and made a production of wiping the smile away. The woman plays me like a hillbilly fiddle.

"Do we have a list to work from, Boss?" John asked.

"This is the Third World, John. There are no civil service lists." To Bettye, I said, "Do we have any applications on file?"

"I think three, but if I remember correctly, everyone is in the military."

"If you don't mind me saying something," Lonnie Ray interjected. "I got a young cousin who could use a job...If you don't hold that stolen car arrest against him."

"You're a big help," I said.

"I just figured since I'm on the clock, I'd offer a suggestion."

I looked at the ceiling. "I do not want to live any longer. I want to go to sleep and never wake up."

"Oh, Sammy darlin', go eat your lunch, and you'll feel better. I'll pull out the police candidate file and see who we've got."

"I plan on washing down my sandwich with a bottle of single-malt. Maybe when I wake up, all this will be a lousy dream."

"You drink single-malt with your lunch?" Lonnie Ray asked.

I sighed. "Let's take a look at the laptop. I want to see what my seventy-five an hour bought me."

He and I adjourned to my office.

"I hope you don't mind if I eat while you explain," I said.

"Won't bother me."

I took the side chair next to my desk, and he parked it in my big swivel, behind the laptop. I unwrapped the turkey, bacon and Swiss hero I purchased when John and I stopped at Quizno's.

"Have you eaten?" I asked.

"The three doughnuts and half-gallon of coffee should hold me for a while. You really having a glass of single-malt?"

I looked over the top of my sandwich. "Some other time maybe."

"Uh-huh."

"This sandwich is cut. You're welcome to half."

"At seventy-five an hour, I should be buying you lunch."

"I agree. Let's save that for another time, too. Want any of this?"

He shook his head. "I'm good. Gotta watch my girlish figure."

"Tell me about Rosanna's business." I took a big bite of sandwich.

"She was no computer pro, but she did a pretty fair job of creating a system and keeping it private."

"Except from you."

He grinned. "Except from me. I sent all of her spreadsheets to your computer. You can look at them or print them and see a chronological history of her escort business. Interesting notes on some of her customers. No full names or addresses, but most have contact numbers and locations —probably prearranged meeting spots. And some even note a client's *pro-pen-sities*."

I wiped my mouth with a paper napkin. "Very good. You want that fulltime cop job?"

"At seventy-five an hour?"

"Hardly." I walked over to the mini-fridge at the side of the room. "Want a bottle of water?"

He shook his head. "Can't take a cut in pay to carry a gun."

"For seventy-five an hour, I'd want you to drag a howitzer with you."

"So much for my po-leece career."

"You seem to fit in here. I might be calling you to handle more of our high-tech investigations. You up for that."

"Sounds like fun."

I sat down and twisted the cap off a bottle of spring water. "Good.

Now, before I spend lots of time trying to find something in her history files, is there a meeting noted for her approximate date of death?"

"Got a last entry for a customer named Andy."

I placed the sandwich on the spread-out wrapper and stood to look at the screen. "Andy?"

"Like in Jackson."

"Or Sipowicz."

"Who?"

"That was part of your police entrance test. Minus one." I pointed at the laptop. "Look at that, even a time and location. Now, I've just got to locate the mysterious Andy."

"How hard can that be?"

"You have a computerized crystal ball?"

———

L onnie Ray and I walked out to the lobby where I wanted to hand out a few new assignments.

"John, see what you can find on this phone number. It's probably a prepaid cell, but you never know, so go through the motions. We're looking for someone who calls himself Andy—no last name." I handed him a sheet of paper with the phone number and location Rosanna listed on her computer. "Then check out the address. It might be where he met Rosanna. Probably something commercial, but who knows?"

John looked at the paper. "That address looks familiar, Boss. Why do I know that? I think I've written it down before."

"Maybe you meet hookers there?"

"I can't afford hookers on what you pay me."

"Humpf. The 1600 block on McTeer is in county territory."

"Yeah, but I know the address. Lemme check out Soundex."

John tapped the keys, looking for inspiration from his computer.

"Aha!" he said. "You're losin' it, Boss. You know this address like the bottom of your shoe."

Bettye smiled. At my side, Lonnie Ray said, "Huh?"

"He means, like the back of my hand."

"Oh."

John cackled like the village idiot. "Or, Boss, maybe you just want us to think you don't know this address."

"Will you stop acting, and tell me why I know the address?"

"I think you're the one acting, Boss."

"Don't make me come over there, you Irish weasel. I'll strangle you."

Bettye tossed her granny glasses onto her desktop and scowled at me. She was about to go into her den mother mode.

"Just what are you two fussin' about? John, tell him what he wants to know."

"He already knows, Sarge. This is his Academy Award performance. He's a better actor than *Awesome* Wells."

I shook my head. "That's Orson Wells, you nitwit. And if you don't tell me, I'll—"

Bettye cut me short. "Sam...John is just about to tell you. Aren't you, John."

Gallagher kept laughing. "1655 McTeer's Station Pike is that cathouse, Boss. Tell me you didn't remember."

"Any minute now, John Boy, and I'll tell you, you're fired."

"You couldn't live without me, Boss."

Before I could respond to that with another juvenile threat, Lonnie Ray spoke up. "There's a cathouse in Prospect?"

"Technically, it's Maryville," Bettye said. "But it's only a hundred yards outside the Prospect line. Most deputies don't like to answer calls there because they're afraid who they'll find inside. So, a Prospect officer usually takes the call."

"Oh." Lonnie Ray dragged the word out.

"They call it the Frenchman's Holler Social Club," I said. "It's a pretty upscale place—popular with the governing fathers of the county and those from its lesser political subdivisions."

"Sounds too rich for the likes of me," Lonnie said.

I couldn't let that go. "Any guy who makes seventy-five bucks an hour could handle it."

With a Jack O'Lantern smile across the width of his face, John took another turn dumping on me.

"The woman who runs the place is sweet on the Boss. Good-lookin' girl, too. I mean *good-lookin'*."

"John," Bettye said. "Stop teasing. Right now, young man."

He had no intention of stopping his performance. "She's got a great name, huh, Boss? Especially for a madam."

I refused to acknowledge him.

"Oh, come on," Lonnie said. "You can't leave me hangin'. What's her name?"

It was like those two were in cahoots.

"Chastity Puryear," I said.

"A madam named Chastity? That's cool."

I pointed at John. "Lonnie, you're as bad as that Irish fool."

"For seventy-five an hour, I guess I should be at least that bad."

"You think?"

———

I left the PD with Bettye calling the people who submitted job applications to find out if they were still interested, still in the military, and if so, were they low crawling through some filthy village in Afghanistan, drinking beer in Germany or cruising around the Arabian Sea.

John was instructed to adjust his attitude and learn something about Andy's phone number.

Lonnie Ray said he knew a few tricks to get information some cell phone carriers were reluctant to provide without subpoenas. He offered to help John track down Andy and the rest of Rosanna Wakefield's clientele.

I suggested that he not let the pesky U.S. Constitution get in his way.

When they finished all those chores, we still had to find out what made Toby L. Bowman tick.

In the meantime, I planned on visiting the classiest madam in the Smokies and look for clues in the best little whorehouse in Tennessee.

CHAPTER SEVEN

The Frenchman's Holler Social Club is housed in a large antebellum farm house that sits on acres of fallow land, long ago gone back to nature. The three story tan and brown and pale yellow structure was built by Mexican War veteran Barton Puryear, Miss Chastity's ancestor. As the story goes, old Barton tried to make a go at farming, but because Tennessee soil (read red clay into that) can be no more than a hundred years away from turning into solid shale, he abandoned that pursuit and started distilling moonshine of a quality unequalled until the infamous Popcorn Sutton came on the scene in the 1970s. With the profits of his untaxed alcohol business burning a hole in the pocket of his overalls, Barton branched out to providing female companionship to the occupying troops during the Civil War.

When Barton died, later generations of Puryears tried their hands at more legitimate enterprises, but never quite encountered success at the family homestead.

Chastity Puryear hit two jackpots within a year's time back in the 1980s. She inherited the ramshackle home and then when her stockbroker husband died unexpectedly, she collected a two-million-dollar life insurance premium.

Two million bucks bought you a lot of top quality renovations back then, so she modernized the house, delved into family history and realized that the only success in the family came from running a whorehouse.

Chastity has been doing a land office business ever since. The reason she remains un-incarcerated is because many of the county commissioners, local politicos, ranking members of the sheriff's office and other notable residents call the Frenchman's Holler Social Club their watering hole and home away from home.

I pulled into the parking lot and found several of Chastity's employees sitting on the porch, reading magazines and sipping delicate libations.

As I trudged up the six steps, five pairs of eyes focused on me.

A good-looking mulatto girl said, "Hello, Chief Jenkins. Are those county cops still afraid ta come here? They send you ta deal with us women of ill repute?"

I shrugged and stuck my hands in my pockets. "You know, I've been embarrassed twice today because I've forgotten something. Refresh my memory. Tell me your name, and I promise to remember it always."

A couple of the girls giggled. A brunette sitting next to the girl with the café au lait skin slapped her upper arm.

"Don't feel bad, Mr. Jenkins," the mulatto said. "We've never been properly introduced. I've seen you on TV and never forget a good-lookin' man."

I smiled. "You just made an old guy feel young again. But you didn't tell me your name."

"No, I didn't. Can I trust you with that information?"

That sparked a few more giggles.

I held my right hand over my heart. "You can. Discretion is my middle name."

"I believe you, sugar. Call me Ida Lou."

"Nice to meet you, miss."

A pretty blonde who looked no more than twenty sipped from a tall glass of something and spoke up. "It's a little early for socializin', Chief."

"It is, but I'm here on business. Is the CEO of this company around?"

"Kinda thought ya might be lookin' for Miss Chastity," Ida Lou said. "Not sure where, but she's inside."

"Thanks, ladies." If I'd been wearing a cowboy hat, I would have tipped it. "Enjoy your drinks."

I opened the front door with a chorus of giggles behind me. They reminded me of a group of high school girls.

I walked through a houseful of Victorian and Edwardian era antiques. Not seeing the subject of my search, I called out, "Chassy? Are you here?"

I heard, "In the kitchen."

I found her removing an assortment of cocktail glasses from the dishwasher.

From checking out her driver's license information after we first met, I knew that she was fifty-four years old and coincidentally, five foot, four inches tall. I once described her in two words: indecently gorgeous. She had a face that always made me smile and a figure that would make a girl half her age jealous. Chastity's uniform of the day was a white T-shirt more than a bit tighter than what's currently in fashion tucked into cut off jeans that hugged her backside like Saran Wrap and a pair of pink old-fashioned boat sneakers.

She removed the last two glasses from the machine, closed the door and stood straight. Her legs were tanned and looked strong.

"Hello, Chassy."

"Oh, shoot, darlin', ya shoulda called. I look a mess. Ya caught me without my makeup."

She spoke with the soft musical accent of the mountain folk.

I shook my head. "You don't need any makeup."

Her hair was the color of polished rust, and while she usually wears it down three inches below her shoulders, that morning she pulled it back in a ponytail. A few strands, broken loose at both sides, added to her casual beauty. Her bangs were pushed to the left.

She stepped very close to me.

"Aren't you just the sweetest man?"

I smiled again. "All part of the po-leece service."

She shook her head. "What must I do ta git you ta come an' see me more often, Sam Jenkins?"

"How about turn this place into an Italian restaurant and not get mad when I bring my wife?"

She took a half step back, almost stomped her foot and put her hands on her hips, feigning an attitude. "You ask a lot from a girl."

From watching her little act, you wouldn't need to be a trained observer to notice that Chastity decided not to wear a bra that morning. She didn't need it anymore than she needed makeup.

"I came to ask a big favor."

"So, this is business and not pleasure."

"No one said business has to be painful."

She took that half step forward again and touched a little crescent-shaped scar on my cheek, an inch below my left eye.

"I've never noticed that b'fore."

"It gets lost in the wrinkles."

"And how'd ya git it?"

"Someone I was arresting threw a screwdriver at me."

"Oh, Lord have mercy. What did ya do?"

"Something appropriate to a guy who tried to poke out my eye."

"Oh, my. It looks old."

"It happened a long time ago."

She smiled again and gently slapped my chest with her right hand. "Long ago. Sounds like the last time I spent a romantic day with a good-lookin' man."

"If that's true, the men in this area are lacking in the brain department."

"Sam, darlin', I may be in the *business*, but I've never *practiced the trade*...if you unnerstand what I'm sayin'."

"Perfectly."

"But for you, sugar, I'd make an exception."

What would the average middle-aged man say to that?

54

"I'd better ask that favor soon, or I'll have to run away and take a cold shower."

She slapped my chest again. "I don't know why I like ya so much. Ya frustrate the hell outta me." She took an exaggerated deep breath. "Oh, all right, go ahead, and ask your favor."

I told Chastity a little about our first murder, and that we suspected it was committed by the Riverside Strangler.

"So far we've determined that the victim did *practice the trade* in this area and seems to have an extensive client list. I want to show you her picture and ask if you've ever seen her or know the name Rosanna Wakefield."

I handed her the snapshot that Iris Wakefield had given me.

Chastity nodded. "Yes, I've seen her. Come over here, and sit down, Sammy."

We sat on opposite sides of the kitchen table.

"Would you like something to drink?" she asked.

"You've got good taste. What are you having?"

"I picked up a bottle of something they haven't made in almost twenty years. Knowing ya drink scotch, I saved it for ya."

"What an honor. You either think I'm nice or a drunk."

She laughed and touched my cheek as she stood up. "Stick around, darlin', while I git the bottle."

Chassy disappeared for a moment and came back carrying a square, squat bottle. She placed it on the table and fetched two small glasses from a kitchen cabinet.

"It's still early, so I thought a liqueur would be appropriate."

I read the label aloud. "Lochan Ore, by the Chivas Brothers. Is it sweet?"

"Not as sweet as you, baby." She cracked the seal and poured two shots. "Here's to ya."

We touched glasses, and I sipped mine. Chassy waited to see my reaction. "Very nice. Thanks."

"Glad you like it."

"Mmm. Tell me how you know Rosanna Wakefield."

"She asked me for a job."

It pays to know the right people and ask the right questions.

"And?"

"And she didn't call herself Wakefield. Said her name was Rosanna Mistral or some such theatrical nonsense."

"How long did she work here?"

Chassy took a tiny sip of her liqueur and gently set her glass back on the table. "One night."

I raised my eyebrows.

"Oh, she was pretty enough and attracted the boys, but I caught her poppin' some kinda pills. This is not that kinda establishment, Sammy. I told her ta pack up right then and there."

"When was that?"

"Couple years ago. She was over eighteen, but not by much."

"Never saw her again?"

"Nosir."

"I had a guy hack into her computer to find her business files. She went private into the *escort* market."

Chassy made a face. "Huh. Outcall girls."

She made it sound like call girls were on a par with lepers.

"Right. One interesting thing was a notation for the day she disappeared. She scheduled a meeting with a customer she called Andy. The location she listed was here."

"*Here* as in this house?"

"Uh-huh."

"Not in here she didn't."

"Were you here four nights ago?"

"I was."

"Did you see a Rosanna who might have changed her appearance in the last two years?"

"No. I do not let just anybody wander in and out of here and set up shop. I hope you don't think so."

It sounded like Chassy was losing patience with me. I finished my drink.

"Want a refill?"

I smiled. "Sure. Can I try it with a little ice?"

Chassy wrinkled up her nose and frowned, as if I suggested putting ketchup on prime rib.

She snatched my glass, walked to the freezer and picked out a single ice cube. Back at the table, she half filled the half-round footed glass and pushed it toward me.

"Andy?" I said.

She shrugged, and I thought how attractive the T-shirt looked on her. "Maybe. I can't think of one right off hand, but I'll ask the girls if someone might use that as a nickname."

"Thanks. How about your parking lot? Do people use it as a meeting place?"

"I hope not—and not without my permission."

I swished the scotch-flavored liquor around the glass and watched the ice cube spin. "Yet things happen." I took a sip. "That ex-football player still your bouncer?"

"Farley? He is."

"Yeah. Farley Gayton. Does he still make periodic visits outside to check on things?"

"He does."

"This is better cold. I'll bet it's good over vanilla ice cream."

She shook her head. "Oh, Lord have mercy."

"Will you have Farley call me?"

I guess she got over the idea of her expensive liqueur being used as a desert topping and smiled. "'Course I will, sugar. You think this Rosanna met her john here, and after that he killed her?"

"Could be. If I ever find Andy, I'll ask."

CHAPTER EIGHT

When I returned to Prospect PD, I found a beehive of activity. John and Bettye were on the phones, while Lonnie Ray kept finding names for Rosanna's customers.

"I have never had to threaten so many people to get them to cooperate," Bettye said.

"A little embarrassing when you're caught on the customer list of a twenty-year-old prostitute."

"I listened to John *persuade* a few people," she said. "He's good. After that it was easy."

John Gallagher hung up his phone and looked at us. "Did I hear my name mentioned?"

"Yeah. The sergeant said you're good at making threats and violating Constitutional rights."

"Years ago I learned how from my favorite lieutenant."

"Liar. You were on the job long before me."

"Can't fool you, can I, Boss?"

"How have you made out with these *clients*?"

"The married ones volunteered to come in," Bettye said. "They don't want us anywhere close to their homes. We've given them appointments starting tonight. Some others weren't so eager to cooperate, but we've got addresses, and they'll talk to us."

"Good. Anybody sound promising?"

Bettye shrugged, and John shook his head.

"Any leads on this Andy?"

"Nothing," John said. "Lonnie is spending a lot of time on him, but so far hasn't found spit."

"Disappointing. It sounds like Andy knows how to hide."

"Yeah," John said. "Maybe like he knows how to cover up a crime scene."

"Anyone on your list admit being cops? Maybe Andy uses two names."

"I had two Knox County deputies," Bettye said.

"You recognize their names?"

"No. I may be wrong, but they sounded more like embarrassed party boys than promising suspects. They'll be here tonight."

"Remember that ol' boy from Knox County, Detective Windy Hatmaker? He owes me. I'll give him a call about these party boys. Ring Stanley and tell him to plan on spending time in the office tonight. He can help us grill these sex-crazed people."

Bettye grinned. "Already have."

"Good. Now, what do you know about our police applicants?"

"Two are still overseas and not scheduled to get out of the service for a while. One returned a few months ago and got discharged. Terri Donnellson."

"Terrance or Theresa?"

"Terri with an I. She spent four years as an Army MP. Just got a job as a store detective in Knoxville."

"If we have to make a quick choice, it's good to know someone with prior police experience. I hope she has an honorable discharge and didn't pick up any bad habits."

"I can't comment on her habits, but she has an honorable discharge. Got out as a sergeant. She sounded intelligent on the phone."

"When's she coming in?"

She handed me a file folder with Terri Marie Donnellson written on the tab. "Tomorrow at nine. You can read all about her."

———

I n between threatening phone calls, John Gallagher ran a quick background investigation on Toby Lee Bowman, our latest murder victim. While Rosanna Wakefield attended a year of community college learning her bookkeeping and computer skills, Toby quit high school in his junior year. From there, we know he became a favorite of Knoxville PD, the Knox County Sheriff's Office, Oak Ridge PD and the Anderson County sheriff. They bagged him numerous times for soliciting, loitering for sex, shoplifting, drug possession and one minor commercial burglary —things typical of a young man banished from his home and disinherited by his father after Pop learned about his son's homosexuality. On several occasions, twenty-three-year-old Toby checked in as a guest of the Knox and Anderson County jails for a total of almost three years.

John had scheduled a meeting with Toby's mother for the next morning. He volunteered to escort Emma Lee Bowman to the morgue to make a formal identification.

———

A n hour later, while I was calling my wife to break the news that her favorite husband would only be home for dinner and then head back to work to interrogate a long line of men known to patronize a young prostitute, John Gallagher strolled into my office and took a seat in one of my guest chairs. He held a yellow lined pad in one hand and adjusted the red and blue striped tie that ended two buttons north of his belt and rested on his round belly.

I hung up the phone. "What's up, John?"

"I kept digging and got a pretty fair story now on Toby Bowman. You already know about his priors, but I called his mother again and have been on the phone with her for almost an hour. She doesn't know where his cell phone is, and I kinda figure the killer took it, but she's got his laptop. Says it's old, but he left it in his room. He lives with her, but, according to her, he's in and out—gone for days at a time. She confirms that he was still driving the '99 Civic that's on file with Department of Safety. She gave me permission to search Toby's room and agreed to let a couple of evidence technicians toss the place tomorrow when I pick her up. I called Jackie. His LT said he and David could meet me there. They know what to look for."

"Good. I'll let Lonnie Ray handle the computer to maintain continuity. Maybe he'll see some similarity with Rosanna's laptop that would get by us. Give him a call and have him show up here when you think you'll be back."

John nodded. "Mrs. Bowman said she split with her husband 'cause o' how he treated the gay son, but she still had an address and number for him. Name's Arlo."

"Give Arlo a ring and set up an appointment."

"Will do, Boss."

———

I walked into the living room at 9:50. Thanks to Netflix, Kate was watching an episode of The Ladies Number One Detective Agency. Perhaps she was planning on opening a similar business. I hoped she wanted to do it in Tennessee and not Botswana.

"Hello, Sweetie," she said. "Long day?"

"Pain in the ass day. I'm not sure how much we accomplished. These interviews tonight were a bust."

I pushed the pause button on the DVD player's remote.

"Want a drinkie-poo?" Kate asked.

"Sure, and don't be stingy, doll-face. A hardboiled gumshoe like me needs his booze after a tough day o' gettin' beat up and stonewalled."

She answered with her Mae West impersonation. "Sit down, Bogie, and I'll get ya some hooch." As she passed by, Kate ran a hand up my thigh.

Two minutes later and the lady detectives were still on hold.

"We interviewed thirty-three lads who decided to take their love to town. I tried to scatter them around the PD so they wouldn't get embarrassed and clam up if they were seen by other johns. And we didn't want them to get together and conspire to concoct self-serving stories. That was the hard part."

"Did they all come in at once?"

"Of course not. John staggered the appointments. But some came in early, and others left late. It happens."

"And between you, John, and Stanley, you learned nothing?"

"We learned that some were pathetic cases. Some were decent enough guys, and a few were total nitwits. We did not meet one guy who admitted ever having been called Andy. Every time a new body came into the room, John called the number Rosanna Wakefield listed on her computer file for Andy and got nothing. That phone must be turned off or thrown away. Nothing but voice mails that John didn't use."

"So, absolutely no leads?"

"They had either good, solid alibis or stories we could never disprove. Except to eliminate those people, we learned nothing."

She placed her hand on my thigh and squeezed. "Oh well, tomorrow's another day."

"You got that right, Scarlett."

I pushed the resume button and a cute but overweight African female detective continued to question a bartender about someone's claim to have spent the previous night drinking in his bar.

As the scene faded to black, Kate asked, "So, what are you going to do next?"

"That's a pretty skimpy night gown you're wearing. I can think of only one appropriate thing."

CHAPTER NINE

I walked into the PD the next morning at 8:45. Annoyed at having worked late the night before. Annoyed because it was drizzling outside. Beyond annoyed that a monster drop of rainwater from the overhang—probably an entire quarter cup—somehow slapped me on the neck and ran down my back when I tapped in my four digit code at the back door. And I was just sick and tired of trying to investigate two homicides with only three assistants—four if you count Lonnie Ray Wilson—when I really needed sixteen. And I was not in the mood to interview a police applicant when I really wanted to advertise the job and end up with a couple dozen people from which to choose.

I should have known something was unusual when Bettye said, "Good morning, sir," but I wasn't paying attention.

I rubbed a hand over my neck and began telling her, "Damn blob of rainwater ran down my collar and—" when I noticed a young lady sitting in one of the guest chairs along the left wall of the lobby. I stopped kvetching. "Morning, Sarge."

Bettye smiled. "Miss Donnellson got here a little early."

"Uh-huh."

She was staring at me. I looked back. "Hi, I'm Sam Jenkins—in charge of this understaffed, overworked herd of elite law enforcement professionals."

She began to stand. I waved a hand at her.

"Sit. Give me a minute to take my coat off."

She resumed the sitting position.

I did a three-quarter about-face and walked to my office where I took off my raincoat, shook it out and hung it on the back of the door. I stuck my umbrella—the one I had already folded up before the torrent of rainwater cascaded down my neck—against the wall and took a deep breath, wondering if I should pour myself a cup of coffee or return to the reception area and fetch our only job applicant. I chose the latter.

"Ms. Donnellson, come in, please."

She rose from the chair carrying a thin briefcase and a tan raincoat. I extended an arm, pointing her through my office doorway. She entered the room and stalled a few feet in front of my desk.

"Give me your coat," I said.

She looked at me as if I had suggested she remove all her clothes.

"Your coat? I'm going to put it on this chair, and you can sit in this one." I pointed at each respectively. She smiled and handed me the raincoat.

I took the coat with my left hand and extended my right, which she shook.

"Nice to meet you," I said. "Sit, please."

She did, and I began to circumnavigate my desk clockwise, but stopped three-quarters of the way around.

"Would you like coffee? Sergeant Lambert makes a fresh pot every morning."

She shook her head. "No, thank you, sir."

She looked a little nervous.

"That wasn't a test or a trick question. If you'd like coffee, say so. I'll fix you a cup. I worked more than twelve hours yesterday, got a lousy night's sleep and I'm going to have coffee. Sure you don't want one?"

She took a long moment to answer. "Thank you, sir. Black, no sugar, please."

I poured two the same and set one on the edge of my desk in front of her. That done, I walked around my desk and dropped into my big swivel chair.

I shook my head. "I know you've done some police work in the Army, so you'll understand this. I've got two homicides working plus all the other crap that comes in via 9-1-1 and a mayor and city council to placate. It's only me and twelve cops. I need at least three times that many. You sure you want to work here?"

She smiled. "Yes, sir, I do. I need a good job."

Terri Marie Donnellson wore a navy blue pantsuit and a white open collar blouse. She was almost pretty. No, she *was* pretty. She was almost beautiful, but as a package, she was incredibly attractive. Long brown hair that could be pulled back, twisted up and discretely worn under an MP helmet, a clear olive complexion that suggested a Mediterranean heritage, but her family name was clearly Gaelic. Soft and expressive brown eyes. Not quite full lips and prominent cheekbones. But the best part—the imperfection that made her look so much better than an out-of-the-box Barbie doll, was her nose. It looked as if it had been broken and was now set off a sixteenth of an inch to the left. I wanted to know what happened.

"I looked over your application. You're twenty-seven and have been in the Army for four years?"

"Yes, sir. Four years and five months."

"You were an MP?"

"Yes, sir." Terri Marie sat at attention, her knees together, her briefcase on her lap and her hands atop the case. She answered as if she were sitting before a panel of officers who might elect her Soldier of the Month.

"Who were you with?"

"Sir?"

"Tell me with whom you were assigned whilst in Uncle Sam's Army."

"Oh, yes sir, sorry. I was with the 716th MP Battalion"

I noticed her looking over my shoulder at the shadow box behind my desk that held the medals, badges and assorted doo-dads I'd earned during my time in the Army.

"I remember the 716th being in Saigon. A kid I knew from New York was assigned to, I think, Charlie Company, received a Silver Star during Tet of '68."

"Yes, sir, we're very proud of the battalion's service in Vietnam."

She still looked as tight as an Army snare drum.

"Relax, Ms. Donnellson. I may bark on occasion, but I don't bite. Drink your coffee before it gets cold. I spent more than twenty years in the Army system, but I'm not like most of the company commanders you might have met." I shrugged. "I guess that's because I don't choose to behave like the average C.O. and never had a normal company."

Terri took a deep breath and smiled again. Then she picked up her cup and sipped the coffee.

"The 716th is at Fort Campbell now, isn't it?" I asked.

"Yes, sir, it is."

"But I'm guessing you've been overseas."

"Yes, sir. Two deployments to Afghanistan."

"Lucky you."

Another smile and another sip.

"Tell me about your Afghan adventures."

She nodded for a brief moment. "My company was assigned to town patrol during my first tour. The second time there, they chose me to be a provost marshal's investigator."

"A military squad dick?"

"Not exactly, sir. We handled misdemeanors and other investigations not sent to CID."

"Sounds like good duty."

"Yes, sir. I loved that job."

"Yet you finished four years and five months and separated from the Army. Why?"

"I wanted to be a cop, sir."

"You already were."

"Not exactly, sir. I wanted to be a civilian cop. I think there's a big difference. In the Army, they never let you forget you're a soldier first."

"Okay. When did they promote you to sergeant?"

"Just before my second trip to Afghanistan."

"Congratulations. I guess you were a sharp troop."

"Thank you, sir."

I smiled. "Can we cut the crap, Terri?"

Her face almost hit the floor. "Sir?"

"Let's stop the *sir* and *Ms. Donnellson* business. This is not a line company in the Army. We're pretty informal at Prospect PD, and I'm afraid that's my fault. I'm going to call you by your first name, and I suggest that you call me Sam—unless you can't quite get your head around that right away. Then Boss works for me. You look savvy enough to know you should call me Chief or Sir when there's a civilian or some media type within earshot, but at other times, I'd prefer not. But remember, if you ever salute me, I might get capped by a sniper."

She relaxed her shoulders and smiled. "I understand."

"Good. Now, I see you graduated from South College with a BS. What did you get that degree in?"

"Behavioral Sciences."

I grinned. "Sounds like BS to me."

She smiled again. "Maybe fifty percent. The rest was geared toward police work."

"Good. Have you taken any more courses on the GI Bill?"

"A few law classes. I've just started."

"You want to be a lawyer?"

No, sir. I want to be a cop. But I figure if I'm going to enforce the law and face off against a lawyer in court, I need to know at least as much as they do."

"Wow. Good answer. I couldn't agree more." I downed a third of my cup of coffee rather than let it cool off. "Look Terri, if I hire you for this job, it's going to be contingent upon you passing medical and psychological exams, a background investigation and physical agility test. No problem with those, right?"

"No, sir."

"How about a polygraph exam? Any problems you'd rather the rest of the world not learn?"

"No, sir, uh, Chief. I mean, boss."

"Good. You don't look like you would."

She gave me a small smile. "No skeletons."

"You would have to start working here before the tests. Meaning you'd have to quit the job you have now. That work for you?"

"No problem, sir."

"Okay, let's get philosophical for a minute. Why do you want Prospect PD and not the county or the troopers or even the TBI? You'd qualify for any of those."

She dropped her eyes and paused for a moment. "Sir, I guess it's because of you."

I wasn't expecting that. "Explain that one for me."

"I live with my parents and their neighbor knows you. He said I could learn a lot from you—how to be a good cop—a good detective."

"First things first. We don't have detectives in Prospect."

"I know that, sir. But I also know you do all your own investigations."

"That's correct. Who's your source of information?"

"Detective Stallins."

I nodded. "Bo's a good man. He'd be a good investigator anywhere."

"Yes, sir."

"Okay, next question. How'd you break your nose?"

Involuntarily, her hand went up to cover her face. "Oh, you noticed."

"I'm a police chief. I notice everything."

She smiled. "During my first tour over in the sandbox, I was working patrol, and we got a call to a maintenance company's compound. Some GI was cranked on speed and tearing up their day room. We confronted him and out of nowhere, he swung a pool cue at me. I half-blocked it, but when it broke over my forearm, the heavy end caught me in the nose. Bruised my arm and broke my nose. It looks bad, doesn't it?"

"Maybe to you. No one else would notice it."

"You did."

I raised my eyebrows. "I'm exceptional...and modest."

Her smile came back.

"What happened to the speed freak?"

"My partner knocked him down, and I cuffed him."

"Hmmm. What did you want to do?"

The memory generated a frown. "Sir, I wanted to shove that pool cue up his—"

"Gotcha. I'm glad you didn't—or maybe we wouldn't be having this conversation."

"Yes, sir."

"One last thing. Are you part Italian?"

She stiffened up. "Is that relevant, sir?"

I grinned. "No, not in the least, but who cares? Is your mother Italian."

She still looked as stiff as a starched shirt collar. "Sir, why do you ask?"

"Terri, I told you to relax. I'm going to offer you a job. I'm not violating your Constitutional rights. The question has nothing to do with my decision. I'm just nosey."

She gave a sigh of relief. "Yes, sir, she is."

"I only planned on asking if you had any good family recipes. I like to cook, and Mediterranean food is my favorite."

She softened up. "Oh. Okay. Sure. My mom's a great cook. She can fix you right up."

"Okay, we're done here. I assume you still want a job?"

She tried to hide a huge smile but didn't do it well. "Yes, sir, you bet."

"Good. I'm afraid you won't be able to give your current employer a full two weeks' notice, but I'll smooth them over if necessary. Our next pay period starts in eleven days, and we need you here then."

"Great. Thank you...Sir."

"Here's your first assignment. Knock off the Sir, okay?"

"Yes...uh, boss."

"Thanks. And congratulations. I think you'll like working here."

"I know I will."

"Stop and talk with Bettye at the desk before you leave. She's your new first sergeant and den mother and will give you a bunch of paperwork the city needs and make sure when you report for duty you have uniforms and are armed and dangerous."

I stood, and so did she. I walked around my desk and shook her hand. "Thanks for signing on."

"And thank you, again...boss."

———

Terri Donnellson wasn't gone twenty minutes when Mo Rappaport called.

"Sam, I'm sorry for the delay with the Bowman boy's post, but I finally got a table for tomorrow morning. Will you be the one attending?"

"Can't think of anything I'd like more."

"Have I ever told you that sarcasm is one of your strongest attributes?"

"Often."

"Ha. Shall we say nineish?"

"I'll be there with Vicks in my nose."

"Oh, one thing you may want to know beforehand. Earl helped me determine the angles of entry on the three shots in Bowman's body. I hope I don't complicate your life by saying I'm confident there were three shooters. All the entry wounds suggest three people of different height."

The first thing that came to mind was Iris Wakefield's statement about Rosanna thinking *they* would kill her.

"Odd, but probably realistic," I said. "I can't envision one shooter dancing around a body pumping shots into it from different angles and different heights."

"That would be unusual. We'll only know if there was more than one gun after I extract the bullets and a firearms examiner puts them under the microscope."

"Okay, Doctor, I'll see you tomorrow, and I'll bring doughnuts."

"Thank you, boychek. I love those old-fashioned jelly doughnuts you get from that cholesterol factory in Maryville."

CHAPTER TEN

At 1:45, John Gallagher walked back into the PD. I was working the desk while Bettye went home for lunch.

I took an exaggerated look at my watch. "Where the hell have you been?"

John's eyes popped wide. He looked aghast. "Boss, you know where I was."

He set a small beaten-up laptop on his desk.

"You were going to take the Bowman woman to the morgue at nine o'clock. It's almost two."

"Yeah, I did. And I met Shuman and Sparks at Mrs. Bowman's house, and we searched her son's room." He cracked a big smile. "And look what I got."

"I see. When is Lonnie Ray coming to look at it?"

"Tomorrow morning, but we don't need him."

"Oh?"

"Yup. There's no password. Just turn it on, and get in. And—" He drew the word out, "This kid saved all the email responses he got from guys answering his gay ads on Charlie's List."

"No kidding? You've got email addresses?"

"Sure. Even one for Andy."

"For Andy? Just before Toby was killed?"

"No. Six months ago, but maybe *Andy* called him directly for a date and then killed him."

"He used a phone number in his ads?"

"He did. But who knows how many calls he got? And we got no cell phone and no bills. Probably bought prepaid minutes at who knows where—they sell them all over the place." John shrugged. "He's got lots of emails. Never deleted anything. They may be our best bet."

"Hmmm. Maybe. Can you back trace the email addresses to a location?"

John pointed to himself and looked shocked. "Me?"

"No, your second grandson."

"That's why Lonnie Ray is coming in."

"You said we don't need him."

"Well, we don't need him to get the emails."

"That's like saying you don't need Enzo Ferrari to win a race if you have a red car."

"Enzo who?"

I ignored him. "What else did you find in Toby's room?"

"A bunch of gay magazines, a couple o' sex videos—also gay and a closet full o' gay clothes."

I sighed. "What are gay clothes, John?"

"You know, clothes. Gay clothes. Clothes you and I wouldn't wear."

"I wouldn't wear those pastel Palm Beach suits you own."

"Boss, you're killin' me here."

"That's all you've done *all* day?"

"Not exactly."

Before I could scream, the radio crackled, and Bobby John Crockett said he was issuing a traffic ticket to a female motorist.

"Ten-four, five-zero-seven. Time is 13:52. Advise when you go two-seven." I turned away from the radio. "John, remind me why I should or shouldn't go ape-shit and yell at you."

"I was gonna tell you something very important I learned today."

Before I threw a staple gun at Gallagher, Bettye walked in and pushed my chair away from the large drawer where she keeps her purse.

"'Cuse me, darlin', I gotta get in there."

I gave the swivel chair an extra kick to allow her more room.

"What are you two boys doin'?" she asked.

"I was just about to choke Gallagher to death if he doesn't tell me the important information he's withholding."

John stood there grinning like a demented Irish gnome.

"Wait till you hear this, Sarge. Who do you think I saw at the ME's office?"

Bettye beat me to the punch. "Who, John?"

"Lew Schmecke and those two county dicks working on the task force, Artie Bonnet and Leo Turner."

I frowned. "What did they want?"

"They brought the ME an order of *exumption* for one of the older victims."

Bettye smiled. "Exumption?"

"That's exhumation, you...John, do you know just how close to death you are?"

He ignored me. "Now get this. Schmecke, that little toad, says he's been checking over the victim's photos and noticed ligature marks on one girl's neck that looked like thick rope."

"So?"

"So, he says that he used some half-assed—Sorry, Sarge—computer program to scan all the local police officer's profiles, 'cause Leary wants to *further explore* the possibility of somebody in law enforcement being the killer."

"So, what does rope burns have to do with local cops?"

"Schmecke says it looks like hemp, and two cops work side jobs with a tree service. You know, like chopping them down and removing them? Schmecke says tree experts use hemp cause it doesn't stretch. He wants the ME to check for fibers."

I shook my head. "The man's an oaf. What did Morris say to that?"

"Doctor Mo wasn't too happy. He says he would have checked and, if he found any, reported it."

"But some judge signed an exhumation order, and Mo's boss wants to comply?" I suggested.

"Yup."

"Didn't Schmecke, the simpleton, consider how many boaters are in this area and maybe some of them still use old-fashioned hemp dock or anchor lines? Not everybody uses nylon."

"Guess not, Boss."

"Schmecke is a clod."

"Is what he asks even remotely reasonable?" Bettye asked.

I shrugged, reluctant to admit that Schmecke was anything but a halfwit, and I was having doubts about Leary if he had agreed to go along with this gag.

"Anything is a possibility, but I really doubt Mo Rappaport would miss something as blatant as coarse fibers scattered around a strangled victim's throat."

"Doctor Mo is pretty thorough," she said.

I nodded. "Mo is an excellent pathologist."

"You know, Boss, I never did trust those two guys from CID—Bonnet and Turner. Bo Stallins is a good guy and even Lieutenant Jensen and Sergeant Bledsoe are okay, but those other two turn me off."

"They're Leary's pet baboons. And they think they're hot stuff. If they can't knuckle a confession out of a suspect, they're lost in space."

"Can this exhumation and new autopsy hurt anything?" Bettye asked.

"It wastes time. It'll freak out the victim's family. It diverts attention from other more meaningful work, although at this point I'm not sure what that is, and if this ever goes to court, a defense attorney can create doubt about the pathologist's ability if a judge considered it reasonable to give a second look at the body. And most importantly, it's gotten me cheesed off. Now, I hope Morris doesn't have to postpone Toby Bowman's autopsy to work on this exhumed victim."

"I'll call Earl and ask," Bettye said.

"Thanks, Betts. John, get together with Stanley and interview the remaining people from Rosanna's list of *clients* tonight. After Lonnie Ray works up a new list from Toby's computer, there'll be more road work."

"Got it, Boss."

———

I spent a couple hours that afternoon reading Rosanna Wakefield's spreadsheets, looking for an anomaly or outlandishly blatant clue, but nothing jumped off the pages.

At 4:30, Chastity Puryear's bouncer, Farley Gayton, called.

"How many times did you check the parking lot that night?" I asked.

"That's a long time ago, Chief. I do the same thing six nights a week. I look for people hangin' around who shouldn't be there—you know, like maybe PIs lookin' ta take pitchers o' some customer, or a wife lookin' ta confront a husband—like that. I also try ta match up the ve-hickles with the customers—see if somethin' doesn't belong."

"Yeah, Farley, I know. But we're not going back six months here. It was a clear night. And, uh, it was the night the Smokies played a double header, if that helps."

"Hmmm. Wait a minute. Mebbe that does he'p. Lemme think some. Yeah. Mebbe I got somethin'. I thought I knew all the customers that night, but when I made my outside rounds, I saw one SUV that didn't match up. But, I figgered mebbe somebody borrowed a ve-hickle or come with someone I didn't see."

"Bottom-line it for me, Farley. What's the vehicle in question?"

"A big stretch GMC, probably black, but could o' been dark blue or green."

"You get a plate number? Anything special about this GMC?"

"No. And I don't write down no tag numbers. That's jest somethin' I remembered."

"Okay, that's good. This could be helpful. Thanks."

He hung up.

The information was a little less than helpful, but nonetheless interesting. Using the theory that the Strangler may have a connection to law enforcement, big GMC Yukons or Chevy Suburbans—virtually the same vehicles—are used by about all the chief deputies, assistant chief deputies, half the police chiefs, and many of the Feds in the tri-county area. Information like this is helpful but tends to give me a frustration headache.

CHAPTER ELEVEN

The next morning, I met Mo Rappaport in his office at the morgue, intending to observe the Toby Bowman autopsy, which in spite of threatened obstacles, I expected to go off on schedule.

I've always hated autopsies. They smell. If I wanted to see dead people dissected, I would have taken a job as a butcher in a cannibal's commune. But autopsies are part of a cop's job—chain of evidence and all that foolishness.

With long, thin rods, Morris and Earl demonstrated how they concluded that Toby had been shot three times by three different people. While their theory was by no means proof beyond a reasonable doubt, it was sound and logical.

Fast-forwarding through all the cutting and dismantling of young Bowman's body, Doctor Mo extracted three bullets from the decedent. The guess I made at the crime scene was correct. The clean, perfectly circular bullet holes had been punched into Toby Bowman's flesh by .38 Special caliber 148 grain lead wadcutters—inexpensive flat-nosed target ammunition. One well-placed or perhaps lucky shot punctured Toby's heart and killed him almost instantly. Two others were recovered from soft tissue or muscle. They did not encounter any major bone and therefore weren't seriously distorted.

"Let's look at those bullets before we go further," Morris suggested.

Earl took the small tray containing the three lead slugs to a sink and rinsed off the bloody matter. That finished, he handed the triangular-shaped receptacle to me.

In my best Boris Karloff, lisp ridden accent, I said, "May we use your microscope, Doctor Frankenstein?"

"That was good, Samilah, very good. When questioned, most people would say Karloff was Frankenstein, when, as we know, he played the unnamed monster. It was Colin Clive who portrayed Dr. F."

"Fascinating."

Morris smiled. "I know. I love old movies. No comparison to the drek and chazerai they make today."

"I'm so glad I have you here, Morris. Without you, I would never hear Yiddish again."

"I'm pleased to accommodate. And I say that with all sincerity. Now, let's look at the bullets."

He picked the cylinder-shaped projectiles from the tray and laid them side by side under one of those dinner plate-sized illuminated magnifying glasses. I stood in the middle, directly over the glass. After a quick look, I glanced to my left at Morris and to the right at Earl.

"We don't need a firearms examiner, gentlemen. The myopic Mr. Magoo could see those striations match. These were all fired from the same gun. And I'll amaze you even further by saying the left-hand twist suggests the gun was a Colt revolver."

"Now who's fascinating?" Morris asked.

"Nonetheless, we'll get Bill Werner at TBI to provide macroscopic comparison photos of these should I ever get a killer or killers into court with their handgun."

"I'll git 'em delivered," Earl said. "Ya only want Werner ta handle 'em?"

"Bill's the best they've got."

"Gotcha covered, Chief."

Our curiosity satisfied, I followed my versions of Dr. Frankenstein and Igor back to the operating table while they finished Toby Bowman's post mortem examination.

Later, Morris snapped off his rubber gloves and tossed them into a nearby trashcan as Earl wheeled the sewn up Bowman toward a refrigerated locker.

The doctor began rinsing down the stainless steel table surface before he spoke. "So, my friend, what do we know? One gun. Maybe three shooters. No evidence of strangulation. No tampering with the fingerprints. No stab wounds. No apparent signs of human sexual contact or sodomy with a foreign object, but he was a Charlie's List prostitute. Are you thinking copycat?"

I shrugged. "Or smoke screen. Maybe the Strangler is messing with our minds, making it so far from the pattern that we'll think a different killer." I shook my head, not quite agreeing with that possibility. "But serial killers are usually proud of their work and egotistical enough to think they can distract us in other ways. They're usually blatant about leaving their calling cards as taunts. Basically, it beats the shit outta me."

"Sam, I've done what I can. After a few more tests, I'll be finished, and you'll have my reports. In the meantime, you might want to run your thoughts past a forensic psychologist."

I shrugged again. "Couldn't hurt. Know anyone that's good with abnormal criminal psychology?"

Like a Brooklyn yenta, Morris said, "Ah, boychek, have I got a girl for you."

———

On the road back to Prospect PD, I stopped to see Chastity Puryear.

This time, I found her sitting in the kitchen eating a bowl of Greek yogurt topped with chunky tropical fruit.

"Hello, darlin'," she said. "Want some o' this?"

"I have no manly opposition to yogurt, but my lunchtime desires tend more toward stick-to-the-ribs food. I'll pass."

She shook her head and let out something between a sniff and a snort. "Men. You want somethin' ta drink?"

"A beer would be nice."

On the way to the fridge, she kissed my forehead. "Sam Adams suit ya?"

"Sure, I'm patriotic as well as thirsty."

"And you're one of the most clever smartasses I know."

"Thank you, ma'am."

She popped the cap and held up the bottle for me to see. "Want a glass?"

"Of course. I'm patriotic and civilized."

Chastity placed both on the table in front of me and sat behind the wheel of her yogurt bowl. Today she wore khaki shorts and a red tank top. Underwear still seemed to be an option she didn't choose.

"Red is a good color for you."

"Nice o' you ta say so, sweetheart, but if you're gonna make it a habit o' stoppin' ta see me, ya gonna have ta call first. Least I got my makeup on t'day, but I'd rather not let ya see me lookin' like some common housewife on a day she wasn't expectin' the pool boy."

I laughed. "I've met plenty of nice housewives."

She frowned. "I'll bet you have. Whatchew want, sugar?" She didn't sound overly patient.

"Aren't we testy today?"

"I am not. I just...Oh, never mind."

"You look great. No need to change...or fish for compliments."

She finally broke a smile. "I do believe we could be quite happy together."

"Every time I see you, Chassy, I think—if only another time, another place."

"Y'all are such a liar." She ate the last spoonful of her yogurt/fruit concoction.

It was time to focus on po-leece business. "I spoke to Farley."

"And?"

After a sip of Sam Adams Summer Lager, I laid my cards on the table. "The night Rosanna Wakefield disappeared and presumably was murdered, Farley spotted a big black SUV—a stretch Yukon or Chevy Suburban, in your lot. Yet he didn't connect the vehicle with a customer. Thanks to Hollywood, SUVs like that have gotten to be the current vehicles-of-choice with some high-ranking cops. Was there someone in that category here on that night? Someone Farley might not have seen?"

"Sam, honey, I wish you didn't ask questions like that. Two reasons. I hate ta talk about our clients, and it wasn't just yesterday. How'm I s'pposed ta remember?"

"You're not only beautiful, but you're intelligent. You'd remember. And forget about not giving up your clients. It comes with the job when your buddy asks."

"You think I know what kinda cars these people drive?"

"Yeah."

"Oh, good Lord have mercy. I do not know why I do as you ask, Sam Jenkins."

I blinked a few times and tried to look irresistible.

"Oh, well," she said. "There was an important police officer here that night. Are you acquainted with Archie Faber?"

"Not intimately, but I know he's the sheriff's assistant chief deputy of patrol."

"That's him."

"And he drives a big black SUV?"

"You'll have ta ask him, Mr. Po-leece Chief."

———

When I walked into the office, Bettye was typing away on her computer, John was missing, and when I hung my sport jacket on the back of the door to my room, I found Lonnie Ray Wilson clicking away on the keys of Toby Bowman's laptop.

"How are you making out with those email addresses?" I asked.

"So far, a piece of cake. Far as I can tell, these are just a bunch of promiscuous guys. I'm guessing some of them are married switch hitters who should have done more to remain anonymous, but even if they opened clandestine email accounts, they're all mainstream freebies—Hotmail, Yahoo, Gmail. You understand what I'm saying?"

"Uh-huh."

"It's just gonna take time."

"At seventy-five an hour?"

"That's me, boss."

"That old email from *Andy* is important. Anything on that yet?"

"Haven't gotten around to Andy yet, but I'll work up all the angles on him."

"Okay, good. Now I need an educated opinion. John Gallagher heard that the task force is looking at two cops as suspects for the Strangler murders."

Lonnie Ray raised his eyebrows.

"This is all based on the *legendary detective* using a computer program to focus on the theoretic possibility of someone in law enforcement being connected. He's using a computer to profile local cops and match their activities to facts in evidence. Possible? Reliable?"

He took a long moment, then shrugged before answering. "Sure, it's possible. But I'd call it little more than a shot in the dark. Reliable? You'd only know after you made a good arrest. That stuff is for mathematicians. It's all got to do with algorithms and probability and statistics. If you believe it's reliable, ask yourself why aren't the guys with these programs picking winners in every horse race or cleaning up with sports betting. Isn't this what profilers do? You take a bunch of statistics known to be true and come up with common factors, then make assumptions and guesses that your guy fits the overall average. How often are they on target?"

I nodded. "Thanks. Good to hear an expert agrees with me."

I sat down at Gallagher's desk and interrupted Bettye. "John on the road?"

She nodded. "Chasin' down a few people he and Stanley didn't see last night."

"I've got a few calls to make before I know what else I'll be doing."

Bettye gave me her okey dokey, and I called a friend at the DA's office.

"Clete, can you do me a favor on the QT?"

"I really hate it when you start a conversation like that."

Cletus Dunn was the senior investigator for the District Attorney General in Blount County.

"I'd say that you probably don't want to know why I'm asking, but if you did, you couldn't resist getting the scoop."

"Man, this is goin' from bad ta worse, but you're right. Tell me."

I gave him a quick story about the big unattributed black, dark green or navy blue SUV.

"You're lookin' at one o' the bosses at the sheriff's office as bein' the serial killer?"

"Not yet and not exactly. There's no doubt that one of the bosses was at Frenchman's Holler that night doing some *socializing*. My problem comes from the SUV being unaccounted for. The bouncer doesn't put Archie Faber as the driver of that vehicle."

"You caught Archie gettin' his ashes hauled?"

"Hard to imagine that he spent his time there playing Chinese checkers."

"I hear that. Faber is a pretty decent guy."

"Lots of decent guys go looking for a harem outside the house. I'm not his problem, but he'd better keep his wife from finding out. If he was driving the SUV that night and he was otherwise *occupied* inside the club, I've got to look elsewhere."

"Exactly what do you need?"

"Find out what Archie drives as a company car. Also, who at the sheriff's office drives one of those big SUVs. My other questions go beyond easy. Like how many cops in the area drive similar vehicles."

"You ain't lookin' for much." He took a moment to sigh. "Okay, I'll do what I can."

"Thanks, partner."

———

I hoped that Clete Dunn got as lucky as I did with my next phone call. Mo Rappaport's psychologist friend, Dr. Sharon Rubenstein, received an appointment cancellation earlier in the day and could see me at four p.m.

At 3:30, John Gallagher came trotting in, pleased with himself for finishing all the pending interviews on his list and asking if we had been listening to the radio or television.

"We're working, John," I said. "You're the one who integrates radio and TV into your police business."

He shook his head and tried to look offended. "This is police business, Boss. Well, maybe not our business, but it's interesting. How about this? Last night some mope broke into Ryan Leary's SUV and took a duffle bag which just happened to hold his Glock and some other stuff."

"He left a gun in his car?"

"Seems so. But it didn't take a couple of patrolmen long to track down a local burglar and recover the bag. Ever hear of a skell named Farris Tingle?"

I shook my head. "Nice name. Never heard of him. Where's he from?"

"The news guy gave an address on the north end of Maryville. Must have been looking for houses to creep if he was in Leary's neighborhood."

"You know that name, Betts?" I asked.

"I'd remember that one. No, sorry."

John continued. "The news guy showed a film clip from when this Tingle was arraigned. He looked like he fell down Mount Le Conte. I guess either the cops or the dick who caught the case tuned him up."

"With two CID guys permanently on the Strangler task force, the only dicks catching squeals are Hugh Bledsoe, the sergeant, and Bo Stallins. Neither of them are knuckle men."

"Yeah, but it looks like somebody really cleaned this mook's clock."

"I wouldn't put it past Leary himself. Just to satisfy my prurient curiosity, make a call, and see who's handling the case."

"Okay, Boss. If somebody stole my gun, I'd want to lump him up a bit, but I wouldn't want some lawyer to make my defendant the poster boy for police brutality."

"You probably wouldn't leave your gun in the car overnight. I wonder what else was in that bag and why didn't he take it into his house?"

———

D octor Sharon Rubenstein hung her shingle outside one of the offices at Foothills Cooperative Counseling on High Street in Maryville. It took me less than fifteen minutes to drive there.

I waited in a cozy anteroom in a big, converted Victorian house only two blocks from the former county courthouse.

At five after four, a heavyset woman that I guessed to be in her late fifties walked out. She tried her best not to make eye contact with me, perhaps thinking I was there to sell timeshares. Or maybe she was Archie Faber's wife.

Less than two minutes later a woman in her early fifties sauntered into the waiting room. She smiled and tilted her head. "Chief Jenkins?"

I stood and returned the smile. "I am he."

She extended her hand. "Hi, I'm Sharon Rubenstein. Nice to meet you."

"Likewise. Thanks for making time for me."

"Not a problem. Please come through."

She led me to an office in the back corner of the building. The furniture complimented the architecture—Victorian-style upholstered chairs, oak lamp tables, a long oak sideboard and a roll top desk against the wall.

"This is a lovely office," I said. "You've been busy antique shopping."

She smiled like a mother just told her child was beautiful.

"I love antiques, but sometimes wonder if any of the people I see recognize or appreciate them."

"If I were your client, I'd be able to relax in this room...and tell you all my innermost secrets."

She laughed. "Are they exciting?"

Sharon Rubenstein had short red hair, which could really be called orange, a prominent nose, full lips and high Slavic cheekbones. Her knee-length black skirt, white blouse and gray cardigan fit her well, and I guessed she might visit a gym three times a week. I wouldn't have called her classically pretty, but any middle-aged guy would have found her attractive.

"I'm a small town cop. How exciting could I be?"

"I think a man in Tennessee with a downstate New York accent might have had a former life that isn't as quiet as he'd like me to believe he's now living."

"You're pretty sharp for a small town shrink."

She laughed again. "Who's originally from Brooklyn."

We devoted a few more minutes to discussing that before getting down to business.

"Do you want me to act like a traditional profiler and give you a best guess of parameters that might fit your killer or get specific about what's probably going on inside his head?" she asked.

"I've already gotten a lecture about the evils of probability and statistics. Let's go with the mental mechanics of this lunatic."

I peeked at a Regulator wall clock, saw that time was moving along briskly, but still spent time covering the basics of what Sharon wouldn't have known from media coverage.

"Let's narrow the field by fifty percent," she said. "You're looking for a man. If there are two participants acting in concert, one might be a woman, but your *lead* killer is male.

"And he's a very troubled man—troubled in a way you don't cure yourself or with daily medication. Based on what he's done locally, I wouldn't be surprised if you learned that he's done the same or worse elsewhere."

I raised my eyebrows and let out a volume of air.

"Think about it," she said. "We assume he's a local resident. With that comes the possibility of capture because of proximity. If he ever travelled, he'd be a new face in town and after he left that place, only a shadow. Since he knows how to cover his tracks well enough, he may never be associated with his deeds in other locales."

"Wow. I wanted a solution. You complicated my life."

She smiled. "If you ever locate this person, you might want to find out where he vacations or visits and check with the police there for similar unsolved murders."

"That's an obvious, but unlikable idea."

She half shrugged. "How much effort is put into finding the killers of one or two prostitutes in big cities?" she asked. "This man is smart. He knows that he might well be able to feed his addiction in an efficient way, should time and circumstances permit."

I shook my head.

"He probably started with an addiction to pornography. After enough time looking at porn and masturbating, it becomes less and less satisfying. Think of it like a combination of physically and psychologically addictive drugs. The more your tolerance builds the more volume you need to feel that kick you crave. So it is with porn."

"Addiction?" I sounded beyond disgusted.

She flipped her hands up and to the sides. "Yes, addiction. Addicted to sex and murder. For some, the act of killing is orgasmic. If he figuratively rapes them first—they're prostitutes, but in his mind it might be rape—then killing them is a bonus. He leaves a happy man. Of course, the interim between killings may be saturated with self-loathing, but nonetheless, he returns to what he needs most."

"I'd rather admit to gasping for a drink."

"Most of us would. But I'm sure this man progressed from simple porn to sado-masochistic porn and even to snuff porn. Once he watched enough snuff films, I'm guessing he wanted to try it himself."

"What about a second killer or an accomplice?"

"That's very possible. Generally speaking, people tend to associate with likeminded individuals. Thankfully, this trait usually manifests itself with more socially acceptable pastimes. But with two sexual deviants? Why not? It's happened before."

"Yikes."

She chuckled. "Yikes, indeed. Now, I'm anticipating your next question. How do you recruit an assistant for something like this or how do two weirdoes meet and strike up a partnership?"

"Is *weirdo* an acceptable psychological term?"

"For me it is. Look, who knows how a pair of—what shall we call them—homicidal bi-sexual pedophiles meet? Your imagination is the limit. But don't let anyone tell you that some strange cosmic force doesn't allow them to recognize each other. I've run across that many, many times. People say opposites attract, but let me tell you, those outside the mainstream with a commonality attract like moths to a flame. Somehow, they recognize each other. Believe that."

"So, theoretically," I said, "they meet somewhere, somehow and engage in a conversation that leads them to this common ground. Somehow they grow closer and venture out together to patronize young male or female prostitutes, possibly for threesomes. Then somewhere along the line, one of the partners explains that "snuff sex" provides the ultimate orgasm. And off they go?"

She nodded thoughtfully. "Quite possibly."

I threw my hands up about shoulder high. "Well hell. That makes my life easy."

Her eyes lit up, and her smile widened. "You get what you pay for."

"Yeah." I shook my head. "I appreciate your help. No one ever said a cop was put on earth to live a carefree life."

"That's a stoic and healthy way to look at it. Do you have any more questions?"

I sighed. "Sure. Why do people get meaningless tattoos, and why does my neighbor need nine cats?"

She laughed and shook her head. "Tough questions. I'm still trying to figure out why my young niece dyed her hair blue."

"Okay, I know when I'm beat."

She stood up and smoothed down her skirt. "While I'd love to sit here and explore the universe of mental disorders with you, I do have a five o'clock customer."

"I understand. Schedules are schedules. But I've always wanted to subscribe to Dial-A-Shrink. If I need more meaningful help, are you game?"

She extended her hand, and we shook again. "If I didn't answer your calls, I'd be just another lonely middle-aged psychotherapist. So, you bet, I'm your girl."

———

The next morning, I dropped into a chair next to Clete Dunn's desk in a third floor room shared by two other investigators and several ADAs. The room looked relatively new like most of the Justice Center, but Spartan compared to the FBI's field office in Knoxville.

"You're on the road early t'day," he said.

Clete was in his mid-fifties, had mostly gray hair, short, parted on the left and combed in a Joe College style across his forehead. He could have lost fifteen pounds but was far from out of shape. He wore a short sleeve white shirt, solid light blue tie and gray slacks.

"I can't understand why," I said. "After I talk with you and drop off the latest case notes to Ryan Leary, we're about dead in the water."

"No new leads?"

"No old or new leads on the Rosanna Wakefield murder. That crime scene was so well sanitized I truly believe a cop stuck his fingers into that pie."

"I hate to hear things like that. Cops all over are taking cheap shots from every big mouth activist out there."

"Like the right Reverend Hal Crofton and his cronies."

Clete closed his eyes briefly and shook his head. "Don't even mention that name."

"It's too bad humps like Crofton and the public in general put their mouths in gear before they know any relative facts or get a basic knowledge of the law."

He gritted his teeth. "That would be too much to ask…Please don't get me started."

I smiled. "Okay. I'm off the soapbox."

"How 'bout your second murder?"

"The male prostitute? That one's simple. Nothing makes any sense except a person in his occupation is always at risk. His being a Charlie's List hooker is all that ties him to the other Strangler victims. We've conducted dozens of interviews and came up with zilch. I can't even give you a juicy tidbit that I haven't already told the media."

"Don't know what ta tell ya, Sam. But I did run down a list of big SUVs in the law enforcement community. I got ya department owned vehickles only. You're gonna have ta get your man to work on privately-owned SUVs in a cop's household."

I nodded, and he handed me several sheets of paper.

"Archie Faber drives a black Crown Victoria," he said, "Which hasn't been in for repairs or service lately. And he wasn't drivin' a loaner SUV that night. The top sheet's got the names of a few people at the sheriff's office who drive those big tubs. And it includes your buddy Ryan Leary."

I nodded again. "They are the police executive's current ride-of-choice."

"Yep. Toss in my boss, the DA himself and the other pages show smaller PDs who run an SUV or two. I didn't list any marked vehickles or get inta the Feds."

"That's great. Thanks, Clete."

"Other than that, I got no good advice for ya."

"Good advice is currently at a premium." I shrugged. "I might resort to using a Ouija board or getting help from that good-looking fortune teller with the business up on Alcoa Highway."

"Anybody asks ya where ya got the info on their ve-hickles, tell 'em from that Gypsy's crystal ball and forget I had anythin' ta do with it."

Chief Deputy Ryan Leary hung his hat on the second floor of the Justice Center in a corner office overlooking a newly constructed Georgian-style bank headquarters, US Highway 321 and Blount Memorial Hospital. Ryan occupied a chunk of prime real estate. The task force and Lew Schmecke, legendary detective, were set up in a large utility room down the hall.

I dropped a folder with copies of my two cases on Ryan's desk.

"Not a hell of a lot there," I said as I sat in one of his guest chairs and sighed. "Besides the basics, there's a list of anyone we interviewed, so you can try to get a match with names that have shown up before. Other than that...I don't see squat."

"I'll give this to Lew. He's brought in a couple of his computer experts. They may turn up something."

Keep dreaming, sport. I'm complaining about paying Lonnie Ray seventy-five bucks an hour. What is that bottom feeder Schmecke charging you?

"Let's hope so," I said.

He thumbed through the reports and tossed the folder into his out box. "One male and one female? Both hookers? Both young?"

"Yep. I'll assume Wakefield, the female, was done by the Strangler. Bowman, the male, I'm not so sure. Unless the Strangler is trying to throw us a curve."

He nodded, looking thoughtful.

I interrupted his thinking. "I heard Schmecke and two of your guys are exhuming a body?"

"Uh-huh. Victim number four."

"And you're looking at a pair of local cops?"

He nodded. "One from Alcoa and one from Maryville."

Ryan needed to tell me more. "Do I know them?"

"Peyton Longshore from Alcoa and Alfred Fenceline from Maryville."

"Longshore and Fenceline? Those are real names?"

He laughed, but still looked tired and frustrated. "I'll get one of the boys to fax you what we've got so far."

I couldn't keep the skepticism from my voice. "Do they look promising?"

"Still waiting for the results of the new autopsy."

That wasn't much of an answer.

———

I hadn't exaggerated when I spoke to Clete Dunn. I literally had nothing more to do on the cases.

In the early afternoon, Lonnie Ray Wilson walked into my office.

"Hey," he said, a little sheepishly.

"How's it goin'."

He shrugged. "Listen, I'm not going to charge you for yesterday."

I frowned and dropped the pen I had been using onto my blotter. "Why?"

"I couldn't produce. Sorry."

"Ah, typical male performance anxiety."

He grinned, but didn't look amused.

"I thought I could have tracked that guy Andy down. I wanted to explain."

"Sit. Speak. You want coffee?"

Lonnie shook his head. "No thanks on the coffee." He dropped into a guest chair and crossed his legs. "I found a trail, but couldn't settle on a definite beginning or end. And, even if I could, I doubt the provider would give us any information."

"That's not cricket."

"It's the way those people are. And based on where they are I don't think anyone around here could do anything about it."

"Really?"

"I started out with an IP from Amsterdam. From there, I got bounced to Romania, then Turkey, Latvia, the Philippines...you don't want me to keep going. Either this guy was well versed in covering his cyber ass or he paid for someone else to route his business around the world."

"I hate these progressive criminals."

"Yeah, not like cruisin' the streets looking for bad guys, is it?"

I shook my head. "Not even close. It sounds like Andy has something he wants hidden."

"You don't do something like this to keep your mother from learning you visit porn sites."

"I wish I knew how to find Andy."

"I don't know how else I can help with that. So the time is on the house."

"Nonsense. You worked. You get paid. That's the way it goes. We've all come up dry with these cases. That's police work."

"I just don't feel right about it."

"Don't sweat it. I might be calling you for something else. Repay me by making Prospect PD a priority customer."

"You got a deal."

———

The six o'clock news brought a surprise. Kate and I had finished dinner and were sitting in the living room sipping the remains of a bottle of New Zealand sauvignon blanc, watching TV before attacking the dinner dishes.

Jack Larsen, one of the co-anchors from WNXX, shocked me.

"Lawyers for Farris Tingle," he said, "the accused Maryville man arrested for stealing a duffle bag from Blount County Chief Deputy Sheriff Ryan Leary's department SUV has filed a Federal lawsuit against Leary, Sheriff Joe Don Hartung and several detectives and deputies. Tingle alleges being beaten, tortured, intimidated and threatened after his arrest.

"Mr. Tingle, currently free on bail, has charges of grand larceny, criminal mischief and resisting arrest pending in Blount County

Criminal Court. He and his lawyers held a press conference at the Federal building on Locust Street in Knoxville only a half-hour ago."

The video shifted to a crowd on the steps of the Federal building. A seedy-looking article, who I assumed was Farris Tingle, stood behind and to the left of a Blount County public defender named Scottie Ringgold. At Ringgold's side, and the center of attention, stood a slick operator named Perry Chalmers, a five-hundred-dollar an hour shyster who usually produced positive results for the parties he represented.

The audio came on, and Chalmers used a slightly southern accented and mostly theatrical voice to address a half-dozen reporters backed up by video and still photographers.

"When I heard the circumstances of Mr. Tingle's arrest," he said, "subsequent *questioning* and pre-arraignment incarceration, I called Mr. Ringgold at the public defender's office and offered my services pro bono. Mr. Tingle agreed to accept my assistance."

A reporter shouted, "What was the amount of bail?"

"Mr. Tingle was released on $200,000 bond. His parents used their home as collateral."

"Who beat your client?" yelled another.

"Mr. Tingle, still handcuffed, was initially pummeled by two plainclothes detectives. Later, he was beaten, tortured and threatened by Chief Leary of the Blount County Sheriff's Office."

"What was stolen from Leary's vehicle?" a third asked.

"We've filed a Federal civil rights violation case with the US attorney. Mr. Tingle gave FBI agents a detailed statement that they will use as a basis for their investigation. It's more appropriate that you ask a representative of the Justice Department for further information."

Before another reporter could shout out another question, Chalmers cracked a smile and continued. "I will tell you this. The evidence Mr. Tingle gave is damning. I am confident that the FBI agents will substantiate it all. I think you can expect a number of indictments forthcoming."

Too many reporters yelled the same thing, making it impossible to attribute a question to anyone in particular. "Indictments for what?"

With a grin pumped up to high wattage and his pearly whites showing as sparkly as the grill of a '55 Buick Roadmaster, Chalmers said, "Besides brutalizing Mr. Tingle and attempting to cover up the gross misconduct of these public officials, some *very embarrassing things*. I can only ask you to wait patiently for the results of the investigation."

The two attorneys and Farris Tingle pushed their way down the steps and through the group of reporters to where a late model Lincoln Town Car waited at the curb on Locust Street.

Twenty-year-old Tingle was an unsightly specimen, at about five-eight and maybe a hundred and forty pounds. His dark crew cut hadn't been trimmed in at least a month, and his cheeks hadn't been scratched by a razor in twice as long. What he might have called a beard was nothing more than patchy stubble that looked more like dirt than facial hair. What skin I could see was scattered with tiny red pimples and with abrasions and bruises on his forehead, cheeks and chin. His pasty, ashen complexion suggested more than a passing fancy with methamphetamines.

"That's a good-looking troop," I said.

"Mmm," Kate offered. "Isn't Perry Chalmers a pretty high-priced attorney?"

"Up there with the best. I guess he's looking to write off his time as an advertising expense. He'll get plenty of ink with this case."

"Do you think the chief and two detectives really beat that boy?"

"The *boy* stole a cop's gun from a cop's company car. Leary has a history of *bending* the rules and not shying away from physical contact. What do you think?"

"If he gets through this without losing his job, I think he should keep his hands in his pockets."

"That's a very big *if*. Perry Chalmers does not play by the rules, and the FBI does not whitewash cases against cops, regardless of their rank."

"It's a shame to throw away a big career over losing your temper."

"Who says he lost his temper? Maybe he enjoyed it. Either way, it's a problem cops have faced since the days of the Ancient Egyptian PD."

"Did the pharaoh have an internal affairs bureau?"

"That gives me an idea. I'll write a story for Police Chief Magazine —*The Rat Squad Throughout History.*"

"Oh, that should make you even more popular with police administrators the world over."

"As I used to tell my mother, I wasn't put on earth to be popular, just efficient."

"So, tell me, efficient one, what do you think Perry Chalmers alluded to as being *very embarrassing?*"

"That *is* a very good question, sweetie. Now I have something to do tomorrow. And I just might have an answer for you in twenty-four hours."

CHAPTER TWELVE

J ohn, Bettye and I were huddled around her desk like three running backs, wondering what play to use next.

"Did you hear that lawyer's last comment?" John asked, referring to last night's news conference. "Something *very* embarrassing. Like what?"

"Well, it *is* embarrassing to leave your duty gun in your police car on the night someone breaks into it," Bettye said.

"True," I said, "but Chalmers loves to build media tension before dropping a bomb that could imbed documentary shrapnel in the minds of potential jurors. He's a sleaze, but he's good at his job. There's something else up his sleeve."

"What do you think was in the bag, Boss? What could embarrass Leary?"

"Good question. If we ask our friends at the sheriff's office, we'd only put them on the spot. They'd have to clam up or rat out a co-worker. If I were in Leary's position, John, would you gossip about me to just anyone?"

"Boss, how could you ask that?" He really looked offended.

"See what I mean? You're shocked I would even suggest such a thing."

"Yeah, I see your point."

"The blue wall of silence?" Bettye said.

"Sort of," I said. "We don't know who was present when this alleged beating took place. If I called Shuman or Stallins or whomever snooping around, they'd think one of two things—I'm too damn nosey or I'm fishing for info for my friends at the FBI."

"But you'd never—" she said.

"Well, I am nosey, but Ralph would never ask me to become his snitch—not really."

"You sure, Boss?" John asked.

"Yeah. I trust Ralph. But nothing says I can't ask *him* a few questions."

———

I called Ralph Oliveri's cell phone and got him on the fifth ring.

"Hey," I said, "where are you? You usually pick up immediately."

"I'm driving, and some asshole just cut me off so he could drive into one of the car dealers near the airport. The traffic is ridiculous today."

"You're in Blount County. Coming to see us?"

"I'm working on something."

"Ahh. Some shit about that chief deputy down here, huh?"

"Uh...yeah. I wouldn't want that hanging over me."

"You working on that?"

"Why do you ask?"

"No reason. Just nosey."

"Well, yeah, sorta."

"Part of the team? Who's the lucky primary?"

"You kiddin'? We're just the grunts. They sent a civil rights team from Nashville. That lawyer, Chalmers, arranged for one before he brought his boy in to make the complaint. We've got a supervisor, six agents and an AUSA who'll act as special prosecutor hanging around the office."

"Yikes. They brought in the *pros from Dover*. I guess Leary is screwed."

"I don't know yet. Is he the kind of guy who would torture a prisoner?"

Time to work my magic.

"Ralphie, hang on a minute. I was just shooting the breeze here. You really want to get serious about this?"

"I was just askin'. You got any history with Leary?"

"I guess I'm just a little sensitive because of what happened once."

"Like what?"

"Off the record?"

"You know I shouldn't agree to that."

"Okay. The reason I called—"

"Hey, with all the favors I've done for you, don't you think you owe me a little help here? If you know something, you'd save me lots of work."

"A nudge in the right direction is one thing. Becoming an informant is another."

"I didn't ask you to testify, did I?

"Then is this off the record? I owe you, but—"

He didn't let me finish.

"Yeah, yeah. Make it off the record."

"You sure? I really don't want to be part of an official investigation. I've got too much to do with my homicides and this task force and all."

"Yes. I said off the record."

I cleared my throat. "Leary is no stranger to innovative interrogation techniques. He spent a number of years at the DA's office, you know."

His tone went up a couple of octaves. "Innovative how?"

"Come on, Ralphie, don't get me in the middle."

"Oh, Goddamnit," he said abruptly. "Traffic just stopped. A couple of trailers with two halves of a modular home and their escort cars are making a left turn from the right lane. They won't get across the highway in this lifetime."

"You've got that right. A small, fast car can't make an easy left off Alcoa Highway during the best of times."

I heard a horn blowing in the background.

"Back to my question," Ralph said. "Innovative how? Were you present when he tuned up a suspect?"

"Oh, man, you're gonna put me on the spot." I took a moment to sigh for dramatic effect. "How about this? Tell me what the charges are, and I'll give you an honest opinion if they might be in Leary's repertoire."

"Look, I'm only one of the field men doing roadwork for these Nashville guys. I don't want to jam up another cop, but this guy Tingle made some big accusations. Hang on. We're moving again. I'll get off 129 at Hunt Road. Lemme pull over and talk."

"Take your time, buddy. I'm not going anywhere."

I'm not a religious man, but I was praying Ralph wouldn't ask why I had really called. I hoped he'd forget to ask. After a few moments, he came back on the line.

"Okay," he said. "I'm off the road. Listen, you gotta promise you won't repeat what I say."

"Cross my heart, buddy."

"Tingle says one of the uniformed cops who collared him called the dick on standby—Bo Stallins. Stallins got there and called Leary. I took Stallins' statement yesterday. Then Leary did something odd. He told Stallins he was reassigning the case to two other detectives, Bonnet and Turner."

"That is odd. Those two have been detached from regular CID duty to work on the Riverside Strangler task force."

"See what I mean? According to Tingle's statement, those two took over from Stallins and cleared the squad room. Then they took turns beating on this kid, repeatedly asking him what he did with the rest of the contents of the gym bag. Only the kid swears he took nothing. That wasn't good enough, so they kept on grinding him through the ringer until Leary got there."

"Did the kid know Leary before that night?"

"Not personally, but Leary introduced himself before he disappeared with the gym bag."

"Wait, wait, wait. What do you mean he disappeared with the bag?"

"Just what I said. He was gone for an hour or so and then returned to take a turn smacking Tingle around."

"So he took evidence out of the building? And then comes back to kick the kid's ass?"

"Yeah, but you haven't heard the best part yet."

"Oh, jeez. Maybe I shouldn't hear this, but...go ahead, tell me."

"When Leary returned, he brought the black bag back and gave it to Bonnet. Then he starts what Tingle called torture."

"Do I want to hear this?"

"Hey, paly, you got me goin'. You're in for the long haul." Ralph took a moment to snicker like a little kid divulging a secret to his best friend. "Leary asks Tingle what he saw in the bag. Tingle starts out saying nothing. Leary didn't buy that, so after a half-dozen slaps in the head, the kid says a gun and other stuff. Leary's still not satisfied, so he pulls off Tingle's jeans and Jockey shorts and makes him stand in the middle of the room with his thing hanging out, while Leary asks him the same question over and over. To show he wasn't satisfied with the kid's answers, Leary laid a few shots into the gut. The kid figures six or seven times."

"Meanwhile, the kid is ricocheting off the walls and floor with no drawers on."

"No," Ralph said. "Bonnet and Turner are holding him up like a heavy bag. Now, Leary puts on sap gloves and before each question, he lays some knuckle to the kid's head. After three of those, Tingle gives Leary a more complete inventory."

"Which was?"

"You're gonna love this."

"I doubt it, but go ahead."

"The kid describes a black automatic. Leary carries a .40 caliber Glock, so the kid has credibility. Then he says four or five magazines that he calls full of *nasty* porn."

"Isn't all porn nasty?"

"Yeah, but when Tingle was questioned in our office, it took Marty Saunders fifteen minutes to drag more out of him. *Nasty* to him meant young girls mostly, but a smattering of young boys—mostly Asian. He thinks they were foreign magazines. Besides that, he says there were a bunch of cases holding DVDs with nasty porn flicks."

"How young is young?"

"Very young. All early teens."

Ralph couldn't see me, but I shook my head in disbelief. "What does Leary say about this?"

"He doesn't. He lawyered up. He's using J.R. Tolbert."

"Another big gun. Are you guys betting on Chalmers or Tolbert?"

"If they square off, it will be in civil court. But at the moment, it's a tag team match: Leary and Tolbert versus the FBI and Justice Department."

"Sure. You're going to do him criminally."

"Yeah, we're not Chalmer's PIs. But wait, there's more."

"You're gonna super-size my order if I call within the next five minutes?"

"Ha! How about add to the gym bag three or four vials of what Tingle the meth-head recognized as crack?"

"And Leary didn't immediately jump on a story that this stuff was evidence he just forgot to lock up overnight?"

"Leary wouldn't say spit. His lawyer said Tingle is a liar, and aside from the gun and a few items of gym clothing, there was nothing else in the bag."

"Because when he disappeared, Leary purged the contents."

"Good guess, Sherlock."

"This is some shit, Ralph. Who do you believe?"

"I saw Tingle. Somebody tuned him big time. But look, he's small potatoes, just a local shithead burglar who was looking for a dark house to hit. When he found Leary's open SUV, he grabbed the bag and ran. Unlucky for him, less than fifteen minutes later, a deputy sees him trotting down the road in a neighborhood where there aren't any resident shitheads and stops him. Tingle is nervous and jerky and didn't come up with any reasonable answers, so the deputy calls for backup. Then deputy number two arrives, and they toss Tingle and look in the gym bag and get a surprise. There's an ID tag with a familiar name on it attached to the bag, so they take their perp back to the Justice Center forthwith. Now the dicks and Leary get involved, and we're back to the beginning of my story."

"Two more people involved. What do the uniforms say about the contents of the bag?"

Ralph laughed briefly. "Cops are hot shit when you question them. I've talked to more eloquent dirt bags. Both say all they saw was a gun and didn't look any further. The stories were so similar, I'd swear they studied a script."

"So, if we look to the future in my crystal ball, when they realize that they could go down for hindering prosecution, obstruction and accessories to everything that transpired in the squad room, you figure they'll flip on Leary."

"Don't forget lying to a Federal officer."

"Of course, something we locals can't fall back on. Okay, another felony to add to their resume."

"It won't be long. A couple of guys on the civil rights team are good interrogators."

"And I'm guessing neither of the two cops are close to having enough time on the job to retire and would lose their pension time as well as their freedom."

"You got it. Bonnet and Turner are close, too. Bonnet's got almost twenty from three different jobs, and Turner is a few years short. Let's see what kind of heroes they are."

"Any possibility Tingle is fabricating the porno and drugs to get back at Leary for the beating?"

"Possible, but I doubt it. The bag went to the lab. If they come up with any trace of crack cocaine, Leary is toast."

"Not one of the sheriff's finest hours."

"Not hardly."

––––––––

I f Dr. John H. Watson wrote the next scene in my workday, it might have read like this:

The aging Irish detective burst into the police station in a state of abject flummox. His usually ruddy complexion had turned to a hue of crimson, and his breathing was most labored. Upon meeting with his chief constable, the overwrought sleuth attempted to compose himself, and after no small means of effort, ejaculated, "My dear Jenkins, you shall be most intrigued with the data I gleaned from the miscreant Bowman."

To this, his long time friend and superior officer said, "Good lord, Gallagher, but you're in a state of mental discomfort. Pray relax yourself, and regale me with what promises to be a most singular narrative."

In reality, this is what happened: "Hey, Boss, Boss, you gotta hear this. I talked to that mutt Arlo Bowman, and you won't believe what he said."

"Oh, yeah? What happened?"

"Oh, man, what a hump." John Gallagher looked over at Bettye Lambert apologetically. "Sorry, Sarge, but you hadda meet this guy. Boss, he sounded like a card-carrying *homophiliac*."

I raised my eyebrows. Bettye did her best to hide a smile.

"You sure, John?"

"Yeah, Boss. He as much as said that if he knew his son was gonna turn out to be gay, he woulda drowned him at birth."

"Wow, that's radical parenting."

"And that's not all he said, Boss. It was like talking with some Grand Wizard of the Klan. He said he knew his son was a hooker and hated him even more for that. He said all prostitutes—male or female—should be stoned to death, like it says in the Bible."

"That's pretty harsh for just a misdemeanor." I looked at Bettye. "Does it really say that in the Bible?"

She shrugged. "Don't look at me, darlin'. Ask your friend, the priest."

I looked back at John. "Did he elaborate on that?"

"Not really, Boss. I quizzed him a lot, but he just ranted and raved about homosexuals and whores and how it's getting to be like *Solomon Gaddorah* around here."

Bettye couldn't contain herself. She tried to stifle a laugh, but it came out half way between a snort and a sneeze.

"That's Sodom and Gomorrah, John. Solomon Gaddorah was the prime minister of Israel years ago...or something."

He looked shocked. "Yeah?"

"Yeah. Trust me. I'm sure." I wanted to change the subject. "After all this talk, do you like this guy Arlo for killing his kid? Or even for any of the other murders?"

John wrinkled his forehead and thought for a brief moment. "Maybe his kid, Boss. But he wouldn't know shit...Sorry, Sarge...about cleaning up a crime scene. He was almost out of control talking about Toby, but he didn't mention anything about the other victims."

"Was he fixated on stoning them, or could he be flexible enough to strangle them?"

"Who knows, Boss? A guy like Arlo is crazy enough to do anything."

"Oh, great."

"Could he account for his whereabouts the night his son was murdered?" Bettye asked.

"Says he was in a sports bar up in north Knoxville."

"Must be some class place," I said.

"If guys like Arlo hang out in that bar," John said, "I wouldn't walk in there alone."

———

Later that day, I received an unexpected phone call.

"Hey, yew doin' aw rot t'day?"

I recognized the voice.

"Windy?"

"Yessir. Wendell P. Hatmaker. The one and only Windy, like the hamburgers."

He said the same thing every time he introduced himself.

"I was going to call you about something, but you saved me the dime."

"Well boy howdy, ain't that somethin'? Whatchew up ta?"

"Me? I'm just lounging around up to my eyeballs in a couple of homicides."

"Heard 'bout 'em. Unnerstand y'all are part o' that Strangler task force."

"A small but not insignificant part."

"I'll bet. Hey listen, bud, I gotta talk with ya 'bout your boss on that task force."

"I guess you heard about his troubles with the Feds?"

"Did I ever. Cain't say he's one o' my favorite people, and I'm gonna give ya some free ad-vice 'bout him. Whether ya take it's up ta yew. But what I'm gonna tell ya is gospel—*gar-anteed*."

"That's one hell of a lead in. What do you know about Leary that I don't?"

"Plenny, 'cause we ain't never let none o' this out nowhere. 'Cept fer our boss callin' the sheriff down in Blount County. Other'n that, we've done kept a lid on all this."

"Man, you've got my curiosity in high gear. What's up?"

"I kinda hate doin' this on the phone."

"We're secure down here. You got problems up by you?"

"Ya never know."

"I can meet you somewhere."

"Might be better."

"I'm at your disposal."

"Could meet ya half way."

"There are not many civilized places between Prospect and Knoxville. We've got time before you finish a day tour. Give me thirty minutes, and I'll meet you in the bar at Chesapeake's. I'll buy you a beer and listen."

"Okay. Works fer me."

"Just so I know, are you doing this on your own, or do your bosses want me to get this information?"

"My boss knows, but he ain't said nuthin' ta the sheriff yet."

"I'm guessing this is big stuff."

"Look, Sam, you've done me a couple big favors and ain't never asked fer nuthin' in return. I figger I owe ya. And this might keep ya from snugglin' up too close ta this Leary character."

"You've piqued my interest, partner. I'll see you at Chesapeake's in a half-hour. I'll be the tall, dark and handsome stranger with a rose in his lapel."

"Ha! Not hardly."

―――――

I pulled into the lot for Chesapeake's restaurant and parked next to a lackluster gold-colored unmarked Ford police car that I assumed belonged to Windy Hatmaker.

Inside, I stood next to a two-foot tall by yard wide painting of three Maryland skipjacks docked somewhere on the Eastern Shore and waited for an attractive, middle-aged blonde to return to the hostess station.

"One?" she asked.

"I'm meeting someone at the bar," I said.

She smiled, slid a menu back into the rack and dipped her head a half inch. "Have a nice day."

Between the lobby and the barroom, I passed more nautical artwork depicting the tidewater region. Colored floats and fishnets hung on the rough wood columns, and the soft sounds of the big band era played through hidden speakers.

I found Windy Hatmaker sitting at the bar behind a schooner of lager, talking with the bartender.

I pushed a stool away to give me room next to Windy and spoke to the barman. "Did you check his proof? He looks too old to drink."

The young man who had been drying a highball glass smiled, but didn't comment.

Windy said, "Hey, whaddaya say, big feller? Yer rot on time."

"That's me, Johnny on the spot."

I laid a twenty on the bar. "Can I have a pint of Black Bear? And when my father here finishes this one, bring him another."

"Yes, sir," the barman said and moved toward the draught handles.

"Let's grab a table so you can tell me all your secrets," I suggested.

Windy slipped off the barstool. "Lead the way, *Keemo-Sabby*."

I picked up the glass of dark ale the bartender dropped off, the change from my twenty and left a couple bucks tip. We took a round table in the back corner of the lounge.

"Okay, I'm all ears," I said, dropping into a heavy wooden captain's chair.

"Ya prob'ly ain't gonna believe this," he began. "Well, mebbe ya will, now that this druggie burglar is makin' a detailed statement against Leary. Best I kin tell ya is yer new boss ain't no stranger up here in north Knoxville."

Windy Hatmaker was in his mid-fifties and medium-sized except for a double chin and basketball tummy. His clothes always looked like he bought them at the Salvation Army on half-price day. His uniform of the day was a green and black hound's tooth sport jacket over a white shirt, striped tie and brown slacks. He wore his wavy gray-streaked, reddish brown hair combed straight back.

"Let's call Leary my temporary associate, shall we? Now, your statement sounds like it deserves an explanation." I ended my line with a long drink from the glass of walnut-colored ale.

"You hear anythin' about Leary's girlfriend?"

I shook my head.

"She's a young junkie whore. Not bad lookin', but got lots o' wear and tear on her."

"How young is young?"

"She must be 'bout twenny-three, twenny-four now, but could pass fer younger with plenty o' makeup. But they's been t'gether fer years now. She's jest a juvenile when they tied up—gar-ranteed."

"Well, if he likes them that young, maybe this girl is getting close to her expiration date."

"Ha. But she probably ain't goin' nowheres 'cause she's got him by the short hairs after all he's been doin' fer her. Got her a sheet full o' solicitin' and possession arrests. Pled out on all o' them. Paid her fines. Mighta been on probation some. She likes ta drop Leary's name when she gets arrested. Says they's in love. Musta been grabbed and let go a lot more times than she was arrested. You know how some cops are."

I set my glass on the table with a click. "I'm sure Leary's wife would love to hear this story."

Windy snorted. "Oh, yeah. But this one I'm tellin' ya about ain't Leary's only extracurricular interest. He's been grabbed himself plenty o' times for patronizin'. Propositioned an undercover more'n once."

I shook my head, not totally able to believe what I was hearing. "Outstanding professionalism."

"I hear that. But buyin' hookers ain't all he's inta. Been caught couple times tryin' ta cop dope for his girlfriend."

"And he always gets off."

"'Course we let him go. Would you arrest the chief deputy from the neighborin' county?"

I didn't answer that, but I did sip more ale.

Windy continued. "But I kin tell ya there's plenty o' hard feelin's over him. Last time he got caught buyin' dope fer his squeeze, my lieutenant complained ta the sheriff. Then, our boss called Leary's boss and more or less said, either can him or keep him outta Knox County, 'cause next time we'll lock his ass up."

"That must have gone over like a lead balloon in Blount County."

"Be my guess, but we ain't seen him since."

"What kinda drugs are you talking about? Grass or real dope?"

"Shoot, not grass. She wants crack mostly and good ol' smack fer those special occasions. This ain't no foolin' around."

"What a jerk. I'm surprised this hasn't leaked out."

"I'm not. We done got told, 'Fergit everythin'. The press gets hold o' this and there's only one place it come from, and if no one 'fesses up, everyone o' us gets the sack. Cain't think o' one guy in CID who would want ta go back inta uniform or worse fer somethin' like this."

"Fear is a good motivator."

"You better believe that."

"And Blount County just lets this happen?"

"Yes and no. I heard a while back somebody brought Leary up on charges."

"What happened?"

"That I don't know, but he got promoted and he's still around. You figger it out."

———

The next morning, I called my buddy at the Blount County DA's office.

"Cletus, old friend, I'd like to buy you a cup of something at the Vienna Coffee House."

"Why do I not like the sound of that?"

"Hey, I'm good company."

"If only that were true. What might ya be needin'?"

"Just to pick your brain for a few minutes."

"Better not take out too much. I don't have lots ta spread around."

At 10:30, we found a table in an out of the way spot in a place almost half-full of young mommies and mature socialites. I had picked up a mug of black coffee at the counter, and Clete ordered a light and sweet.

"You worked with Ryan Leary for a few years," I said. "Ever hear of him being charged with conduct unbecoming?"

Clete gave me a dose of the evil eye. "Who told you that?"

"A little bird whispered in my ear."

"I'll bet." He took a sip of coffee. "Yeah, I remember that." He went back to the coffee.

I raised my eyebrows and spread my hands to my sides. "I'm not asking just to satisfy my morbid curiosity."

He nodded. "When Leary made lieutenant, he was assigned as chief investigator at my office."

"The job you were slated to get."

"The job I got when he left. The job I would have gotten back then if he hadn't stayed in the office."

"And sometime during his tenure as your boss, something happened."

"Exactly. He'd been keepin' company with a female of dubious reputation and tender years."

"A junior hooker?"

"A fifteen year old runaway hooker druggie."

"I thought he'd have more class."

"Yeah? Think again."

"What happened?"

"Remember the old chief deputy, Marty Hudnall?"

"I know the name."

"Well, he found out about Leary's antics and handled the investigation himself. IDed the bimbo, substantiated everything and charged Leary with conduct unbecoming."

He stopped for another sip of his sickly sweet coffee.

"And?"

"And Leary got a simple written rep which has since disappeared from his personnel file. And the DA stepped in and made nice for everyone. And Marty is now retired, and Leary has his job."

"Because of the DA?"

Clete nodded. "Ain't politics grand?"

"This conduct unbecoming thing didn't quite get scandal status. Before that, did Leary talk about catting around? Was he one of those swordsmen who kisses and tells everyone?"

"Look, I've known him for years—long before he got to be the chief investigator. He was quite proud of his ways with the ladies. I mean what kind of a guy goes on sex vacations?"

That shocked me. "Huh?"

"Don't look so surprised. He used to tell anyone he worked with about going ta Thailand ta sample the exotic wares, if ya know what I mean. Went more than once. Other stuff, too."

"And he told these stories to anyone he partnered up with?"

"Uh-huh."

I went back to shaking my head. "Did it sound like he went alone or took his wife?"

"Took his wife?"

"Yeah. Maybe they're swappers or swingers or generally into kinky stuff as a couple. It happens."

"Lord have mercy." Clete picked up where I left off shaking his head. "He never said he went with his wife. I just assumed he did these things on his own. You know, tell her he's going hunting in Alabama and ends up in Bangkok, screwing whatever he can find."

"Well, there is that possibility."

CHAPTER THIRTEEN

A t 9:30 the next morning, Bettye made a new pot of coffee, John opened a box of Entenmann's doughnut holes, and I dragged two armchairs into my office from the lobby to supplement the pair of guest chairs already there. Stan Rose walked in five minutes later, swinging an LA Dodgers cap on his index finger.

We sat for a moment before I dropped my theory on them.

"I've got a far-out idea on our Riverside Strangler."

Stan raised his eyebrows. Bettye stopped writing on the yellow pad lying on her lap and looked at me over the half lenses of her granny glasses. John licked honey glaze off his thumb after popping a doughnut hole into his mouth.

"Something happened between last night and this morning that gave you this idea?" Bettye asked.

"Yes and no. After my conversation with Clete Dunn, I got a nagging thought. At 3:49 this morning, I woke up with a working theory."

"Divine intervention?" Stanley asked.

"More like a subliminal infusion," I said. "I think it's brilliant, so there's no way I'll share credit with a deity. I'll tell you this. You guys are not going to like it. And I can't even come close to proving it, but all our circumstantial factors fit like a latex glove."

"Don't keep us in suspense, Boss," John said as he reached for another doughnut hole.

He smiled, and I scowled at his dietary habits.

"Let me start snapping together the puzzle pieces, and you may agree that Ryan Leary is the killer."

John stopped chewing and coughed—not exactly choking on his doughnut, but definitely caught off guard.

"You don't do anything half way, do you?" Stan said. It sounded more like a statement than a question.

I shrugged.

"Sammy, darlin', you know I'd never second guess you, but—"

"I know. I know. I'm not going to call a press conference or even share this possibility with anyone but you guys. Let me explain why I came to this conclusion then give me your thoughts."

No one said anything for a long moment.

John broke the ice. "Shoot, Boss. We're all ears."

"Okay. All the murders are sexually oriented, and according to my new friend, the shrink, sexually motivated—literally. She says this guy can't control himself. He *needs* this snuff sex to feel a temporary satisfaction. He's a sex junkie. He's totally abhorrent in that department. And she thinks he's smarter than the average miscreant we encounter. For us, it's like trying to catch a professional hit man who ain't no slouch."

"This is like something out of a Frederick Forsythe novel," Stan said.

"Not far from it," I said.

"I'm not a Leary fan, Boss, but why him?" John asked. "Those porn videos that were supposedly in his duffle bag aren't exactly smoking guns."

"You're correct, but as we're accumulating circumstantial evidence, they do go on the plus pile. Now, let me expand on Leary's sexual preferences. I've heard that he's made no secret of the fact that he's spared no time or expense on recreational kinky sex."

Bettye shook her head. "I can't wait to hear this."

"As with many guys, and cops in particular, who fancy themselves a stud, Leary made casual office conversation...No, I'm guessing he bragged about taking sex junkets to Thailand—highlighted by *young* and lovely Siamese girls. With an emphasis on *young*."

"Talk about sleazy," Bettye said.

"Hard to believe Leary would tell other people about that," Stan said. "And it wasn't just a onetime thing?"

"Supposedly not. It goes back to his days as a DA's investigator."

"Maybe he thinks he's something out of Hollywood," John said. "Everybody knows that *Thighland* is the sex capitol of the world."

"These trips are certainly not what the average Blount County resident takes," Bettye offered.

I raised my eyebrows. "Are you sure?"

She gave me a dirty look.

"So, Boss, we've got an embarrassing collection of porn—supposedly," John said. "But we've only got a junkie burglar's word on that. And now rumors that Leary likes degenerate vacations. That's it?"

"No, John, give me a break. There was an unaccounted-for black suburban seen at Frenchman's Holler the night Rosanna Wakefield got killed. Leary drives one of those."

"Can't be the only one," Stan said.

"As a matter of fact, no." I picked up the list of stretch SUVs driven by police personnel. "Sticking with the assumption that a cop may be the killer, here's a list of PD Suburbans. So Leary's not alone with that. We've only got to narrow down the vehicle in question to his—if it was."

"Is there more?" Bettye asked.

"Those were just a few of the heavies, and I've got a bit more from one of my confidential sources, but before I get to that, let's stay with the basic premise that the killer is an experienced investigator of major crimes—one who knows what to look for and how to sanitize a crime scene."

John showed me the malevolent grin he uses when he wants to look like an evil leprechaun. "We could say that about you, Boss."

"See why I hate you, John?"

Bettye and Stan snickered.

"Normally, John, I'd chase you into the parking lot with a fire ax if you said something like that. But this is serious business, so I'll wait until later to kill you. I need your input first."

"I'm just trying to be part of your *rainstorming* process, Boss."

"And we all just appreciate the shit out if it, John."

"Leary being basically bulletproof always bothered me," Stanley said. "Word is, he's gotten away with more than the average guy who stretches the rules."

"He is the DA's pet," Bettye said.

"We're also thinking about a pair of killers, Boss. You think the DA might be Leary's accomplice?"

I shook my head. "That's pretty far out. Two dominant personalities. You'd think there would be some serious conflicts. And do we know anything about Calvin Pitts' sexual preferences?"

Everyone shook their heads.

"Hard to believe Pitts would make the same water cooler conversation as Leary," Stan said.

"Yeah," I said. "If there are two, I'm inclined to think Leary would have a helper and not a full partner."

"Sounds about right," Stan said. "Can you get more input from your friend, the shrink?"

"She says yes. But at this time, I don't want to spread my theory around too far."

"Talk *hypotheoretically* to her, Boss," John suggested.

I rolled my eyes but let that go. Bettye and Stan smiled, but didn't encourage him by laughing.

"I could, but let's go back to that other biggie I said I learned. And this is a documented fact."

I elaborated on the saga told to me by Windy Hatmaker and how Cletus Dunn confirmed it.

"Lord have mercy," Bettye said. "Little girls in Thailand, 'nasty pornography' in his duffle bag and now a young prostitute with a drug habit. How does he keep his job?"

"Good question. Another thing that bothers me is how he's repeatedly refused any FBI assistance—even though the Strangler task force is virtually dead in the water."

John smiled. "He did hire the 'legendary detective' to help out."

"I'm not sure Schmecke is a hindrance, but I've got serious doubts about his being much help."

"You think Leary refused Federal help because he doesn't want outside investigators to find more about the killer?" Stan asked.

"If my theory is correct—yeah. I'm not a big fan of our G-men, but they do have resources and funding far beyond mortal cops."

"Sammy," Bettye said, "you've messed with a few pretty high-powered public officials before, but this would be something else."

———

B y the time we finished our brainstorming session, John had eaten more than half the doughnut holes, and everyone left with a few jobs.

John would pursue the possibility that Toby Bowman's death might not be attributable to the Riverside Strangler and look at Arlo as our prime suspect.

Bettye would continue to work with Lonnie Ray Wilson and attempt to backtrack any of the victims to Leary.

Stan would have the unenviable job of surreptitiously probing the Blount County deputies for additional information or just rumors about Leary's peccadilloes.

I would revisit Sharon Rubenstein and run a few hypothetical questions past her and broach a new topic—one that might net me information a witness might not know he possessed.

CHAPTER FOURTEEN

D r. Rubenstein told me she finished her appointments at five p.m. and asked for another fifteen minutes to tidy up her office before taking on my job. Gallant gentleman that I am, and considering my consultations were 'on the arm' as a favor to me and our mutual friend, Mo Rappaport, I offered to buy Sharon dinner.

She liked the idea of the Cholan Garden, a Southeast Asian restaurant in Maryville. She knew they served excellent food and the high-backed booths offered us privacy to discuss Ryan Leary's future.

Without mentioning the chief deputy by name, I ran my theory past her and outlined all the embarrassing details of Leary's kinky propensities while waiting for our Tom Yum soup.

The doctor wore a silky blue print dress belted at the waist. It fit so well, she could have been an advertisement on how good girls over fifty could look if they wanted to.

"Is this Ryan Leary we're talking about?" she asked.

"What makes you ask that?"

"You're more transparent than you think."

I shrugged. "Oh, well. I really shouldn't say."

"I think you just did."

"Who, me?"

She made a face. "So, he has a history of violence against suspects beyond the allegations we've just heard about?"

"Are we operating under the same doctor's confidentiality business a regular client can expect?"

"I'm the soul of discretion, dahling. Whatever you say is perfectly confidential. My lips are sealed." She did the locking her lips thing children do when they want you to think they can keep a secret.

"Good. Okay. One reliable source said, 'When we saw Ryan Leary show up with his boys, we expected some kind of trouble.' So, yeah, he has an established reputation as not only a knuckle-man, but one who also relies on intimidation and humiliation to get cooperation from a suspect."

"Such as?"

"Making uncooperative subjects stand in a squad room naked from the waist down while being questioned or tuned up."

She waved a hand dismissively. "That's neither unique nor innovative, but under most circumstances effective—almost Gestapo-like."

"Maybe Leary wears a black leather trench coat during the colder months. I'll check."

She smiled. "You do that, sweetheart. Look, I think your theory is pretty good, but after all these years of watching Law & Order, even I know you couldn't get an indictment on what you've got."

"Yeah. I don't need Jack McCoy to remind me of that."

"Any physical evidence linking him to even one of the murders?"

I didn't answer, while a waitress dropped off our soup—two bowls chockfull of an orangey broth with mushrooms and chicken.

The waitress checked the level of our tea pot before saying in heavily accented English, "Your dinner will be out in ten minutes, maybe fifteen."

"Thanks," I said, and she shuffled off toward the kitchen.

Sharon had ordered mu-shu chicken, and I couldn't resist the marinated Vietnamese shrimp with spicy vegetables.

"Physical evidence? Ha, we haven't got a clue," I said, continuing our conversation of moments ago. "And unless Leary is hiding something from the rest of the task force, there is none. Nothing. Bupkis."

She smiled again. "Not many Tennessee cops speak Yiddish. It's refreshing."

"Yeah, that's me, the Yiddish speaking detective, the guy with no evidence and so far, no witnesses to speak of—except one guy who claims he can't remember much." I shrugged and took a spoonful of soup without slurping. "But he's all I've got, an interesting guy from an even more interesting spot."

I dove back into the Tom Yum Gai, but Sharon wouldn't leave me in peace.

"Oh, come on. You can't set your hooks like that and not explain more. Who and what is so interesting?"

I explained about the Rosanna Wakefield meeting place at Frenchman's Holler.

She looked genuinely surprised. "I didn't know we had a proper bordello in Blount County."

"Then I guess you don't have many local politicians or police administrators as clients who divulge their innermost and sexy secrets."

"Police administrators?" Sharon raised her eyebrows to the top floor.

I grinned like a bad little boy. "Present company excepted, of course."

"Of course. But what about our person of interest? Is he a regular?"

"According to the proprietress, no." I shrugged. "Her employees are older than those who attract Mr. Leary."

"And she's reliable?"

"I think so."

She gave me a look full of unspoken questions. "Hmmm."

"Farley Gayton is a guy who would like to keep his shady but well-paying job and go through life not getting involved. I think he'd be diligent looking for something that threatened his boss and her operation but wouldn't pay close attention to the finer points I'd consider good po-leece observation."

"If you think he saw something, but just breezed past it, maybe he could be coaxed into a better recall."

I felt a crooked smile cross my face. "I remember a few enemy agents 'coaxed' into providing information with the help of a field phone and pair of alligator clips during my army days. I can't exactly ask someone to do that."

She had finished her soup and placed the spoon between the cup and saucer. "We can probably come up with more humane ways to *coax* information out of someone. I'm assuming that if your man did see something and just passed on by, as you say, I might be able to help his recall while under hypnosis."

"I was hoping you'd say something like that." I racked up my spoon and pushed the soup cup to the side. "You'd swing a pocket watch and say, 'Look deeply into my eyes. You're getting drowsy, very drowsy?'"

Sharon smiled, the way shrinks smile when a client says something dreadfully inane. "Were you trying to imitate Sigmund Freud's Vienna accent? You sounded more like Bella Lugosi."

I frowned and tried to look offended. "You get my point."

"I do. But I'm not quite that theatrical. Look on the positive side. If he can't remember something germane to your case, maybe I can get him to stop smoking."

———

Getting Farley Gayton enthused about being hypnotized was no walk in the park. I arrived at Frenchman's Holler at ten the next morning and didn't leave until 11:30. Finally, Chastity Puryear helped, and we set up an appointment for 5:15 the next day.

That left me with a half day to kill before I went home. I was facing a brick wall at my end of the investigation and didn't fancy spending time with mundane chores. I was just about to call Ralph Oliveri to see if I could expect any information from him when Bettye walked into my office.

"Someone from Greg Bivins' Gun Shop called. The Glock you ordered for Terri Donnellson is in."

"How's she doing with her tests?"

"The medical results are back. Everything okay there. The psychologist hasn't submitted his report, but from what I understand, if there was a problem we'd get a quick call."

"Good. I'll call the sheriff and schedule a polygraph exam."

"Are you going to give her an agility test?"

"I suppose we have to. Stanley would seem like the man to do that. Give the middle school a ring and ask to use their athletic field for an hour or so."

Okey dokey. When do you want her to start?"

"Soon as possible. But we don't want the payroll clerks to get their knickers in a spin. So, I guess we should time it to coincide with one of the pay periods."

"I'll find out what day suits them."

"Good, and since an Academy class is a couple months away, I guess we should get her checked out with her new shootin' iron before she hits the road. Ronnie will love me to death for covering his liability issues."

"You going to do that?" Bettye asked.

"Why me? How about sending her to the county range and let their firearms guys do it?"

"We just got a notice. They closed the range for two weeks to mine out the lead from the target line."

"Rats. That's damn inconvenient. You're a good shot. Teach her what a practical police course is like. She's been qualified with the army. Should be a piece of cake."

"I don't doubt Terri's abilities, but aren't you the guy who always mentions *our* liability?"

"You're not going to let me off the hook, are you?"

"You are the only one here that's attended the FBI Advanced Firearms School. And like you always say, 'Give me enough time and ammunition and I can teach a chimpanzee how to shoot.'"

"True enough, doll-face. Me and Bogie will mosey over and see those gunsels on Chapman Highway and pick up Terri's new roscoe. Tell her to call me before five, and we'll plan something for early morning, day after tomorrow. Got that, sister?"

Bettye nodded.

"Swell."

"Who shall I tell her to expect, Sam Spade or Philip Marlowe?"

———

Farley Gayton was a big, good-looking kid in his mid-twenties. His short brown hair, stylishly combed to a point in the center of his head, suggested a teenage mentality, but Farley was no dope. Those in the know about college sports said he could have made a name for himself as a defensive end had he not lost his UT football scholarship because of a DUI conviction during game season. At six-two and weighing a little over two and a quarter, Farley had a pair of shoulders that could support a small overpass on Interstate 40. Chastity Puryear preferred that I call him her security consultant rather than bouncer or hired muscle.

The big kid sat in a comfortable chair in front of Sharon Rubenstein's desk. I stood a few feet to his right and Sharon no more than two feet in front of him.

I never doubted that Farley would be fearless when chasing an offensive receiver or rousting an unruly drunk, but the look on his face suggested that Dr. Rubenstein had him on the verge of soiling his undies.

"Relax, Farley," she said. "Let your shoulders drop. That's good. Now, relax your neck. Loosen up. This won't hurt." Her voice could have soothed a savage beast. "Look at the pendant, and let your mind go blank. Just watch the pendant spin. And spin, And spin."

She was twisting the chain of a snowflake-shaped crystal charm about the size of a quarter between her thumb and forefinger.

"Watch the colors. See the sparkles. Look deeply into the crystal. Relax. Let yourself float. Time to relax and go to sleep. Let go now. Let yourself sleep."

I almost nodded off listening to her. Farley's eyes closed, and his head listed to the left about twenty degrees. The whole process took less than a minute.

"He's a good subject," she said, looking at me.

"You must be a blast at cocktail parties."

She smiled and refocused on Farley.

"Farley, I'm going to ask you to think back to the night we spoke about, the night when you saw the big black or blue SUV. Can we do that?"

"Yes, ma'am."

"Did you see any people in the parking lot?"

"Uh-uh, no people."

"Why did you notice the SUV?"

He sighed slightly before speaking. His breathing appeared shallow. "I count cars. Match them to people."

"Did the SUV belong to one of the customers?"

"Don't think so."

"Did you see the front or rear of the SUV?"

"Front. It was backed into a spot."

"Did you see a license plate?"

"No, didn't walk around back."

Tennessee vehicles only display a rear plate.

Sharon turned to me with disappointment all over her face.

"May I?" I asked.

She nodded. "Yes. Speak softly."

"Farley," I said, "let's look at the SUV carefully. First, look at the whole vehicle. Get a big picture in your mind. What color is it?"

Farley sighed. His head rolled no more than an inch to the right, then back to the left. "Black."

"Was the SUV clean or dirty?"

No hesitation. "Shiny clean."

"Good. Now narrow your focus to the front grill. What do you remember?"

A few seconds passed. "Big chrome. Showy. GMC letters in the middle."

"Very good. Now raise your attention and look at the windshield. Were there any stickers or anything hanging from the mirror? Focus only on the windshield."

"No. Nothin'."

I felt a stab of disappointment.

"Did you look at the side of the vehicle?"

He nodded slowly. "Uh-huh."

"Did you look inside?"

"Mmm. Tan inside. Light brown?"

"Did you see anything else? A briefcase? A water bottle? Anything?"

A few more protracted seconds passed. "A radio."

"Just a radio?"

"A police radio. With a microphone."

"Very good. What else?"

Farley took a breath, and furrows appeared on his forehead. It looked like he was thinking.

"Mmm. Half a cigar in an open ashtray."

"Okay, good. What else in the car? In the back seats, maybe?"

His eyebrows moved up and down. "No. Don't remember."

"That's okay. Let's take a step back and look at the side of the vehicle. Driver's side or passenger's side?"

"Driver's."

"Start at the front and move back *very* slowly. Go *very* slowly and look at everything. Every detail. Go *very* slowly."

"Uh-huh."

"Do you see any dents or scratches?"

"No damage." He paused. "But one's missing."

"What's missing?"

"A letter."

"A letter?"

His head moved a little, almost a nod. "YUKO. It said YUKO, not YUKON. And then XL."

"Good. Very good. What else do you remember?"

His face gyrated again as if he was struggling to remember something.

"Nothin'. Just YUKO XL."

I looked at Sharon and smiled.

"You're pretty good at this," she whispered.

"I'm a police chief. I'm good at everything."

"Oy."

"I think Farley is my star witness. Is he finished?"

"I'd say so. I'll bring him back."

She touched Farley's hand gently. "Farley, I'm going to count to three and snap my fingers. When you hear the snap, you'll wake up and feel rested. You'll feel very good, as if you had eight hours sleep. Okay now— one, two, three." Snap.

Farley's eyes opened, he blinked, and his head moved around slowly. His eyes rolled a little, and then he focused on Sharon. Then he looked at me.

"Hey," he said, "How'd I do?"

"You're on my all-star team, kid."

———

At ten to nine the next morning, I took the back steps to the PD two at a time feeling full of piss and vinegar and prepared to turn my investigation into high gear again. Bettye had been at work for an hour, and John Gallagher also arrived a little early. They sat at their desks when I popped into the reception area.

"Mornin', Sammy," Bettye said.

"Hey, Boss, howz it goin'," John asked.

"Hello, Blondie. Aren't you gorgeous today? And John Boy, it's goin' a hundred miles an hour. I think we're in like Flynn with this Strangler thing. Who's going to court today?"

Bettye wheeled her chair around a-hundred-and-eighty degrees and grabbed a clipboard from the wall behind her desk.

"Court?"

"Yeah. I need someone reliable at the Justice Center who's got a legitimate purpose for being there."

"Junior's got a couple of traffic cases and has to report in at 9:30. Then, Harley is a witness at a civil trial on a car versus pedestrian injury case at 1:30."

"Junior should be on his way there now."

"He should."

"Super. Hit him with a 10-13 forthwith on the radio. I need a phone call before he walks into the building."

Bettye hung the clipboard back on its hook and made the radio call to Junior Huskey in unit 501.

"What's up, Boss?" John asked.

"Later. Let me get Junior squared away and see if he can give me what I need, and I'll tell you all about it. This should be good. I hope."

Sixty seconds hadn't passed when the main number on Bettye's phone console rang. She answered, spoke a few words and handed the phone to me. "Your boy answered the call."

"Hey, kid," I said. "I love a guy who knows the meaning of forthwith."

"Whatcha need, boss-man?"

"A little surreptitious undercover work. Got a camera with you?"

Junior sighed. "Man, you are in the dark ages, ain't ya? These smart phones all got cameras, boss—yours too."

"Huh. I knew that, smartass. Do me a big favor. Before you go into court, park in the back lot where the county guys leave their cars. Then look for the black SUV Chief Deputy Leary drives. He's got a reserved spot next to the back door. Look for the sign and have your camera ready and take a photo from the left rear quarter showing the plate number and the entire driver's side. Then take a shot of the chrome letters just forward of the front door. A letter should be missing. Instead of saying YUKON XL, it should be YUKO—no N—XL. Then a third shot showing the grill and GMC logo. You follow?"

"Sure. I'm guessin' you don't want nobody seein' me do this."

"That's essential."

"You gonna tell me what's goin' on?"

"Yes, but not now. If you're captured, they can't torture the details of the mission out of you. By the way, do you have a cyanide capsule handy?"

"Oh, Lord have mercy. Okay, gotcha. Soon as I git inta the buildin', I'll call and then send ya the pitchers."

"You can do that, huh? I don't have to wait? Cool. You've got the technology, kid."

"Yessir, shore do."

"Now, cross your fingers, and hope Leary's SUV is missing that letter."

"Boss, I ain't got no idea what yer talkin' about, but I'll git 'er done."

Fifteen minutes later, Junior called and shortly thereafter, he emailed three pictures to my computer.

"Ha!" I shouted.

Bettye was walking by and stuck her head into my office. "What are you screamin' about, Sam Jenkins?"

"Look at this. Get in here. Call John in. He's gotta see this, too. We've got him!"

Bettye and John stood behind me as I clicked through the photos.

"See this one? The chrome bars across the grill with GMC in the middle. That means it's a premier edition Yukon. Now look at this—a letter is missing from the word Yukon. And last, here's the rear tying in the license plate and the left side where the thing says YUKO XL. This is good stuff."

I looked at their blank stares and figured I should calm down and should have prefaced my show-and-tell with a complete account of Farley Gayton's recollection under hypnosis.

"Don't you think we need more than that to arrest Leary, Boss?"

I let my shoulder drop a couple inches for dramatic effect. "Of course, but this is the first piece of physical evidence we've got. This puts Leary's SUV at Frenchman's Holler the night Rosanna Wakefield met 'Andy' there. Let him explain that one away."

"You think a guy like Leary will 'fess up when you confront him with this?" Bettye asked.

"He'll tell you to go f...pound salt, Boss," John added.

"No, Betts, maybe not. And yes, John, he'd probably say what you were thinking. But when I get more information from his computer and link him to 'Andy', we'll have him by the...we'll have him in a bad position."

Bettye smiled at my enthusiasm. "Didn't Lonnie Ray have a big problem tying into Andy's emails?"

"He did, but after he hacks into Leary's computer at the sheriff's office, I'll bet he finds all kinds of useful stuff."

Bettye shook her head and frowned. "Oh, Lord have mercy, Sam. Even I know that's not legal."

"Maybe we'll see you at the Supreme Court, huh, Boss?"

"Have faith, guys. And think unconventionally. I'm just gettin' started."

———

L onnie Ray Wilson spread out his equipment on my desk and sat behind something that looked like a laptop on steroids.

"That's one hell of a machine you've got there, son."

"When you want me to get into exotic computer work, I'd rather use my stuff," he said matter-of-factly.

"I understand. I just hope you know I don't evacuate my desk and office for just anyone."

He exaggerated his Ebonics act. "Dat 'cause you don't know diddly squat 'bout computers, boss."

"*Diddly squat* is an exaggeration. I'd prefer to say I'm a step above clueless. But, the fact remains, I treat you good and pay seventy-five bucks an hour."

Lonnie gave a silent snort. "Cheap when you consider I could get thrown in jail for what you want me to do."

"Another exaggeration. I'll tell anyone who catches you that you're authorized."

"Who by?"

"By whom." I corrected his usage. "By yours truly."

"Great. We can get adjoining cells. You figger they'll let us play cards through the bars?"

"Pfui. You get me the info I need, and I'll make you a star."

"Sure as hell ain't gonna make me any friends at the sheriff's office."

I shrugged. "Yeah, neither will I. But we might get to put away a serial killer. We going to talk about this, or are you going to start hacking?"

"Yas, suh, I be ready ta start hackin'. Now close da dough, and don't let it hit yo ass on da way out."

"Do I get a discount for taking this abuse?"

"Not hardly. Now leave me be."

————

Having been dispossessed from my own office, I wandered around looking for something to do. I made a couple phone calls, thought about a report the mayor wanted, for which I had no enthusiasm, and ended up dropping into the side chair next to Bettye's desk.

"Are you eating in or going out today?" I asked.

She smiled and for some reason looked pleased with herself.

"It's only quarter to twelve. I assume being bored makes you extra hungry?"

I shrugged. "I could eat something. But back to my question. What are you doing for lunch?"

"I brought a container of yogurt."

I shook my head. "All that bacteria is no good for you. You should eat real food."

"If I ate like you, I'd look like the Goodyear blimp."

"Impossible. Where's Gallagher?"

"In the squad room trying to pin a murder on Arlo Bowman and eat lunch at the same time."

"Hmmm. Want Chinese for lunch? I'm buying."

She sighed. "Oh, all right, if Mr. Lum can make me that thing he calls Buddhist's delight."

"You're an Episcopalian. Eat something substantial."

"I do not want you callin' me Sergeant Goodyear."

Before I could counter that with a good reason for her to order one of the new Thai curries old man Lum had added to his menu, the frenzied cry of our honorary detective broke my concentration.

"Boss! Sarge! Come look at this. Hurry up. Boss, get in here. Quick!"

Bettye and I abandoned our seats and scurried down the hall to the squad room to find John sitting in front of the TV.

"For chrissakes, John, will you stop watching TV on company time?" I said.

"Can it, Boss. Watch. Watch. They're taking Leary out in cuffs."

Sure enough, a TV cameraman had captured Ralph Oliveri and Marty Saunders from the good old FBI in Knoxville walking a handcuffed Ryan Leary from the back door of the justice center to a waiting Crown Victoria. Three other suits followed. Two looked like agents and one must have been the AUSA assigned to lead the violation of civil rights investigation. He had that over-educated, lean and hungry look about him.

"I'll be damned," I said.

"Will you look at that?" Bettye added.

And John stuck in, "Some shit, huh, Boss? Uh, sorry, Sarge."

CHAPTER FIFTEEN

Being the world-class detective I fancy myself, it didn't take me long to learn exactly what happened to Ryan Leary.

The Feds had worked fast and efficiently. A team of first-rate interrogators scooped up detectives Artie Bonnet and Leo Turner, isolated them and laid out their probable future, if they continued to play dumb about the Farris Tingle beating.

While these slick operators held that pair incommunicado, FBI computer geeks scoured personal and departmental emails while communications technicians tracked down every telephone call made between Leary and his minions since young Tingle, the junkie burglar, swiped Leary's gym bag from the infamous black SUV.

Establishing a line of communication for times that coincided with the incidents Tingle described to investigators put Bonnet and Turner in a strong circumstantial jackpot neither could explain away.

As I've always said, dishonest cops are their own worst enemies, and those two were no exception. Knowing that the jig was up and threatened with loss of their pensions and freedom, the pair independently rolled over and formally gave up their boss in written statements. Everything they said jibed with Tingle's allegations. A Federal judge loved the thoroughness of the investigation and issued a warrant for Leary's arrest on several serious federal crimes.

For the time being, Leary was out on a very high conditional bail and wearing a monitored ankle bracelet to keep him under house arrest. However, Dayton Corliss, the AUSA in charge of the posse assigned to take down Ryan Leary, was no slouch and wanted an extra pound of flesh. He asked for pre-trial incarceration based on the assumption that Leary would potentially intimidate or otherwise tamper with the witnesses who could testify against him. This not only included Bonnet and Turner, but the two uniformed deputies involved with the apprehension of Farris Tingle, who also rolled over on everyone quicker than you can say, 'Your pensions are sliding into the cesspool, gentlemen.'

The judge granted J.R. Tolbert's motion for a bail hearing set seven days later. If Tolbert could convince the judge Leary was not a risk to confront the witnesses, he'd most likely remain under house arrest. If not, Ryan would spend his pre-trial days in administrative segregation at some Federal slammer.

Either scenario worked for me. All I had to do was convince the hamstrung Leary to live with the charges for beating Farris Tingle and confess to killing nine people.

———

Before the ink could dry on the video tape of Ryan Leary's perp march out of the Justice Center in handcuffs, my phone rang. Sheriff Joe Don Hartung had a proposition for me.

"Sam, I'm assumin' you've heard what's happenin' ta Ryan."

Having less faith in his chief deputy than the sheriff, I tap-danced around committing myself to backing a fellow cop.

"I did," was the best I would offer.

"I jest don't know what to say. I'm hopin' that Ryan's lawyer can git this ironed out quick-like. I jest hate this, I surely do."

Because it makes you look like a horse's ass or because you really believe Leary is innocent?

"Uh-huh."

"Sam, this puts us in a bad position."

You think?

"Everybody from the newspapers ta the governor is askin' when we're gonna find this Riverside Strangler," he said. "And now that Ryan ain't gonna be here and his two detectives are, uh, on administrative leave, I don't know what ta do." Joe Don sounded distraught.

Isn't that why you have the 'legendary detective' on board?

"I'm guessing Turner and Bonnet are going to be indefinitely indisposed?"

The sheriff sighed and sounded as if the fate of the free world was his responsibility. "Afraid so."

"Sounds like you've got both feet in a bucket of chicken manure."

"Ta say the least."

"So, what's your plan?"

"Uh, I was hopin' that, uh, that is ta say, uh, I wanted ta ask ya I, uh... Shoot, Sam, would you take over the Strangler task force?"

Should I be flattered or see this as it probably was—an opportunity to dump a floundering investigation on an outsider? What to do? What to do?

"Look, Joe D, I appreciate the fact that you have confidence in me, but I couldn't possibly take on that job and continue to run Prospect PD concurrently."

And implement my plan to nail your chief deputy for all those pesky unsolved murders.

I tried a different approach. "I know the FBI has offered Ryan assistance with the cases several times. I suggest you call Carl Harmon. He'll fix you up with a team of investigators."

And he'll probably shitcan Lew Schmecke and his tribe of assistant legendary private eyes.

"Sam, I'm sure you can understand how I'd hate to call in Federal people for a local case." He sounded like he'd rather cut off his left arm.

"I do, but under the circumstances, you don't have much choice."

"Oh, Lord have mercy."

———

After kissing off Joe Don Hartung and preparing to tell Bettye and John how little time we had to nail down a case against Leary, Lonnie Ray Wilson stepped out from behind my desk with great vigor.

"Hot damn, but I'm in."

I stepped over to the doorway to my office. "What's that mean?"

"Means I broke into Leary's computer at the sheriff's office. But that was the easy part. Combing through his hard drive for deleted emails and other files took all my time."

"And?"

"And the best part was an email forwarded to himself."

"I don't understand."

"He sent something from his work computer to his home PC. And that allowed me to hack into all his private stuff. *All* his stuff." He had a grin that would have made the Cheshire Cat jealous.

"Will you get to the point?"

Lonnie sighed like he was speaking to a total moron. "He forwarded the email to *Andy's account*—which is on his home computer."

"Aha."

"You bet. Having an origin made it easy to get into his private stuff. I couldn't do it before because the damn thing bounced all over the world. But now I've got Andy."

"So Ryan Leary *is* Andy? You're sure?"

"No doubt in my mind."

"Can you access all the Andy emails?"

"I can, but I gotta do it before somebody deletes anything."

"What are you waiting for?"

"It's downloading as we speak."

"Okay, another seventy-five bucks well spent."

"A bargain."

"What kind of email did he forward?"

"Something from an account with a user name of Stones."

"Stones?"

"Uh-huh. Kinda cryptic, but I'll let you read it. Maybe it'll mean something to you."

"Could you pin down a better ID for Stones?"

"Not yet. He's also got his stuff bouncing from one IP to another, from one continent to another."

Lonnie Ray was still smiling. "But I'm still working on Leary's hard drive. If I can keep it up without interruption, there may be more stuff you can use."

"I'm glad you're optimistic. And do what you've gotta do."

"I'll get on it."

"Even if you locate Stones, I've still got to dream up a way to use this rather damning, but illegally gotten information, in court."

————

Lonnie obtained the link between ryanleary@BCSO.com and andy1796@gconnect.net without benefit of a warrant to intrude on Leary's private property. The Fourth Amendment promised to scream from the sidelines about my methods. No court would allow me to introduce anything I had into evidence, and J.R. Tolbert would certainly move to exclude it as 'fruit of the poisoned tree'.

Having no more technical knowledge of a computer's innards than Francis the Talking Mule, I could think for a hundred years and never come up with a plausible explanation that eventually we would have found that link under what a court would call 'inevitable discovery'.

So, I had to engineer a way to effectively bamboozle the only other law enforcement agency who had legal access to Leary's computer from a totally unrelated case—my local and friendly G-men.

————

I called Ralph Oliveri.

"Are you alone?" I asked.

"I'm at my desk in the squad room, but you knew that because you called me."

"I mean can anyone hear you?"

"Probably not. I don't know. Why?"

"I want to drop something on you that will make you an all-star."

"Oh, here we go. What do you want?"

"I want you to catch the Riverside Strangler, and I'll tell you how."

"If you know how, why do you need me?"

"That's what has to remain our little secret—for the moment. I don't want to do this over the phone."

"Okay, you want to come here?"

"Not yet. And, as I said, we can't talk on the phone."

"Why all the intrigue? What's going on?"

"I discovered the link I needed, using, uh, a little unconventional investigative procedure."

Ralph snorted. "You illegally obtained evidence. What else is new? How can I magically make it admissible?"

"That's what I'll explain—in private."

"It's four o'clock. Even if you jumped in the car right now, by the time you got here, we'd be ready to close up shop for the day."

"Can you get Carl to stick around tonight for a little OT?"

"I've got plans tonight."

"Oh, for chrissakes. I'm going to hand you the case of the century, and you've got a date."

"What do you think we could do with your brilliant plan tonight?"

I took a long moment to think about that. "You're right. This will involve other personnel. How about tomorrow? I'll take you and Carl to lunch, bare my soul and we'll work out a plan."

"Wait a minute. Lemme look at my calendar and ask the boss."

I waited. The seconds passed by interminably. Well, maybe not.

"I'm back," Ralph said. "We're good. Where and when?"

I thought for a moment. "How about Puleo's on North Peters Road? They'll give us a table away from the crowd for privacy. I'll be there at 11:45."

"Yeah, good. I like their lasagna."

"The lasagna is good, but you should try the shrimp and grits."

"I don't eat grits."

"Eat anything you want, but if you never try the shrimp and grits, you're a putz."

"Up yours. I'll see you tomorrow."

———

Bettye was sitting at her desk, and John was standing at a file cabinet against the back wall of the reception area.

"I'm going to Knoxville tomorrow to see Ralph and Carl Harmon at noon. Maybe I can get the Feds to manipulate a little of the evidence they have access to and get what we know about Leary admissible."

"You were going to take Terri to qualify tomorrow at ten," Bettye reminded me.

"Rats. That's too late. I won't be able to give her a fair shake and get to Knoxville in time. Call her back and tell her to meet me at 8:30."

"Do you know how difficult you make my life?"

"What other boss would allow you to talk like that?"

She fluttered her eyelashes and smiled.

———

At 8:15 the next morning, I pulled up to the locked gate at the Fraternal Order of Police range. Terry Donnellson was already waiting in her racing green Mini Cooper.

As I would have done, she parked her car facing the entrance to see who drove in after her.

I got out of the Ford, walked toward the gate and tapped on the hood of her car.

"Morning," I said.

She slipped a bookmark between the pages to save her place and rolled down a window.

"Morning, boss."

I pointed at the gate. "I'll open up. Follow me down range. You'll see the parking area."

She flipped me a casual salute and sent the car window back up. I dialed up the four-digit combination to the padlock, unraveled the chain and swung the gate to the side.

The range sat in a natural bowl-shaped hollow. Steep mounds with trees and scrub brush everywhere created a partial perimeter for the target line on three sides. Old creosote coated utility poles lying on their sides separated the parking area from the fifty yard line of the range.

I got out of my car as Terri stepped out of the Mini. She looked like a calendar girl for Guns & Ammo magazine. She wore her dark hair in a ponytail, topped off by a sage green camo Army ranger cap. The rest of her outfit consisted of large aviator-style sunglasses, a gray *Re-Up Army* T-shirt and washed off blue jeans. She carried her gear in a small black duffle bag.

"Not the most sophisticated range facility," I said, "but it works."

"Better looking than some of the ranges I re-qualified on overseas," she said.

"Okay, then this should be like a vacation at a gun spa."

I handed her a black plastic box that looked like something provided by Tupperware. "Here's your Glock. Regardless of what you may have heard about polymer frame guns, it's a good weapon. Just don't use it to clock a skell with an extremely hard head. The slide might pop off the frame."

"Say again?" She looked surprised.

"It's not made to replace the blackjack. Shoot with it. Don't use it as a club."

Her big brown eyes looked like small saucers. "Uh, yes, sir."

Then I handed her a shopping bag.

"Here's your duty holster, Sam Browne belt, handcuffs and all the crap you've got to hang around you. Put it together at home. I assume you've got a preference on what goes where. For right now, slide the magazine pouch onto your pants belt." I handed her a high riding off-duty style holster. "This is an extra I had. Use it today and until you get your own. Then give it back. I've got the targets and ammo. You ready to go?"

"That's it? No class?"

I grinned. "You were a soldier. You qualified with a Beretta and the M-4. What do you want, a brass band?"

"Uh, no, sir."

"Good. Wait for me to tell you what to do. Then we'll wing it."

I placed a canvas bag of ammunition on a former telephone company overhead wire spool turned on its side to be used as a table. I had boxes of .40 caliber rounds for Terri and a box of nine millimeter for my old Glock.

"I'm going down range to staple up a few targets. Don't load your gun until I get back."

"Yes, sir."

I posted four black B-27 silhouette targets on the Homosote backboards resting in metal angle iron frames. Above the three on the left, I used a thick Magic Marker to write a T on each. On the one to the right, I wrote an S.

Back at the table, I spoke to Terri. "Obviously the magazines load the same as the Beretta 92 you're used to. The City of Prospect has provided you with three—one for the gun and two for your pouches. Load them up, and we'll see how you like the gun."

Terri snapped ten rounds into each magazine. I took longer cramming sixteen bullets into two of the magazines for my Glock. I didn't want to get the Smith & Wesson revolver that I usually carried dirty.

Terri waited until I finished and stood by prepared to hear my instructions.

"The big difference between the Beretta and the Glock is the double action only feature. Once you rack a round into the chamber, it's ready to go. No safety. No external hammer. I ordered your gun with a 'New

York' trigger. That means it's a bit safer than the standard Glock arrangement. You have a smooth single stage pull of eight pounds to fire your gun. The other is a putzy trigger safety to encounter and then only five pounds of pull before it goes off. Too many cops have shot subjects with that hair trigger. This one is better."

She looked and sounded all business. "Yes, sir."

I put on a pair of shooting glasses and screwed in a pair of earplugs. "Okay. Let's get started. Put your ears on."

She took a pair of soundproof earmuffs from her black bag and secured them onto her head.

I spoke a little louder than usual. "Walk to the twenty-five yard line with your three magazines, one in your hand and two in your pouches."

She began the trek, and I followed.

She stood behind a 2x6 wooden barricade sitting inside a piece of PVC pipe buried in the ground.

"Now we're going to do it by the numbers," I said. "I'll give you the command to load your magazine, and you seat it into the butt of your gun. Then I'll say, prepare your weapon, and you rack a round into the chamber and holster a loaded weapon. Then I'll give you the okay to draw the pistol, and at your own speed, fire three rounds at the X-ring. No time limit and use a two hand hold. Use the barricade to steady your aim. After the third shot, holster the weapon. Any questions?"

"In the Army we usually warmed up by shooting a few rounds of bull's-eye."

"Yeah, that's the Army. Far as I'm concerned, bull's eye shooting is for sissies. I like to keep it real and stick to combat shooting. That way if you ever have to testify about how you're trained, your testimony shows them we don't look at this as a sport. Anything else?"

"No, sir."

"Okay. Ready on the right. Ready on the left. Ready on the firing line. Load 'em up."

Terri took the magazine from her front pocket and slapped it into the butt of the Glock like she knew exactly what she was doing.

"Prepare to fire."

With the muzzle end of her gun pointing down range, she pulled the slide to the rear, released it, let it slam home and holstered the gun.

"No time limit. When you're ready, fire three rounds and holster."

She drew the weapon, tightened her grip, rested the palm of her left hand against the barricade with her thumb sticking out parallel to the ground and cradled the wrist of her shooting hand on top of the thumb. She took a deep breath, let half out and squeezed off one round. With both eyes open she looked at the target, saw the round hit low and to the left in the nine ring. She shook her head, tightened up her stance and in a few seconds fired another round. That hit about an inch to the left of the first shot, straddling the eight/nine rings. Once more and the round cut paper between the first two. She holstered the Glock and turned toward me.

"What do you think?" I asked.

"Not so good."

"Not in a match, but in real life, you blew out his spleen."

She laughed and removed her earmuffs.

"Just my opinion," I said, "but you're 'heeling' the gun and trying to pick the time your shot goes off. When you do that, you 'push' the shot low and to the left."

She frowned.

"I watched you. You're squeezing the trigger and that's good. But just before you complete the trigger squeeze, you tighten your grip. The extra pressure from the heel of your right hand on the grip causes the shot to go left. And when you like your sight picture, you get impatient and want the gun to go off when you think the sights and X-ring are perfectly aligned. So, you give the trigger a little extra squeeze. Being right handed, your shot gets pushed to about eight o'clock on the target. Sound about right?"

She shrugged. "I guess. That's where the rounds hit."

"So relax. You're not getting graded, and I'm not going to bite you. We're just getting you familiar with the gun. When you get to the police academy or shoot on the county range, you can impress those officers and show them how a former Army cop can do it."

She smiled and nodded.

"For today, cool off. Let me talk you through the fundamentals, and you'll squeeze off some good shots."

"Okay, boss."

"My first recommendation is to forget that old-fashioned way you cradle your gun at the barricade. That went out of style before J. Edgar Hoover bought his first Tommy gun. With the slide travelling back and forth on top of a light weight frame and the recoil of the hot ammo, you need more grip on the gun."

She nodded again, but looked like she wasn't sure of a good alternative.

"Wrap your left hand around your right, but keep it well below the slide. You know it's tight enough when the polymer crumbles in your palm."

She grinned at my exaggeration.

"Then, just lightly rest your knuckles against the wood. That's all you need. My gun's unloaded. I'll show you what I mean."

I demonstrated and re-holstered.

"Okay," she said. "I'll try that."

"Let me talk you through this. Don't do anything but listen to me, and do what I tell you. Above all, do not pick a time when you want the shot to go off. Let it surprise you. Got it?"

She half smiled but looked a little apprehensive. "Roger that, sir."

"Look, Terri, I'm not your opponent here. I'm your partner, not your boss. Right now, I'm acting like your coach. I want you to be happy with the targets you shoot. I know you can qualify with that gun. I want you to do it well. Relax. I'll say it once more. This is not a test. It's practice."

She nodded and adjusted her earphones.

"You're still loaded. Un-holster your weapon and point it down range. Get your grip. Get your stance."

She braced the pistol against the barricade as I suggested.

"Ready on the right. Ready on the left, and all that jazz. Now listen carefully. Align your sights and set the front one at center mass on the target. Now forget the target. I want that black silhouette to gray out and get fuzzy. You can't get a sharp picture of the sights and the target at the same time. *Do not* look for the X-ring. Stare at the front sight, and keep it aligned with the rear. Take a breath and let half of it out. Start your squeeze. Slowly. Nice and smooth. Look at the front sight as if it was mounted on a railroad track and the more you squeeze the closer it gets to you. *Squeeze* that trigger back toward you. Watch the sight coming at you. *Squeeze*."

Bang! The shot rang out.

"Do not look for where that shot landed."

She flinched.

"Hear me?"

She nodded, almost frozen in position.

"Get right back on your sights. It's not your job to score your target. Your job is to kill that guy down range. Take another breath, and listen..."

I went through the same drill. A second and then a third shot went off.

"Okay, holster your weapon. We're going down range to take a look."

We walked the seventy-five feet to the target line. Seven yards from the silhouette, I looked over at Terri. A big smile crossed her face.

"Not bad," I said. "What do you think?"

"No complaints from me, boss. I guess you've taught people how to shoot before?"

"Once or twice." *Oh, modest me.*

Her three shots were all in the ten ring.

"Pretty good, considering you're not familiar with this piece of Austrian plastic. Let's do it all over again, but you talk yourself through it. I'll watch."

At 10:45 I was satisfied that Terri Donnellson could handle her Glock safely and efficiently.

"Not bad for an ex-Army cop. I have no doubt you'll do well at the range. I've got plenty of money in the budget for practice ammo. Whenever you get the urge to pop some caps, let me know. From what I've seen today, I wouldn't be surprised if you didn't come back from the academy with an expert bar."

"I guess you've got one."

"I seem to have a natural knack for this," I said. "I shoot distinguished expert." I smiled. "And I'm too old to act modest and not mention that."

She smiled, too. "I guess that tells me."

"No, I'll show you. It's my turn. I don't want you thinking I'm one of those guys who can teach but not do. Let's go to the twenty-five yard line and put our ears on."

I squared off seventy-five feet from my target, drew my Glock and took an unsupported 'point shoulder' stance. I took a breath and rapped off sixteen shots. The slide locked back. I released the magazine, pulled it free and stuck it in my pocket. I rammed in a fresh magazine, released the slide, seated a round and holstered my gun.

"Damn," she said, "is that thing full auto? I never heard someone fire that fast."

"No, it's just broken in. Let's take a look."

About ten feet from the silhouette Terri said, "Holy sh— Wow, you blew out the X-ring. What have you got, three, no four tens? It looks like one big hole."

"Shucks, ma'am, weren't nuthin'.'"

"Yeah, right. I guess I'll listen to your advice from now on."

"Smart girl. I knew I had a good reason for hiring you."

"Yeah. Thank you for that."

"I don't hand out jobs. You earned it."

She nodded. "I'm anxious to start working a real job again."

"I guess collaring teenage shoplifters isn't the most interesting aspect of law enforcement, is it?"

"I understand the teenagers. It's the seventy-five-year-old kleptomaniacs that depress me."

I laughed. "Have you picked up your uniforms yet?"

"Got them the other day."

"Good. We'll see you at eight o'clock Monday morning. Bettye will get you started in the office, and then she'll probably find someone to take you out on the road for the afternoon."

"Is Sergeant Lambert sort of your XO?"

"I don't really have an executive officer on the table of organization, but I guess she acts like it. And she's the boss while I'm gone. Stan Rose runs the show from four to twelve. He's the official road sergeant. And then there's John Gallagher. Except for Vern Hobbs, John's got more time on the job than anyone else. He was a good detective back in New York. If you ever learn his brand of English, listen to him. You'll learn lots about investigations."

"I think I'm going to like Prospect PD."

"You will."

I looked at my watch.

"Let's clean up. I've got to get up to Knoxville and charm a couple of Feds into a big favor."

CHAPTER SIXTEEN

O liveri and Harmon were already at Puleo's Grill when I walked in. After telling the hostess who I intended to meet, she escorted me to a booth away from the other occupied tables and against the back wall of the main dining room.

"Gentlemen," I said as I sat.

"Nice of you to dress for the occasion," the snide Italian said.

I wore Khakis, sneakers and a plaid sport shirt. The Feds were in uniform: Wall Street gray suits, white shirts and somber ties.

"I spent the morning with a new recruit. I wanted to familiarize her with the Glock before sending her out on patrol."

I opened the menu, but already knew what I'd order.

"Your recruit is a her?" Ralph asked.

"Yeah. A former MP. She seems like a sharp kid."

Before Ralph could wander off on the unrelated topic of Terri Donnellson, Carl spoke up.

"Ralph says you have new info on the Riverside Strangler that you'd like some help with?"

"I do. Very new and very good information."

"Can I assume you know that I received a call from Sheriff Hartung requesting our assistance on his task force?"

"Not officially. He spoke to me about the task force after Ryan Leary was taken into custody. I suggested that your help was long overdue and that he should let you take the lead."

He nodded. "If your new information is extremely good, why not make the arrest yourself?"

I raised my eyebrows. "Ahh. How I obtained the information would tend to preclude its use in court and without it, I'm no closer to an arrest than I was two days ago."

A waitress stopped at the table to take our orders. Ralph insisted on the lasagna. Carl wanted chicken picatta, and I, of course, chose the shrimp and andouille sausage in tasso sauce over a mound of cheese grits.

After the waitress left, Carl continued. He kept his delivery objective, but the look on his face told me he wasn't pleased to hear what I was saying. "Why do you think we could use this illegally obtained evidence?"

"Simple. If I whisper in your ear and tell you where and what to look for in a batch of *legally* obtained evidence you already have, no one will ever know it wasn't an inevitable discovery. All you have to do is take young Oliveri here," I pointed at Ralph with a knife I just used to spread a little butter on a small piece of bread, "who has been working on the Leary brutality case and assign him to the Strangler task force."

Carl narrowed his eyes, and deep lines wrinkled his forehead. It made me think he worried a lot.

"I'm not sure I understand."

"I'll explain all the details, but basically, Ralph has...or should have already seen the evidence, only he probably didn't know what he was looking at."

"Wait. Wait. Are you telling me—?"

I nodded. "Ryan Leary is the killer. Or at least one of them."

"Madonna mi!" Ralph said, and almost choked on a slice of homemade bread.

Carl shook his head in disbelief. "Sam, you had better be sure on this."

"Oh, I'm sure about Leary. Only I'm not sure Ralphie has already seen the evidence. But someone working the Leary case has. That's a minor logistical technicality you can work out. The point is...no one on your end would have seen the snake in the woodpile because you weren't privy to any task force information. Now that you are, and coincidentally I'm part of that task force, I can present all my circumstantial evidence leading me to theorize that Ryan Leary should be a person of interest." I broke off another piece of bread and dabbed on a tidbit of butter. "I've got at least a reasonable suspicion. When I suggest that you scrutinize his emails, which you already have, during the time *after* his involvement with the thief Farris Tingle, you'll be amazed when one of your agents remembers seeing an email from a sender with a screen name of 'Stones' mentioning a subject called 'Andy' forwarded from Ryan's sheriff's office computer to his personal email account on his home computer. Coincidentally, the email account for 'Andy' can be traced to Ryan's computer."

I popped the piece of bread into my mouth and chewed for a moment.

"As I'll tell you after we are sitting together as part of the task force, 'Andy' is a key lead in the Rosanna Wakefield murder. She made an appointment to meet with 'Andy' the night she was killed. The meeting was scheduled to take place in the parking lot of the greatest little whorehouse in Tennessee, where I can, with great certainty, place Ryan Leary's vehicle. Let's let him start explaining away those circumstances."

Carl rubbed a hand across his forehead and didn't look happy. "My God, what are we talking about? Nine murders?"

I nodded. "If he goes for everything, nine is the magic number."

"We'll have to get together with Dayton Corliss as soon as possible and whatever local AUSA who will be advising the task force."

I added, "I hesitate to say this, but you may want to keep the Blount County District Attorney in the dark about this as long as possible. He's got a real chummy history with Leary."

Carl shook his head, showing the frustration of a pitcher who missed a perfect game by one walk. "We don't need a complication like that."

The waitress dropped off two glasses of red wine for Ralph and me and a vodka martini for Carl.

Ralph raised his glass. "Salute."

Carl said, "Success," and drained half in one gulp.

"We certainly live in interesting times," was my contribution.

———

The Justice Department's office complex didn't let me down. It was at least as posh as the place where the FBI agents hung their fedoras two floors below at 710 Locust Street in Knoxville, where I began my morning having a brief powwow with Carl Harmon, Ralph Oliveri and his partner, Bonnie Rowatt. Five minutes before the appointed hour, we took the elevator up to Heidi Piper's suite where she and Dayton Corliss waited.

Six modern armchairs had been set in a circle in front of Heidi's desk. There was enough room for us to play badminton, but we'd settle for a conference on the Riverside Strangler.

The circular arrangement immediately reminded me of two things: The way King Arthur and his knights discussed matters in and around Camelot, and since the Feds were heavily involved, a somewhat derogatory term used for certain Chinese get-togethers, upon which I won't elaborate. I hoped our meeting stuck more to the Arthurian standards.

Before Heidi's secretary left the room, she asked if anyone wanted coffee. Corliss already had a cup. Carl and Heidi said yes. Ralph, Bonnie and I were nos. I didn't think a request for scotch was an option.

Before settling into our seats, Carl handled the introductions. "Sam, this is Heidi Piper, a supervising AUSA for the Knoxville district. She will be advising the Strangler task force."

"We've met," she said and extended a hand. "Sam handed us a rather colorful Eastern European hood who provided information for our people in New York and New Jersey. Nice to see you again."

I smiled like a visiting diplomat. "My pleasure."

Heidi was a tall and trim brunette who pulled her hair back in a low-slung ponytail. Her uniform of the day was a burgundy pantsuit over a white blouse.

"And this is Dayton Corliss," Carl said. "As you know, he's come from Nashville to lead the investigation into the brutality complaint against Ryan Leary."

"Good morning," I said and did the handshake thing again.

Corliss was a few inches short of six foot and in good enough shape to make me think he stopped off to play squash with the boys at least three times a week. His expensive-looking pearl gray suit screamed government yuppie.

But, I thought, he shouldn't feel too superior because in only two-inch heels, Heidi had him by half an inch and was a hell of a lot better looking.

The coffee arrived, and we all sat to discuss the preliminaries.

After fifteen minutes of listening to me, Heidi asked, "Who did you use to *infiltrate* Leary's computers?"

"His name is Lonnie Ray Wilson. He works out of Maryville."

"Would he be willing to meet with our technicians after we establish that the data we already have would lead us to believe Leary might be the killer?"

"For seventy-five bucks an hour, Lonnie will tell your fortune with a computerized Ouija board."

Corliss sounded a little skeptical. "Is this man reliable?"

"I think so. Have your techs speak with him and let them determine his expertise. He's realistic and seems honest. He worked diligently, and at one point when he didn't achieve the results he expected, he offered to waive the day's pay. I'm no computer whiz, but I'm satisfied with what he's achieved."

Corliss nodded, but he didn't look very proud of Lonnie Ray or me. "I still don't like the way you obtained this information tying Leary to the murders."

I shrugged. "Neither do I, but the direct approach of going at 'Andy's' email account straight on netted me and the entire task force—including the *legendary detective* Lew Schmecke and his cyber PIs—nothing more than a computer trip around the world. Using a back door represented either knowing something or letting the killer continue to march."

Corliss screwed up his face as if he still didn't give my cunning plan much hope.

"Do you feel comfortable with this approach, Heidi?"

She nodded. "If we handle it properly and the data we obtained legally provides the same link, yes. We're under no obligation to ever mention Sam's foray into Leary's computers." She turned to me. "I know you're not going to be a problem, but will this Wilson keep his mouth shut?"

"I believe so. Confidentiality is part of his regular business. But I'll insure that he does."

Heidi was glancing at a document but tilted her exceptionally dark brown eyes up at me. "Should we know how you intend to do that?"

I smiled. "I don't ask how you supervise Ralph Oliveri. I'll take care of Lonnie Ray my way."

Carl broke in just as Corliss was about to say something. "Then our best bet is to assemble our task force and revisit all the information on record. We'll look at Sam's two cases first. They're the most recent. He can brief us on everything and end up with his suspicions of Leary, leaving out any mention of what he saw on Leary's computers. I'll make sure someone who worked on the civil rights case is present to hear your theory." Then he did something I'd never seen him do before. Carl actually smiled and winked at me. "With luck, that agent will remember seeing a reference to an email from 'Andy'. Then off we go."

He made our little game of role-play sound so easy.

CHAPTER SEVENTEEN

O n Monday morning, Terri Donnellson began working for Prospect PD. Mayor Ronnie Shields swore her in. She signed an oath of office that Trudy Connor notarized. John Gallagher handled all the new employee paperwork, and Bettye constructed a personnel folder that she would send upstairs to Human Resources.

Simultaneously, an FBI investigative team descended on the Blount County Justice Center and assumed responsibility for the Riverside Strangler task force. Detective Sergeant Hugh Bledsoe was the only county officer permanently assigned. Detectives Artie Bonnet and Leo Turner had been relieved of duty and placed on indefinite suspension.

A squad of Federal computer geeks sat with Lew Schemcke and his three private eyes attempting to learn if the legendary detective had found anything germane to the killings.

On Tuesday, I showed up and, for the record, began discussing my two cases with Carl Harmon, Heidi Piper, Bonnie Rowatt and Ralph Oliveri. Senior Special Agent Marty Saunders assumed the role of second in command and worked with four agents on the other seven murders.

At around three p.m., I got around to mentioning 'Andy', how we legally obtained that information before Lonnie Ray hacked Leary's computers and my suspicions about Ryan Leary based on several pieces of important, but circumstantial evidence.

For the record, Bonnie stated that during her time assigned to the civil rights team, she had occasion to work on analyzing information taken from Ryan Leary's departmental computer. Although it appeared to have no bearing on Leary's communication with other officers regarding the Farris Tingle beating, she remembered a fairly cryptic email from the screen name 'Stones' mentioning 'Andy' in the text and that it was routed from Leary's departmental computer to his home PC.

That was the magic ingredient. With that convenient revelation, I worked with Heidi Piper who prepared an application to extend our search to electronic data already in custody pursuant to their earlier search warrant.

At 1:30 the next day, Carl Harmon called me at Prospect PD to let me know the warrant extension had been signed, and an agent named Al Hahn had just left Knoxville with it in hand.

I pulled into the parking lot of the Justice Center and walked into the building just behind Al who held one of the front doors for me.

"Any problems getting a judge to agree to this?" I asked.

"No, but it's limited to only information dated after that slime ball Tingle boosted the duffle bag from Leary's car."

"We pretty well figured that."

"The judge did mention that if we find usable stuff and can reasonably demonstrate that Leary is linked to the murders, we should apply for a search of his work and home computers going back to the date of the first death."

"Mighty nice of him."

"Isn't it though?"

"Like no one else would have thought of that."

Al Hahn laughed. "That's why he's a judge and we're only gumshoes."

W e weren't upstairs in the task force room ten minutes when Dayton Corliss, two field agents and two technicians walked in. The assembled crowd made the large room feel small. If nothing else, the FBI likes to overwhelm everyone with their manpower commitments.

While Heidi, Carl, Corliss and Alex Rand, the supervising agent of the civil rights team, discussed strategy, and a platoon of computer technicians attacked Leary's hard drive, Ralph, Bonnie and I adjourned to the coffee room.

Bonnie poured herself a steaming cup as Ralph and I waited our turns.

I said, "Now that we've got legal evidence linking Leary to 'Andy' and sooner or later, some computer guy will probably find 'Stones', I can't help thinking that some non-electronic tangible evidence would be nice to have—something to actually place Leary at the scene of at least one of the murders."

"And how do you plan on finding that, Sherlock?" Ralph asked.

Bonnie spoke before I could answer. "Leary was careful to lawyer up quickly on the brutality charges."

"Okay. Tolbert won't let him talk about these murders if we name him as a suspect. I know that. Ryan won't give us spit. So while the heavies sit on their asses down the hall making their war plans, let's go out, and see what we can find. I've got an idea where to start."

B efore I could elaborate on my potentially brilliant strategy, Heidi Piper stepped into the coffee room. "Sam, can you call the IT man who helped you *find* the evidence against Leary? Our guys want to pick his brain. They figure he can save them hours of work."

"Sure, just have your check book handy. He'll work for anybody, but his seventy-five an hour is non-negotiable."

"I've got plenty of vouchers."

"Our tax dollars at work."

"You bet."

"Hey, I was just thinking about the bag of goodies that creep Tingle glommed from Leary's SUV. As you recall, the same SUV that we think 'Andy' used to meet Rosanna Wakefield."

Heidi frowned, and her eyes narrowed. She looked interested.

"Corliss and his boys have established with certainty that once Leary showed up at the Justice Center the night Tingle got collared, he took custody of the gym bag," I said. "Bonnet and Turner confirm that, as do the uniformed cops who made the arrest. Then Leary and the bag disappeared for an hour, undoubtedly to *sanitize* the embarrassing contents. All along, we've thought it was to lose the porno discs and drugs. In the big scheme of things, this porn represents a 'so what'. If the FBI attempted to do something about all the porn found in PDs around the country, they'd be busy for a thousand years. And the drugs could have been explained away as sloppy evidence handling. Surely Bonnet and Turner would have lied to back up their boss's tall tale. But Leary put himself on the line when he removed evidence from the police facility. He's no fool. There might have been something *really* embarrassing in that bag."

"And how do you intend to learn what?" Heidi asked.

"I asked the same thing two minutes ago," Ralph added.

"There's only one starting point—Farris Tingle. Are you okay with the three of us talking with him?"

Heidi shrugged. "I can't see it doing any harm. But agents from the civil rights team interviewed the hell out of the kid. Why do you think you can get more out of him?"

"We won't be shotgunning questions at him about getting beaten and tortured. We're looking for something specific related to something beyond the scope of the civil rights investigation. And just recently I was told that I had a knack for extracting things buried inside a person's head."

She frowned again. "I hope you're not planning another end run around the Constitution with hopes that I can make whatever you find admissible."

"Now you've hurt my feelings. I had assumed that young Tingle would have his lawyer present while we spoke."

"Okay. I can see Corliss getting his shorts in an uproar over you backtracking his case, but go ahead, I'll cover that."

"You'd have to give that mope a pass on anything criminal he admits for his lawyer to produce him as a witness. But it would be worth lots if pimply-faced Farris saw a bloody knife in the bag that he has yet to mention."

"Or something else." Heidi nodded. "More physical evidence would be very nice."

"We need a hard object to shake up the jury," I said. "People don't often feel outrage looking at a stack of emails."

"Mmm. I'll call Chalmers for you."

———

Perry Chalmers was an oily specimen in a three-thousand-dollar suit. His offices looked like the interior of the Governor's Palace at Colonial Williamsburg.

Farris Tingle had yet to collect anything from either Ryan Leary or Blount County in his pending brutality suit settlement. He didn't come even remotely close to having spent one percent of Chalmers' worth on the hoof for his wardrobe of faded blue jeans and a long-sleeved T-shirt.

Chalmers' tongue and groove paneled office was large enough to hold a desk upon which a talented pilot could land a Chinook helicopter. Then you could toss in two walls of built-in bookcases, full of leather bound volumes, and still have space for a conference area with two leather covered sofas. Add to the picture four wing-back chairs and a four foot square cocktail table with Queen Anne legs and you might infer I was impressed by the furnishings.

Bonnie and Ralph sat on one couch. I used a chair on the north end of an antique Persian rug, while Chalmers and Tingle perched on chairs to the south.

"You people hope to learn something more about the contents of the bag Farris removed from Mr. Leary's vehicle?" Chalmers asked.

He was careful not to say that Farris took, grabbed or stole the bag.

I nodded. "We do. And we'll be giving you information explaining why we need to go over that inventory in great detail that must remain one-hundred-percent confidential. Just to put your mind at ease, nothing we learn from Farris at this point would have any negative impact on his civil case against Leary."

Furrows appeared on Chalmers' forehead. He looked intrigued, but sat patiently, nodding very slightly.

"Special Agent Rowatt is an attorney herself, and she'll be asking you both to agree to some very specific stipulations. You will be the only people given these facts, so once you agree, you, of course, understand that should this information leak to the press or be divulged to anyone else, you or your client could be charged with lying to a Federal officer. And since we will be pursuing a secondary criminal case having nothing to do with Mr. Tingle, hindering prosecution and other counts to be determined later. If you wish to proceed, I'll pass the torch to Agent Rowatt."

Chalmers' frown intensified. Tingle sat in the horribly expensive leather covered chair showing no more intelligence than a piece of shelf fungus.

"Ms. Piper has agreed to grant Mr. Tingle immunity on any issues that might come to light during this conversation," Chalmers said. "Are you aware of that, and do you agree to that stipulation?"

"I certainly do," I said and extended a hand toward my Federal colleagues.

"I speak for the FBI," Ralph said. "Mr. Tingle doesn't contest stealing the duffle bag. We doubt anything he could say would place him in any further jeopardy."

Chalmers' face relaxed. "Then we agree. What do you have to say, Ms. Rowatt?"

Bonnie straightened up a smidge, crossed her right leg over the left and ended up showing about three inches of thigh below her maroon skirt. "First, I want it understood that none of us represent Ryan Leary's interests in his capacity as a defendant in the Federal violation of civil rights case based on Mr. Tingle's complaint or as respondent to the civil suit we understand you are initiating on behalf of your client."

Chalmers dipped his head an inch. "Understood."

"Mr. Tingle must understand he is not a suspect. We wish to question him as a possible witness, or at least someone who might be able to furnish useful information—a friend of the court, so to speak."

Chalmers nodded again.

Tingle shot his lawyer a concerned look. "Huh?"

Chalmers raised a hand a few inches off the arm of the chair. "We're good here, Farris."

Tingle wiggled around in his chair.

"Next, as Chief Jenkins has stipulated, what we tell you must remain in this room. No one, especially the media, is to hear anything from you. His mention of a criminal prosecution for a violation of that confidentiality is not a threat. It's a certainty. Please be sure your client understands that.

"Lastly, if Mr. Tingle admits to some minor violation of law while answering our questions, he will be granted immunity from prosecution in either a state or Federal court."

"What about major crimes? Your definition is a little ambiguous."

Bonnie, never one to mask her emotions, rolled her eyes. "As I said, he's not a suspect in anything. He's being asked for help. But, in addition to immunity, we're prepared to offer him a recommendation of no jail time for his pending case of theft from Ryan Leary's SUV. Short of admitting to murder, yes, he gets a pass."

"You're asking for help," Chalmers said. "How about a walk on the larceny charge? Save me time and aggravation. Farris was tortured by Leary and his men. I'll get it thrown out anyway. I'm doing this pro bono. My time is money. Throw me a bone here."

Bonnie shifted into top gear. "Mr. Chalmers, you're getting priceless publicity for your expenditure of time. The beating took place after he was apprehended and in custody. No one attempted to beat a confession out of him. He wasn't in any way coerced into admitting his guilt. The police had him cold—caught with the proceeds. The beating occurred because Leary, and the detectives to a lesser degree, were looking to keep Mr. Tingle's mouth shut about the contents of Leary's bag. We're looking at two separate incidents."

Chalmers chewed on the side of his lower lip but said nothing. Tingle looked like he was contemplating an epileptic fit.

Bonnie kept charging ahead. "We'll win you a civil rights conviction. And with that, may I add, we'll be handing you a victory in your civil suit. With our zealous assistance, Mr. Tingle will be a wealthy man. But without us going to bat for him with the court, he might have to wait to spend his newly awarded money after doing felony time in a Tennessee prison for grand larceny. As you remember, the bag he stole contained drugs and a loaded firearm."

Tingle looked at Chalmers like his hopes and dreams of a swimming pool full of greenbacks might be circling the drain.

"Okay," Chalmers said abruptly. "We agree to all. I'm going to trust you people here—don't disappoint me."

I saw an opportune spot to stick in my two cents. "And tell Farris not to disappoint us. We need the whole truth. No evasions. No half truths. And no lies."

The bastard had the nerve to look shocked. "Why would you expect him to lie?"

"Come on, counselor, and no offence, Farris, but he's a known burglar and a drug addict. He doesn't have a reputation for doing good amongst humanity."

"Farris will tell you the whole truth."

———

Everyone spent a few brief moments looking at each other.

"Since I assume we'll be here for some time," Chalmers said, "would anyone of you like a beverage? Coffee? Tea? Something else?"

I shook my head as did Bonnie. Ralph answered for us. "We're good. Thanks."

However, Farris wasn't. "I wouldn't mind havin' me a soda."

I sighed. Ralph momentarily closed his eyes and shook his head, and Bonnie did her eye rolling thing once again. I thought that perhaps the entire human race bored her.

Chalmers looked a bit put out, but he had offered and would accommodate his client. "All right, Farris. I'll get you a soda."

He stood up and walked toward his desk, the one large enough to get its own zip code, and the phone.

"A *Mella Yella* if ya got one," Tingle said. It was the first time he smiled since we arrived.

"I don't know if we have that, Farris," Chalmers said. "I'll get you something good."

"Okay, but I don't like no Dr. Pepper. Gives me the burps."

Chalmers smiled. Or was it a sneer? He nodded and lifted the phone.

"Look, Farris," I said. "I want to remind you, you're not being looked at for committing a crime. We're asking for your help. I'm not blowing smoke at you, son, I think you can help us. I think you may have seen something we'd find useful. And I want to help you remember what you actually saw because you may have forgotten after Leary and his two detectives tuned you up. Understand?"

Chalmers had finished on the phone and walked back to the chair he'd been using.

"What's this you've been saying?"

"I told Farris we're not trying to hurt him, only assist him in remembering something that may help us."

Chalmers forced a phony smile. "Umm. Wonderful. I applaud your generosity, but let's go back to the reason you're here and the information you're so afraid may leak to the media."

I thought we might have skated past that one, but Chalmers was no slouch.

Ralph spoke up. "We believe Ryan Leary may have committed another crime. We think he may have done something to someone else—

worse than the beating he gave Farris. We'd like to find more evidence to substantiate that."

Chalmers' eyebrows went up two inches, and a big smile crossed his face. "And you want me to forget I heard about this? If Leary has beaten other subjects, I'd love to introduce it at trial and establish a pattern of behavior."

Bonnie answered that. "Relax, counselor. If we're successful in establishing Leary's guilt here, you can use whatever you know to establish your fair preponderance of guilt. We wouldn't begrudge you that. It's something you'd learn from the news. Now, let's get back to having Mr. Tingle help us out."

Chalmers wouldn't let up. "What do you think Leary did?"

"Something more than he did to your client," Ralph said. "Look, your representation during the civil rights portion of this affair may be pro bono, but you can't expect us to believe you aren't operating on a contingency with the civil trial. You have a vested interest in us learning as much derogatory information about Leary as possible. We win, you win, and certainly Mr. Tingle goes home with more money than he ever envisioned in his entire life."

"Point taken, Mr. Oliveri." The lawyer thought for a long moment. "You think Leary killed someone. You have no complainant. You have a body?"

We didn't answer for an equally long moment, but I felt compelled to break the ice. "And what you envision would look great in civil court, wouldn't it? So, let's get to it, and if Farris comes up with something good, you both hit pay dirt."

CHAPTER EIGHTEEN

P erry Chalmers' secretary, an almost pretty, well-dressed brunette of around forty-five, walked in after knocking. She handed Farris Tingle a twelve-ounce plastic bottle of Mountain Dew and set a glass tumbler on a soapstone coaster lying on the big cocktail table that separated us all.

"I'm sorry, sir," she said to Tingle. "I couldn't find a Mello Yello. I hope this will do."

Farris smiled, showing a missing canine on the top left. I wondered if Ryan Leary had knocked it out.

"Oh, yes, ma'am," he said. "That'll be fine. Thank ya."

The secretary left. Farris twisted off the cap and took a long drink from the spout.

"Tastes better from the bottle," he said.

"Farris," I said, "Let me tell you a little about what we're going to do."

He stared at me without blinking, his eyes open very wide, accompanied by an otherwise blank expression.

"I'm interested in what you saw in the black SUV and what you found in the duffle bag."

As he nodded, his entire upper body moved forward and back. He looked like something out of a carnival sideshow.

"If you don't mind, sit on the couch next to my chair. Being closer works better."

He frowned and looked to Chalmers for approval. Chalmers nodded. Farris still looked apprehensive.

"It's okay. I'm not going to hit you," I said.

His head pivoted, again looking to Chalmers for instruction.

"Go ahead. Sit next to him," the lawyer said.

Tingle placed his sweaty soda bottle on the wooden tabletop next to the coaster and moved himself to the sofa on my right. Chalmers gave his client a dirty look and swapped the wet bottle for the dry glass sitting on the soapstone. He pulled a clean handkerchief from his back pants pocket and wiped the ring of moisture from the mellow glow of the waxed walnut tabletop.

I shifted my chair forty-five degrees to face Tingle.

"To make this easy on you, Farris, don't look at anyone or anything in the room. Just look at me, or if it helps you relax and remember, close your eyes. Mr. Chalmers will be right here if you need him."

The kid nodded.

"Now, let's go back to the night you found the black bag. Where was the bag in the SUV?"

"Back seat."

"Did you see anything else in the SUV?"

"Nosir."

"Nothing?"

"Don't remember."

"The door was unlocked, and you picked up the bag?"

"Uh-huh."

"Did you open it then?"

"'Course not."

Farris was a man of few words. I wanted to smack him.

"Tell me what you did."

"Walked away."

"You didn't run?"

"Wouldn't do that."

"Where did you go?"

He shifted his eyes to Chalmers and waited. Chalmers nodded, looking a little impatient. Then Farris looked over toward Ralph and Bonnie. His eyes remained there for a moment. I assumed to check out Bonnie's legs. I snapped my fingers.

"Come on back, Farris. Look at me."

I repeated my last question. "Where'd you go next?"

"'Bout a block away. There's a vacant lot with trees."

"And you opened the bag?"

"Uh-huh."

"It was night. How did you see?"

"Got me a l'il flashlight." He said that as if only a fool would need to ask. The need to smack him came back to me.

"Tell me what you saw in the bag."

"Sir, I done tol' ya this b'fore."

"I know. Indulge me. Let's hear it again."

When Farris first sat on the sofa, he had crossed his legs and as we spoke, his raised foot jiggled to the rhythm of an unheard tune. As his foot moved, he tapped the first two fingers of his left hand on his thigh.

"Well, I seen them porno DVDs."

"They were in plastic cases?"

"Yessir, all of 'em."

"How many?"

"Don't know. A bunch."

"How many is a bunch?"

"Not sure."

"More than three?"

"Uh-huh."

I was getting impatient. Farris kept jiggling and tapping away.

"Fifty?" I asked.

"Not that many. Ten or twelve, mebbe."

"What else did you find?"

"Crack."

"Little vials?"

"Not so li'l. Bigger, like a dealer might have. Couple o' fifty dollar vials, couple o' hunnert dollar each."

"How many?'

"I didn't take none."

I kept my voice soft, without a hint of accusation. "I didn't say you did. How many did you find?"

He began blinking rapidly. "Six."

"That many large vials cost a lot of money."

"Yessir, lots. Didn't take none, though."

"I know you didn't. You once said that you saw a black handgun. Is that correct?"

"Uh-huh, but didn't touch it. Don't know nuthin' 'bout guns."

I nodded, and we went through a few more inconsequential items we already knew about.

"Now close your eyes, Farris, and think hard." And forget about Bonnie's thighs. "Focus on the black bag, just as you saw it that night. What else was in that bag?"

His shoulders tensed up, and he straightened a bit from the slouching position he'd been in. He stopped jiggling his foot and tapping on his leg. He opened his eyes.

"Nuthin'."

I don't claim to be a human lie detector, but it's not difficult to read someone's body language—especially if they tell a whopper.

I slid my chair a foot closer to Farris and leaned in. "I want you to think hard now. Focus on the inside of the bag. What else did you see? Was there a knife? Were there any more drugs?"

Those two prompts didn't get a rise from him. In fact, he relaxed a little, and his left index finger began tapping his thigh again.

"Think hard, son. If you help us find what we're looking for it could mean you'll get lots of money in your civil suit. Give us a hand, and you could be a rich man."

Tingle frowned to where his eyes were only slits. I could almost smell

170

the gears inside his head grinding. Another gentle nudge might just tip him over the edge.

"Was there something in the bag that you may have taken out—by accident? Something you put in your pocket and didn't remember until just now? What else was in the bag?"

The finger stopped. He uncrossed his legs and straightened up in the chair, sitting forward, looking at me defiantly.

"I tol' ya, sir. I didn't see nuthin' more."

"You look like you're getting upset, Farris. If you took something from the bag, it's okay. You won't be punished for it. Mr. Leary will not harm you. I won't harm you. Tell me what you saw."

Farris began blinking again, like a flashing strobe light. He shot a look at Chalmers, who sat there impassively, and then jerked his head back to me.

"Counselor," I said, "it seems as if your client has something to say, but he's reluctant. A little help, please."

The lawyer gestured with his hand. "Come over here, Farris."

The boy stood.

Chalmers gestured again and then pointed to the chair next to his. "Sit."

They spoke in whispers for a very long moment.

Chalmers leaned away from Tingle and straightened his tie. "Go back and tell the man."

Farris returned to the couch. He sighed. "A cell phone."

My eyes popped wide. I gave Ralph and Bonnie a quick look.

"A cell phone was in the bag?"

"Yessir."

"Where is it now?"

"I ditched it."

"Why?"

"Figgered it might have a GPS chip, and somebody'd track me."

Farris Tingle was obviously more tech savvy than I might have thought.

"Where did you ditch it?"

"The woods where I checked the bag."

"Was there anything else besides the phone that you found in the bag and haven't mentioned yet?"

"Nosir."

I looked at Chalmers. "Would you mind if we took Mr. Tingle to the woods to retrieve this cell phone?"

Chalmers shook his head and shrugged. "Be my guest."

"Will you be coming with us?"

Not exactly dripping with enthusiasm, Chalmers said, "Let me know what happens."

———

I called the PD and asked Bettye to send John Gallagher and two cops to meet us at the wooded lot near Ryan Leary's home to help secure the area and search for the cell phone Farris said he tossed away.

Thirty-five minutes later, I pulled up behind a Prospect PD cruiser parked across from the vacant land. John and POs Lenny Alcock and Billy Puckett stood on the blacktop leaning against the sector car. Ralph parked his silver Ford behind my car. He, Bonnie and Tingle stepped out.

"Okay, Farris," I said, "What are we looking for?"

"Cheap l'il cell phone. One o' them Walmart specials."

"About where do you think it landed?"

"Not sure." He stepped into the woods, weaving his way between the scrub foliage and pointed to a spot fifteen to twenty feet from the roadway. "I was 'bout here and tossed it back there someplace."

"Okay, guys, let's spread out, and take a look."

"Hang on, Boss," John said. "I got an idea and something that might help."

He took a pink smart phone from his pocket, played around with it for a few moments and made a production of pushing a button. From fifty feet inside the woods the stylized ring of a cell phone sounded off.

Gallagher got a stupid grin on his face. "There ya go, Boss. Easy, huh?"

I scowled at him. "Yeah, John. Good work." I turned toward Alcock and Puckett. "Guys, find that phone."

The two uniformed cops carefully walked toward the ring. I looked back at John.

"What?" he said as if I had a problem. "I took Rosanna Wakefield's phone out of property. I hit the redial when I saw 'Andy's' number and *wah-la*. Ain't technology great?"

———

Ralph and Bonnie returned Farris Tingle to his attorney's office and took the cell phone to an FBI evidence recovery team technician to be dusted for fingerprints. That done, they turned the phone over to a communications specialist working with the Strangler task force. Ralph said he'd call with the results.

At quarter to five, my phone rang.

"They lifted a beauty off the battery," Ralph said, sounding especially upbeat. "Our latents guy took care of the search work and matched it to Leary. Charlie, the commo guy, says that phone is a treasure chest of numbers and texts. In short, paly, Leary is dog chow."

"Is Heidi getting a warrant?"

"Of course. Bonnie hand carried the application to our favorite judge —a guy who always keeps his mouth shut."

"Good. Is Heidi going to call J.R. Tolbert and have him surrender his client?"

"That was mentioned, but Corliss stuck his nose in and suggested that we just take Leary off at his house. Heidi is more civilized than Corliss, but everyone else liked the idea so much, she agreed."

"Sounds like Corliss is good for something."

"He's not so bad, just a real mover and shaker. The kind of guy you never turn your back on."

"I know the type."

"We should have that warrant back shortly—before six anyway. The judge won't file anything until tomorrow. We'll pick him up in the morning."

"Good. Want company?"

"I thought you'd be interested, so I asked. Mizz Piper approves your presence."

"Nice of her," I said sarcastically. "Listen, save the SWAT team and battalion of agents for something else. You and Bonnie meet me here tomorrow. I'll get a bunch of cops to cover the back door and we'll have him in cuffs lickety split."

"Okay, I can sell that."

———

At nine the next morning, Ralph and Bonnie walked briskly into Prospect PD wearing their fighting clothes and FBI raid jackets—navy blue windbreakers with large yellow letters front and back and the FBI seal over their hearts.

I had arranged to have Stan Rose and two off-duty cops in to assist with the arrest.

Bettye was sitting at my desk while Terri Donnellson took a turn answering the phone and dispatching the radio cars. John Gallagher was drinking coffee, itching to hit the road with me.

We pulled up in front of Leary's house at 9:20. John, Stanley and the two uniforms jogged to cover the sides and back. Bonnie, Ralph and I approached the front door. I pressed an illuminated doorbell button. Chimes sounded off within the house.

We waited a long moment—nothing. I tried again. After another few moments, still nothing.

"That bastard," I said.

"I've got his number," Ralph said and tapped it into his cell phone and let it ring. After a short wait, He shook his head. "Seven rings and it went to voice mail."

I began to percolate. "He's breaking chops." I pounded on the door. "Ryan, it's Sam Jenkins. Answer the door."

"Save your breath," Bonnie said. "He's either not here or not coming out. Maybe someone tipped him off."

"Who's monitoring his ankle transmitter?" I asked.

"Federal court officers," Ralph said.

"You have their number?"

"Yeah."

He called them.

Two minutes later: "They say the device is inside, and the strap has not been cut."

"So, he's playing with us. His SUV is in the driveway. Hang on."

I called Stan Rose on his cell phone. "Is there a door or back window to the garage?"

"Yeah, back door and side window. What do you need?"

"Look inside. Any cars?"

"Standby."

Moments later: "Silver Corvette and an empty space. His wife work?"

"At the county mayor's office. I'll have Bettye track her down. Meantime, send John up front."

I telephoned Bettye and asked her to confirm Mrs. Leary's whereabouts, but not tell her we were about to collar her husband for murder. As I hung up, John Gallagher stopped next to us.

"I want the two cops to keep a watch on this place while you impound Leary's SUV," I said. "Call Fleenor's Body Shop. He'll have a flatbed here in ten minutes. Then call Earl Biggins and have him secure the SUV in our garage."

"Okay, Boss."

"When the wrecker leaves, send one cop to the sheriff's motor pool and ask their car man for the spare set of keys for Earl."

John nodded.

"Then you and the other cop park down the street and make sure Leary stays put."

"Wanna let us in on what's going on?" Ralph asked.

"We're going to make Leary come out."

"I'll call Heidi," he said. "She can get a "no knock" endorsement on the warrant. If Leary wants to play cute, we'll kick the door in."

"And how long will that take? We'll have to come back later today or tomorrow," I added.

"You're always impatient. What do you have in mind?"

"We'll be back here in less than an hour and ready to go."

"And do what?" Bonnie asked.

"Leary has a big libido. We'll cast a sexy lure and catch the big fish."

———

Before going back to the PD, I stopped at Walking Horse Realty on the town square to see my neighbor, Glenda Mae Waddell. A small bell tinkled as I opened the front door.

"Hey, Maezy, what's goin' on?"

"Hey ya se'f, Sammy. To what do I owe this pleasure?"

"I need a favor."

She batted the lashes over her grey-blue eyes and demurely pated her short blonde hair. "Why, sugar, what is it you wont?" Mae is a shameless flirt.

"Raise your right hand."

"Okay." And she did.

"Say I do."

She smiled. "I do what, darlin'?"

"You're deputized. Now help me do some po-leece work."

"Shoot, Sammy, I thought...Well, doesn't matter what I thought, does it?"

I didn't answer that. "Do you know Ryan Leary?"

"I've seen him on the TV news. Got himse'f inta some real trouble, hasn't he?"

"Yep. But you don't know him personally?"

"No."

"Does he know you?"

"Me? I don't think so."

"Okay. I need a dozen of your business cards."

"Sure. Why?"

"Brand new deputy detectives shouldn't ask questions."

———

I found Ralph and Bonnie standing in the lobby meeting Terri Donnellson and speaking with Bettye.

"Hello, troops," I said.

"Hi, boss," Terri said.

Bettye asked, "Sammy darlin', what are you up to? I know that look."

Ralph and Bonnie looked at me like I had two heads, probably wondering why I'd greet them again after leaving them only twenty minutes earlier.

"Terri, you ever do any undercover work in the MPs?"

"Uh, only once. It wasn't much. CID needed a female decoy in an NCO club."

"Good. How far away do you live?"

"Ten minutes or so."

"Also good. I want you to go home and change into civilian clothes. Have you got a short skirt and high heels?"

A slight frown crossed her forehead. "Uh, sure."

"How about a real slinky blouse? Maybe something low cut."

Bettye broke in, protecting one of her new children. "Sam Jenkins, what's goin' on?"

"Elementary, my dear Sergeant. We're going to capitalize on Ryan Leary's penchant for good-looking young women."

Bettye tilted her head and raised a single eyebrow. She only does that to fascinate me.

"Officer Donnellson is going to pose as a real estate broker looking for listings. Leary's neighborhood is full of big, expensive houses where, no doubt, everyone in the home has to work to pay their ridiculous mortgages. So, Terri probably won't encounter any homeowners—except Leary who's under house arrest. But he may not answer the door until Terri fakes having car trouble. Then she'll go back and keep banging on his door until he can't resist the young lady on his door step. With luck, he'll make himself available to be collared—the easy way or the hard way, his choice."

"Uh, hey, paly, do we get any say about this?" Ralph asked.

"Of course, Ralph. You get the arrest. The FBI comes out smelling like a French bimbo, Leary goes to jail, the Internet hookers of East Tennessee are once again safe, and we clear maybe nine homicides. Cool, huh?"

He threw his hands up. "Why do I get involved with you?"

"We're goombahs. You know you love it. Shut up already."

"Nuts."

I laughed. "Hey, Betts, do you still own that blue mini-van?"

"Not for a couple years. Why?"

"I want a van with a sliding side door. Anyone in the building have one?"

She thought for a moment. "I've seen Ted Hanshe, the man who has a contract with the city to do plumbing work, around for a couple days now. He drives a van."

"Yeah, Ted Hanshe, the auxiliary cop. He works church traffic details on Sundays. He's good. Where is he?"

"Somewhere on the second floor."

"I'll find him. In the meantime, Terri, go home, change, and hurry back. Bring your own car. We can't have you using a marked PD to do your real estate business."

Ted Hanshe wasn't difficult to find. I followed the noise to the ladies room, found an open door and a pair of legs poking out from one of the stalls.

"Teddy, that you banging around in here?"

"Yeah, who wants to know?" Ted was another transplant from

somewhere in the northeast who brought his plumbing business with him.

"Me, Sam Jenkins, your sometimes fearless leader. Got a minute?"

He untangled himself from behind the toilet, got to his feet and stepped out wiping his hand on his pants legs.

"Whaddaya say, Chief?" He extended his hand and shrugged. "It's almost clean."

We shook hands, and I got down to business.

"You got a few minutes to sign in as a part-time cop today? I need you and your van and promise a little excitement."

Ted was stocky but not fat and had a thick head of salt and pepper hair. His gray work shirt showed Hanshe and Sons Plumbing embroidered over the left pocket.

"Yeah, I'm about done in this room. Who do I have to kill?"

"Nothing that drastic. A couple of Feds and I want to arrest an uncooperative subject. You drive the van, and we'll grab the guy and toss him into the back. Kind of like a snatch and grab operation. Interested?"

A big smile crossed his very Irish face. "You bet. But you gotta give me a few minutes to clear some tools outta the van."

"No problem. We're waiting for our undercover cop to get back wearing her civvies."

———

Terri showed up at 12:30. I missed lunch and was not a happy police chief. Bettye would also miss her hour off while we were out playing fugitive squad. But she didn't care because she'd eat a container of low fat, low carb, low calorie yogurt at her desk. Ralph looked like he was gasping for a meal and a glass of beer, and Bonnie showed no emotion.

We all met Ted Hanshe and Stan Rose in the parking lot. Terri followed us, driving her Mini Cooper, to the street where we found Leary's cell phone. John Gallagher and Bobby John Crockett met us there.

After a short council of war, Terri took off to begin her portrayal of Glenda Mae Waddell, real estate broker. Ted Hanshe drove the van with Stanley riding shotgun while Ralph and I hid in the back. He parked the van three doors down from Leary's place. Bonnie and the other three parked the remaining vehicles out of sight, but close enough to Leary's house to assist if necessary.

Terri had changed into a red skirt that stopped four inches above her knees. That was topped off with a white scoop-neck blouse that showed enough cleavage to drive the likes of Ryan Leary into a frenzy but would still be appropriate for a young realtor who wanted to look professional, but cash in on her sex appeal. A natural tan linen jacket covered all that and looked very businesslike.

She parked her Mini directly across from Leary's house and conspicuously began knocking on front doors. When no one answered, she tucked a business card between the door and the frame. She worked her way down one side of the street and up the other. When she knocked on Leary's door, he peeked out the window and asked what she wanted.

"Afternoon, sir. I's wonderin' if y'all would like ta sell yer beautiful house? I've got interested buyers, jest needin' a home like yours. And, sir, they got plenty o' cash fer a down payment and won't have a problem gettin' a mortgage."

She really played up the southern belle act for him.

"We're not looking to sell," he said.

"Oh, shoot. I's hopin' I'd find someone interested in sellin'. Like I said, I got a few buyers really wantin' inta this neighborhood. Kin I jest leave ya with my card? If ya know of anyone who wants ta sell and ya steer 'em in my direction, I'd be sure ta mention ya in the contract and pay y'all a nice finder's fee."

A few moments later, Leary opened the door and took the card Terri handed him—after thoroughly checking out her appearance and smiling like a copperhead eyeing up a juicy mouse.

After hitting about a dozen houses, Terri walked back to her car. And she played it perfectly in case Leary had been watching. She appeared to be turning the ignition key, but nothing happened. She slapped the steering wheel and looked angry. She got out of the car, slammed the door and attempted to make a cell phone call. Having no luck there, she stomped across the street and again knocked on Leary's door. Soon enough he answered.

"I'm sorry ta bother ya again," she said, "but my car won't start. I turn the key and get nothin'. On top o' that, my cell phone is dead. I mean, like completely dead."

"You want to call a tow truck?"

She gave him an inviting smile. "I'd like ta jest drive away. My car was perfectly okay a few minutes ago. Do ya know anythin' about motors or cars or whatever?"

Leary looked her over again and smiled. "Yeah, maybe." Then he stuck his head out the door and checked up one side of the street and down the other—probably looking for police cars.

Seeing only a white plumber's van and nothing suspicious, he shrugged. "You don't hear the engine turn over at all?"

"No, sir, nothin'. I mean like really nothin'."

"Is the battery old?"

She shook her head. "It's only a two-year-old car."

"Okay. Maybe one of your wires popped off a terminal. I'll take a look. Release the hood for me."

They walked away from the house toward Terri's car.

On the way, Terri touched his arm. "Oh, you're so sweet."

With her high heels clicking on the blacktop and her backside swaying enough to keep Leary interested, she led him to the waiting Mini.

As soon as Leary lifted the hood and stuck his head into the engine compartment, Ted Hanshe slapped the shift lever into gear and gently drove down the block. As he came parallel to Terri's car, he jammed on the brakes and screeched to a stop. Ralph and I slid open the side door and jumped from the van. I slammed the hood down on Leary and twisted his left arm behind his back. While Ralph cuffed that hand, I pulled the right into place to receive the second handcuff.

Together, we stood Leary upright, Ralph holding one arm and me the other. We pushed him through the van's doorway and jumped in after him. It only took seconds.

Ralph slammed the door closed, and Teddy hit the gas. As the van lurched forward, we all jockeyed for a secure position. Leary blinked several times and looked at me.

"What the fuck is this? What's going on?"

"FBI," Ralph said. "We have a warrant for your arrest."

"I know you," Leary said, looking at Ralph. "We've done this before. I'm already under house arrest. What's the problem? What's this warrant business?"

"The warrant is for murder, Ryan," I said. "It's all over."

"Sam, you're fuckin' crazy. This is bullshit."

"No, it's not. We have your emails. We have your cell phone. You're 'Andy'. It's over."

He let out a long breath and nodded. "I want to call my lawyer."

CHAPTER NINETEEN

Ralph, Bonnie and I took Leary into our squad room and closed the door. Stan Rose and Ted Hanshe walked to the lobby to give Bettye an account of what happened on the street. I knew I could trust Stanley to filter out the things my beloved administrative officer would raise her eyebrow over, but I never got the chance to instruct Teddy to keep the details of our swashbuckling and sometimes unconventional operations to a bare minimum. Terri drove her 'disabled' Mini Cooper back by herself.

Ralph unhooked the handcuffs from behind Leary's back and locked him to the steel ring bolted to the side of a desk.

"Why am I here?" Leary asked as he rubbed his free wrist with his shackled hand.

"Out of deference to you," I said. "Would you rather we walked you through the halls of the Justice Center in cuffs?"

His face changed from a tight look of defiance to a more relaxed, resigned expression. He shrugged. "No, thank you."

"In the van you said lawyer," Ralph added. "There's a phone."

"Okay, but can we talk first?"

Always thinking like an attorney, Bonnie said, "Sure, if you sign a waiver of counsel *first*."

Leary attempted to make light of her thoroughness. "Come on, we're just talking here."

I knew where he was trying to go. "Horseshit. Sign the paper, and we'll talk all you want."

Leary flipped his free hand up to shoulder height in a gesture of resignation. "Okay, okay. Gimme the form."

I walked over to the shelves where all our paperwork resided, grabbed the appropriate document and handed it to Bonnie. She placed it on the desktop next to Leary and handed him a pen.

He scribbled a signature on the dotted line. "There. Signed, sealed and delivered."

"Good," I said. "You want to talk, it's your dime."

"Who's got the case, you or the FBI?"

I raised my eyebrows and looked at Ralph.

"The FBI has taken over responsibility for the Task Force," he said.

A sly smile and look of chagrin took over Leary's face. "Ahh, the *task force*." He spent a long moment nodding. "Who's the AUSA in charge?"

"Heidi Piper," Ralph said.

Ryan looked at me. "I doubt you'd have gotten involved in that spectacular little street arrest unless you had a good reason."

"We weren't shooting in the dark, partner. We've got a warrant and a real good case."

"Then get Heidi down here," Leary said. "I think we might have a deal."

"A deal for what?" Ralph asked, showing a great deal of attitude. "We've got your balls in a vice. Why should we deal?"

"Simple. I won't claim to be totally innocent or uninvolved, but I want the death penalty off the agenda. Then I'll give you the guy everyone has been calling the Riverside Strangler."

"Gimme a break, Ryan," Ralph said. "We've got you. We've got everything. You're toast. You're the man. You're guilty. End of story."

Leary shook his head with a bit of vigor. "Hold your horses, cowboy.

Yeah, I'm guilty—of something, but not of what you think. You wanna hear what I've got to say, or you wanna just stick it up my ass and not get the real killer?"

"We'll listen," I said, "but quit dancing. What's the story?"

"The story, Sam, is I'll give you the guy you want and the evidence you need to convict him—if we make a deal. It's simple. I don't want to die, and I have no problem pointing you in the right direction."

I was interested but losing patience. "And at whom will we be looking?"

Leary grinned. "Someone important...very important."

Ralph showed his annoyance. "Come on, pal, you're not writing a cliffhanger episode for some second rate TV show. Who's so special?"

Leary wouldn't budge. "Get Heidi down here. I'll call my lawyer. Then, when we're all sittin' around the campfire, I'll tell ya what ya want to know."

———

Before we had pulled into the parking lot of the municipal building, Ralph had called Carl Harmon, who in turn said he would call Heidi Piper. So, they were already on the road travelling toward Prospect as fast as their little Government Issue tires could carry them out of Knoxville. When Ralph called a second time, Carl said they were about fifteen minutes away.

Leary called his lawyer, J.R. Tolbert, but learned that J.R. was in court. Tolbert's office manager promised to send an associate immediately and have Tolbert drag his ass to Prospect PD as quickly as possible.

In the interim, Ryan seemed amenable to chat.

"Look, Ryan," I said, "There's no reason we can't do this in a civilized fashion. It's after noon. Have you eaten?"

"Not since breakfast. But as you may assume, I'm not really in a festive mood lookin' for snacks."

"Suit yourself. But you're not going anywhere, and I believe it'll be a long time until they serve chow at the Federal lock-up."

"I'm guessin' you people want to eat?" he asked.

Bonnie shrugged. Ralph nodded. I spoke.

"I'm always hungry, and we can get Chinese delivered."

"Yeah, okay."

"You need a menu?"

"You're hot shit," he said. "You want to put me away for life and buy me Chinese food."

"I have my good points."

He nodded. "How about sweet and sour chicken?"

"Wouldn't be my choice, but what the hell? Ralph, there's a menu in the top right drawer of my desk. After you and Bonnie make a choice, ask Bettye to call with Ryan's order and add home-style tofu for me. I'll spring, of course."

Ralph frowned. "Tofu? You gotta be kidding."

I scowled. "Make the list, and get lost, kid."

Leary chuckled. He was beginning to loosen up. "While we're waiting, I wouldn't mind something to drink."

"I haven't got any sweet tea for you Tennessee boys."

"I had something stronger in mind."

"I haven't drunk any bourbon since 1969. Scotch suit you?"

"Scotch'll do."

"Ralph, hang on. It sounds like we're going to have cocktails before lunch."

"Sure your lawyer will approve of us getting you half loaded before you make a statement?" Ralph asked.

"I'm goin' to have a drink or two, not get fallin' down drunk."

"Okay," I said, "will one of you mind going into the bottom right draw of my desk and getting the bottle of Glenfiddich? Glasses are in the cabinet below the coffee maker. There should be ice in the mini-fridge. Feel free to indulge if you'd like."

Ralph looked at Bonnie. "Come on, I'll give you a hand."

She shook her head and addressed me. "He's right, you are hot shit. I graduate from Law School and the FBI academy to be a cocktail waitress."

She turned and walked out. Ralph followed.

"Some ass on that one," Leary observed.

"Yeah. Good-looking girl," I said. "Good cop, too—for an FBI agent and lawyer."

He chuckled again. "You know, I told—" Leary frowned and paused. "I told the guy I'm going to tell you about, not to get anywhere near Prospect. I just knew that if you caught a case, you'd be like a nasty pit-bull until you cleared it."

I shrugged. "Sorry."

"No, you're not."

I smiled. "No, I'm not. So, are you saying you were only an accomplice and didn't commit any of the murders?"

"Let's wait until J.R. gets here."

I nodded. "You took one hell of a risk. I mean, the stuff you did in Knoxville with your girlfriend was bad enough. And telling people about your sex junkets to Thailand wasn't exactly your most brilliant moment. But what the hell did this person provide or offer or hang over your head to get you to participate in all this?"

Leary let out a long breath before answering. "My life as you see it."

———

B onnie returned with the bottle of whisky and a pint of spring water. Ralph was right behind her carrying four glasses.

"I hope neither of you *gentlemen* needs rocks," she said sarcastically. "I really didn't feel like scaring up an ice bucket, and I'd like to finish my drink before his lawyer and my boss get here."

"Not a problem, miss," Leary said.

Bonnie frowned at the word *miss*.

"Thanks, Bonnie," I said. "I think you'll like the single-malt with just a splash of water."

She uncorked the bottle and handed it to me. "I can't believe you're doing this. I mean, the man's a serial killer."

"Last week we were all friends and colleagues. Today, that changed.

Ryan says he'll make our professional lives easy. Why hate someone when it's not necessary?"

I poured four shots of scotch, drizzled a little water into mine and asked if Leary wanted any. He shook his head. I handed him a glass first, then one to Bonnie and finally to Ralph. Bonnie picked up the water, added more than necessary and passed it to Ralph.

"Bottoms up, folks."

Everyone took sips.

"Since you're cooperating and behaving yourself, Ryan," I said, "I'm happy to deal with you without rancor. On the other hand, I could hate Lew Schmecke without much effort."

Leary was in mid sip when he laughed and almost choked on the scotch. "That's why I hired him. I figgered you wouldn't like Lew and maybe his presence might keep you away from the task force."

"Very clever. I hope Schmecke is the guy you're going to flip on."

He took another drink of scotch and laughed again. "No such luck."

We finished our drinks, and Bonnie gathered up three glasses. "Would you like another?" she asked Leary.

"Damn straight," he said with a smile.

Bonnie didn't return the pleasantry. I guess Ryan's charm wasn't working on her. She left his glass, the Scotch and the water and left the room.

Leary took a healthy pull on his drink. "Oh, yeah, great ass."

———

It wasn't five minutes later when Bettye led Carl Harmon and Heidi Piper into the squad room.

"Isn't this cozy?" Heidi said. "A picnic?"

Carl looked at Ralph and Bonnie like a wicked stepfather.

I stood to greet our new guests. "I believe you both know Ryan Leary. He's had a tough morning and has a long day ahead of him. I offered him a drink before we ordered a Chinese lunch."

Heidi nodded, but didn't even come close to smiling. "Chinese food and Scotch. Interesting combination. Have you ordered the food yet?"

"Waited for you two and Mr. Tolbert's associate."

"I was a little up tight," Leary said. "The Scotch helped. Are you ready to talk deal?"

That seemed to soften up Heidi a bit. "Aren't you waiting for your attorney?" she asked.

"They're sending an associate. Tolbert is in court. We'll wait for him, but I know what I want to say."

Five minutes and almost all of Leary's Scotch later, Tolbert's hired hand, a fifty-something-year-old guy named Arthur Hellman showed up. I figured him a little long in the tooth to still be an associate and not a partner somewhere, but Arthur didn't look like a fool.

"I hope you haven't made a statement yet, Mr. Leary." Hellman said.

Leary looked at him as if he was a foolish child. "I pay you people for legal representation, but don't think I'm stupid. I told them I'd cooperate, but I waited for you."

Hellman set an oxblood-colored leather brief case on the desk and looked at Heidi. "What are you prepared to offer?"

Heidi yanked the handbag off her shoulder and tossed it on another desk. "How the hell should I know? I've got who we think is the Riverside Strangler in cuffs—based on lots of solid evidence, and you act like you've got an inside straight to play. He's the one who asked for a deal. I can go back to Knoxville and still finish my day quite happy."

"Hold on now, Arthur," Leary said. "Let me do this."

"I advise you to say nothing until they agree to a deal."

"Lord have mercy, man. I gotta tell them what I'll give up b'fore they move an inch. Understand? It's how it works."

Hellman was about to speak, but Heidi beat him to the punch.

"I understand you're claiming someone else is the actual killer. What exactly was your part in all this?"

"Reasonable question," Leary said. "And I'll tell ya." He shifted in the chair and took another drink of scotch. "I'm willin' to admit bein' an accomplice to the murder of the Wakefield girl—Rosanna or Mysty or whatever she called herself on Charlie's List—Sam's case. I'll also tell you about the other seven victims in the county and a few more I know about in other jurisdictions that I had nothin' ta do with." His speech was beginning to show the effects of the Glenfiddich. "But I know the details. Lotsa details. For all this, I want the other seven murders written off my slate—cleared administratively—and whatever sentence Mr. Tolbert negotiates here to run concurrently with the fifty-four months AUSA Corliss offered in the Farris Tingle case. That sound reasonable?"

Before Heidi could comment, I interjected, "You said seven other murders. There are eight more attributed to the Riverside Strangler."

Leary shook his head. "Seven is the number. Sorry ta disappoint ya, Sam, but I don't know anythin' about that young male prostitute o' yours."

CHAPTER TWENTY

L eary's statement took the wind out of my sails and the face of Arlo Bowman flashed into my mind.

Heidi Piper caused my wandering mind to snap back to the present.

"I certainly hope this actual killer is as interesting as you, Mr. Leary."

"Oh, don't you worry, Miss Piper. Y'all will love what I've got ta say." He punctuated his statement with a smile and a sip of Scotch.

We didn't have to wait another two minutes before a squad room phone rang. Ralph picked it up, listened for a minute and handed the receiver to me.

"Chief," Bettye said, "a Mr. Tolbert is here representing Ryan Leary."

"Be right there."

I met Tolbert in the lobby. I hadn't run his particulars but guessed him to be about sixty and an inch or two over six feet. I won't say he was thin, but he made a string bean look fat. His light tan suit, which might have cost as much as a good late model Cadillac, had been cut to make his Ichabod Crane-like body appear more physically imposing. That might have worked in a courtroom, but J.R. should never argue a case at a nudist resort.

We shook hands, and he smiled. His gossamer thin white hair sparkled beneath the overhead lighting.

"Ryan is in the squad room," I said. "Let's take a walk back."

"Have you questioned him yet?"

"He's made conversation but waited for you."

"Good. I assume Arthur Hellman is here."

"Also in the squad room."

As soon as Tolbert and I entered the crowded room, he looked at Leary. "Chief, are those handcuffs necessary?"

I shrugged. "Protocol. Your client didn't object."

"Don't sweat it, J.R.," Leary said. "I don't object ta bein' cuffed to a desk when the man is giving me Scotch that cost more 'an fifty dollars a bottle."

Tolbert looked at me. "He might not object, but I do. Can we remove them, please?"

I shot Heidi a quick look. In essence, she was the boss. She gave me a curt nod, and I pulled a ring of keys from my back pocket and stepped toward Leary. "I can always shoot him if he runs."

Leary laughed. "I believe you would. And I *was* a friend."

I unlocked the cuff from around his wrist. "I make it quick and painless for friends."

He laughed again, and I removed the second cuff from the steel ring.

"May we speak to Mr. Leary in private?" Tolbert asked of no one in particular.

"Sure," I said. "Use the room across the hall. We'll stay here."

Ralph escorted them out, and Heidi asked, "What's in that room?"

"It's the juvenile room, just a table and chairs. Oh, yeah, and a one way mirror if you're as unethical as me."

"Maybe next time."

Twenty-five minutes later, the trio strolled back into the squad room. Leary sat in the same chair he had vacated earlier. "You gonna cuff me again?" he asked and forced a grin.

"We'll skip that because you're a friend. But just so you know, while you were gone, I filled my hollow points with garlic butter."

Bonnie rolled her eyes, and Ralph shook his head. I didn't get a chance to check on Carl Harmon before Tolbert spoke up. "Okay, Ms. Piper, how about a nice bundle and a plea?"

"What do you have in mind?" she asked.

The negotiations had begun.

"Shall we say seven and a half to fifteen in a minimum security Federal facility?"

Ralph couldn't keep his mouth shut. "With that sentence, he'll never do more than the seven and a half. For eight murders and torturing that kid? Madone!"

Heidi ignored Oliveri and addressed Tolbert. "I was more inclined to say twenty-five to life with possible parole. And I could find him a bunk in one of our Federal country clubs."

The Tennessee horse trader in Tolbert emerged. "When you hear what he has to say, I'm sure you'll agree to a clean cut fifteen years." He took a moment to smile. "You'll like what you hear."

Heidi looked at me. I shrugged.

"How old are you Ryan?" I asked.

"Fifty-three."

I turned the Heidi. "He'll get out at sixty-eight and be virtually unemployable. Your call, counselor. I could live with him collecting some of the social security he's already paid in."

Ralph stifled a snort.

Heidi said, "His story must lead to an arrest. I don't want to start chasing some phantom all over the country."

"No phantom," Tolbert said. "Your Riverside Strangler is a very local and prominent person. You can have him under arrest by tomorrow if you wish."

———

"Okay, he does the full fifteen," Heidi said. "But Mr. Leary allocutes, outlines every murder in Blount County, gives what he knows about the crimes in other jurisdictions and leads us to any evidence we need. Now, who's the celebrity killer?"

Tolbert extended a hand toward the seated Leary. "Tell them, Ryan."

Leary let out a large volume of air. "Our very own district attorney general."

"Jeez," Ralph said.

Bonnie and I exchanged looks.

"Calvin Pitts?" Heidi didn't exactly gasp, but I had no doubt she wasn't expecting that.

"This promises to be quite a melodramatic saga," I said. "Heidi, do you want to get a recorder working?"

She nodded. "That's a good idea."

Bonnie made an offer. "I'll call the office and get a team here with video gear."

Heidi nodded, and Bonnie left the room.

I looked at Tolbert. "It's getting late, and we're far from finished. Everyone, your client included, must be hungry. We were about to order Chinese food. Do you mind slumming with us law enforcement types, counselor? Lunch is on the city of Prospect."

"Don't mind at all, Chief. I assume you have a menu?"

"Do I ever."

"Great. It's nice doing business like civilized people. Uh, do you think I could have a bit of that fifty-dollar Scotch?"

"Absolutely." I made a forty-five degree turn. "How about you, Heidi? Carl? Scotch?"

"Do you have any ice?" she asked.

"I think that can be arranged."

"Good. I'll have a double."

I laughed. "Ralph, you're custodian of the Glenfiddich. A couple more glasses, please."

Leary chimed in, "Mind if I have another?"

To which Tolbert said, "After your statement, Ryan. After your statement."

———

Forty-five minutes and one Chinese lunch later, two agents showed up with a fairly unsophisticated looking video recorder and tripod that they set up in my office. Before we adjourned there, Ralph and I brought in the requisite number of chairs needed to accommodate all the players and spectators. Then we settled in to watch the Heidi and Ryan show.

The spectacle dragged on for several hours. We took a few breaks, but Leary kept on going like the Energizer Bunny. His memory was exceptional, and he provided enough detail that no one doubted the accuracy of his information.

In addition to the eight murders in Blount County, he brought up three in Asheville on the North Carolina side of the Smokies, two more in Chattanooga and two on the outskirts of Atlanta. He ended with a suggestion.

"Ask Cal. He might be in a talkin' mood. He might jus' give ya more if ya make it worth his while." Leary spoke as if we were interested in buying a used car inventory to start a new dealership.

"I'll ask," Heidi said. "But I honestly don't know if anyone is too eager to provide him with much wiggle room."

Leary shrugged. "Your case, not mine. I just thought givin' the families o' his victims a little closure would be nice." He looked at his lawyer. "I'm about done here, J.R. Mind if I have that Scotch now?"

A nice gesture, I thought, but ironic coming from Leary.

Tolbert nodded. "Yes, Ryan, you may have a Scotch now. And, Chief, may I trouble you for another. It's very good, you know."

"Ralph, would you do the honors? And help yourself to one. Bonnie, Heidi, Carl, raise your hand if you'd like some before Ryan drinks it all."

Leary laughed as Ralph poured two fingers of amber liquid into Ryan's now empty glass.

"I have a question," I said, looking straight into Ryan Leary's eyes. "You've provided all the factual data necessary for the new task force to wrap up a neat package. Mind addressing a few background areas to satisfy my curiosity?"

Leary switched his eyes to J.R. Tolbert.

The lawyer nodded. "Go ahead. If I want you to stop talking, I'll let you know."

"First thing," I said. "Let's go back to why you brought in Lew Schmecke?"

Leary laughed a little too loudly. Apparently the Glenfiddich had loosened up his inhibitions.

"I learned a little about him—what some other cops from New York thought about Lew. I mentioned you and heard you knew of him from years ago and had a little history—nothing major, but basically, I figgered he'd piss you off and keep you away from the task force."

"You've already said that."

He nodded and hit his drink again before continuing.

"I told Cal not to go anywhere near Prospect with his pastime. I didn't want you to work a case. I told him what you'd be like if you got going. But, no, he wouldn't listen. Cal thought he knew more than anyone. Look what it got him."

"And that's it? Schmecke would keep me away from your investigations? There's got to be more."

He shrugged. "After Carl offered FBI he'p a second time, Joe Don started gettin' impatient—said the county mayor had been pushin' for some results. Schmecke had a reputation, deserved or not, of someone who cared. Lew was a TV star. He was my alternative to the FBI. Nothin' mysterious about it."

I nodded, and wondered if Joe Don Hartung was worth the hundred and fifty grand salary he collected from the Blount County taxpayers every year.

"Next thing. How did you two get tied up?"

Tolbert interrupted. "Ryan, perhaps you shouldn't elaborate on that."

"Come on, counselor, I said this is just to satisfy my curiosity—our curiosity. It's off the record. Ms. Piper has agreed to your sweetheart deal. There won't be a trial."

Tolbert relented. He half closed his eyes and nodded.

Leary looked at Ralph and stuck out his glass. Ralph poured. There wasn't much left in the bottle.

"I was waiting in Cal's office one day early in our relationship. I snooped around a little and found an envelope full of pictures. Good quality, professional porn. He really wasn't hiding them. We struck up a conversation, compared notes and preferences." Leary sort of sagged in his chair with a look of defeat about him. "It was like we were happy to find someone who shared similar interests. Hell, it was like a drunk talking to someone else who's addicted to likker. Common ground. I told him about a trip to Thailand I took and how easy it is to get all kinds of sex over there. He was interested. We went together once. A couple years later, he started a conversation about snuff movies. That wasn't really my thing, but I listened. Then, I guess when he thought the time was right, he spoke to me about snuff sex. After a while, he said there was nothing like it—the ultimate orgasm. He admitted to doing it."

Leary looked at his almost empty glass and swished the remaining Scotch around. I lifted my eyes to see how my FBI colleagues had reacted. The looks on their faces were priceless.

Leary continued. "He asked if I wanted to try." He stopped talking and took a deep breath. "Listen, I might do some things people satisfied with the missionary position wouldn't understand but choking a young pross while I was bangin' her wasn't on my wish list."

"Yet you went along for the ride—so to speak."

"Yeah, look, my job was secure working as a DA's investigator. More than a couple times, I made sure Cal won cases that meant a lot to him. I—"

Tolbert jumped in with both feet. "Ryan, shut up. Stay on topic."

Leary nodded slowly. The liquor had tired him out and probably depressed him enough to make him realize how drastically he had ruined his life.

"Yeah, yer right, J.R. No sense talkin' about my entire life now. Anyways, I would always have a job as long as Cal was DA. And, think about it. As long as he wanted to run, he'd get elected. But I wanted the job of chief deputy." He laughed silently. "Who do you think runs that department?"

"Not much doubt about that," I said.

"Joe D is no cop. Man worked for his daddy before he got elected. Hell, if ol' Delbert Hartung didn't have so much pull, Joe D'd still be workin' for daddy. The man doesn't know the difference between po-leece work and a mule's ass"

I smiled. "That's one way to put it."

"Cal trusted me like nobody else. We shared too much. Finally, he decided he could control *all* law enforcement in the county if I was chief deputy and his inside man."

I raised my eyebrows. "*All* law enforcement?"

Ryan shook his head. "Not you. It's no secret Cal thinks you're a royal pain in his ass."

"Thanks. I didn't know he cared."

Leary shrugged. "So that's it. Cal had his thing. I had mine. It's not like those prostitutes were good solid citizens."

Tolbert drained his second glass of Scotch. "I think you've said enough, Ryan."

But I wasn't prepared to leave it alone.

"The ladies present might object to me asking for more specific details," I said, "but you've hung all the involvement with the killings on Cal Pitts. What makes you think he won't turn on you and say everything was your idea? That he was the follower. The evidence we have or soon collect will put you both at the scenes, but it isn't specific as to which of you did exactly what. You have the more assertive personality, and someone might believe you did more than just contact the prostitutes and clean up the mess. Should we believe you just stood around watching?"

Leary looked at Tolbert, then quickly at Heidi. "The deal is still in place, right? I mean it's etched in stone, right?"

"Are you going to change your story drastically?" Heidi asked.

"Stop, Ryan," Tolbert said. "Tell me what you might say."

"Sure," Leary said and then looked at Heidi and scanned his eyes over the rest of us. "Give us a minute, will ya?"

Five of us stepped to the other side of the room while Leary whispered into Tolbert's ear. A few moments later, Tolbert stood upright.

"We're not talking about anything more than a few additional misdemeanors here. I assume they can be overlooked," Tolbert said.

Heidi said, "Misdemeanors, yes."

Leary sighed, not out of relief from this new agreement, but because he was tired and half-drunk. "I didn't just stand around. Of course not. I did the girls first. Not the guys, just the girls. Cal was the switch hitter. And he liked to watch. Liked me to watch him, too. The rest you know."

"Okay," I said, "but back to my earlier question. What happens if we get into a he said, he said pissing contest? Why won't Pitts tell a jury you're full of shit?"

Leary sat forward and puffed up his chest. "'Cause I got me some insurance."

Tolbert snapped, "Ryan, for God's sake, shut up."

"No, J.R. What does it matter if it comes out now or you drop it on them if Calvin tries to lie his way outta this? Let's get it in the open. I'll do the fifteen years, but I want to sleep easy between now and when this is all over."

Tolbert shook his head resignedly. "It's your life, Ryan."

At first Leary said nothing. The silence in the room was deafening.

"Ryan?" I said.

"Evidence, man, evidence. I used my cell phone to video what Cal did."

"Oh, my God," Heidi said. "Why didn't you tell me this before?"

Leary shrugged. "You never put all your cards on the table. I wanted to hold back a few as double insurance."

"Where's the phone," I asked.

"My house."

"It's not the 'Andy' phone?"

"No, my regular iPhone."

"I assume we have your permission to retrieve it?"

He nodded.

"Mr. Tolbert, will you or Ryan contact Mrs. Leary and tell her what's happened, or shall we?"

"We'll use your phone."

"Good. And he'll sign permission for us to search the house for the iPhone?"

Tolbert and Leary buzzed in each other's ears for a long moment. I assumed discussing the possibility of finding other damning evidence while retrieving the phone.

"Yes. No search will be necessary. He'll instruct you where to find the phone in plain view."

I nodded.

"Ralph, you and Bonnie get over to the Leary house," Carl said. "Be there when Mrs. Leary gets home and take custody of that phone."

CHAPTER TWENTY-ONE

The two agents who brought the video equipment took Leary to Knoxville to process his arrest and lodge him before arraignment.

Ralph and Bonnie drove to the Leary homestead to take custody of the cell phone that Heidi Piper thought was worth its weight in gold.

J.R. Tolbert thanked me for the Scotch and took his briefcase and assistant back to their Knoxville office.

That left Heidi, Carl and me standing in the squad room.

"This will not be a simple case to write up," Heidi said. "And look at the time. I'll have to break my ass to get things ready to present my warrant applications in the morning."

"Can you hold Leary incommunicado until you've got the warrants for Pitts and his house in your hand?" I asked. "The less said, the less chance our DA will hear about his fate before some cop knocks on his door."

"I hope to God no one leaks this story to the press or anyone," she said.

"You don't have to worry about Oliveri or Rowatt," Carl said. "You see any problems on your end, Sam?"

"I've spoken to Stan Rose and Terri Donnellson. They're no problem.

You could threaten to cut out John Gallagher's tongue, and he wouldn't say a word. Ted Hanshe, the auxiliary cop with the van, is a good man. I told him to keep this quiet, but I'll touch base with him again and insure he understands the importance of Mum's the Word."

"Good," Carl said. "And, Heidi, you think you'll be prepared for us to execute the warrants tomorrow?"

"I'll work through the night," she said. "Judge Coker gets in early. I'll be knocking on his door at 9 a.m."

I shrugged. "But let's plan for the worst. We need to track Pitts from now until he's in cuffs. We can't let him do a runner."

"I agree," Carl said. "But we need a couple of really good *pavement artists* to keep him under surveillance."

"You get the personnel. I'll approve any and all overtime necessary," Heidi said.

"I've got a former member of the JTTF in Manhattan with us," Carl said. "He spent five years following suspected terrorists all over the Metro New York area. He's the best I've got."

"Stan Rose was with LAPD's Metro Squad for a couple years," I said, so Carl wouldn't think I needed him to provide all the key personnel. "He's a crackerjack on surveillance. That can be our A team. Two more people as backup should be enough for the likes of Calvin Pitts."

"Okay, two men each. Done," Carl said. "My second man is new to Knoxville, but he's good. I'll have to requisition suitable unmarked vehicles. Pitts would recognize our standard cars."

"No problem," I said. "We can use my people's cars. I'll hand out portable radios and credit cards for gas. Stanley will use his Cadillac. John Gallagher is good at this, and no one would make him as an undercover cop in his rattletrap Saturn."

"Sounds good," Heidi said. "And you two will make this happen?"

I nodded. "I'll tell Stan now. John is at his desk. They can meet up with Carl's guys at the task force office. Pitts lives in Maryville. They can follow him home from the Justice Center."

"It'll take my men a little while to get there from Knoxville. Can you pick up the first contact?" Carl asked.

"I'll send John now. Stan can meet your agents in the task force room. Our radios are on a closed net, so the county dispatcher won't be involved unless our guys switch channels."

"Good," Carl said. "Let's do it."

———

I t would take someone with a sixth sense to recognize middle-aged John Gallagher, sitting in his faded electric blue Saturn as an undercover cop. I established that Calvin Pitts was still in his office when I sent John to tail him. Stanley went back home to get into civilian clothes and pick up his white Caddy.

At a few minutes after four o'clock, I felt like hiding in my office, putting my feet up and having a relaxing and satisfying drink. But thanks to Ryan Leary and his thirsty lawyer, my bottle of Glenfiddich was down to nothing but fumes. And I owed it to Ronnie Shields to let him know what I had accomplished.

I trudged through the marble halls of the municipal building, up the majestic staircase and swung open one of the great plate glass doors to the mayor's anteroom to find Trudy Connor, as usual, mashing the keys of her computer.

She stopped typing and looked at me over the tops of her tinted glasses. I smiled and waited.

"Hello, Mr. Jenkins. You doin' aw right today?"

"Trudy, I'm as good as an old policeman could be after cracking the case of the decade."

She smiled and placed her glasses on her desk. "Well, they," she said in typical Tennessee fashion. And I wondered, as I have for years, who *they* were.

"And I'd like to tell Ronald McDonald all about it."

Her smile turned to a serious frown, a face not unlike something I saw from any one of my grammar school teachers. "Mr. Jenkins, I've asked you not to call the mayor that."

I dipped my head and tried to appear contrite. "My apologies, madam. Is the maharaja available?"

She took a breath and forcefully expelled it in frustration. "Oh, Lord have mercy. I'll have to call Bettye Lambert and see if she can do anything with you."

Trudy picked up her phone, and my grin got a little wider.

"The mayor is free. Y'all can go in now," she said, with no small amount of exasperation.

I found Ronnie behind his desk looking as cool as shaved ice in his gray pinstripe suit. A yellow lined pad lay in front of him, but I knew, from my psychic abilities and what I found while snooping in his desk once, that he had probably just ditched the crossword book he keeps in the top draw.

"Hello, Sam. You doin' aw right t'day?"

"Better than usual and twice as proud."

"Proud o' what?"

"With a little help from the FBI, we've cleared the Riverside Strangler murders. One subject is in custody and one shall soon fall."

"Lord have mercy. When did this happen?"

"We've been busy most of the day. Our one defendant just started the trip to a judge and arraignment. We'll put the arm on the second as soon as our U.S. Attorney obtains a warrant."

"Outstandin', Sam. And you arrested him personally?"

"Technically, the FBI arrested him, but I was there to steer them in the right direction and slap the cuffs on."

"Uh, who was this subject?"

"Sorry to say, the first one arrested was the sheriff's chief deputy, Ryan Leary."

Ronnie's face dropped faster than a barometer before a hurricane.

"Ryan Leary? Lord have mercy. And you're responsible for his arrest?"

"Yes, but as I said, with FBI help. As you know, they took over the task force the other day, and I gave them the information I developed."

Ronnie closed his eyes for a moment and shook his head. He did not look as appropriately pleased as I expected. "Oh, Sam, this is a bad day for Blount County. Ryan Leary is a very important man."

That one annoyed the hell out of me. "*Was* important. There are two ways to look at it, Ronnie. Bad because the county's top sworn officer was involved in eight murders, but then again, he'd already been arrested for beating and torturing a nineteen-year-old shithead in an incident littered with scandal. But pretty damn good because Leary and his partner won't be killing off any more citizens."

"Yes. Right." He still didn't look overjoyed. "Who's the other one you're gonna arrest?"

For some reason, I was reluctant to tell my less than enthusiastic mayor the complete story. "Uh, Leary is playing it cool and close to the vest. He told the AUSA in charge that he'd reveal his accomplice in front of the judge after he got his guaranteed deal on the record. His attorney liked that idea."

"Oh. Think it's anyone we would know?"

I ignored his question. "You don't seem glad to hear that the Riverside Strangler won't be whittling down the population of young hookers any longer."

"Oh, uh, well, o' course I am. It's that, uh, I hate to see a local, uh... public servant arrested fer such a thing. Gives us in Blount County a black eye, so ta speak."

"Yeah, so to speak. Guys like Leary give *all cops* everywhere a black eye."

"When will ya know who the other man is? It is a man, ain't it?"

"Be my guess. But I'll only know when I get a phone call from Ms. Piper."

"She's the U.S. Attorney ya spoke of?"

"She is."

"Well good. Yessir, real fine. Keep me informed so I can tell the council all about this."

I sort of expected a hero's reception but had to take what the mayor offered. "Okay, boss, but I must impress upon you the importance of keeping this operation under wraps until the second subject is in custody. That means I won't be putting out a press release until the Justice Department gives me an okay. We can't even discuss this with other cops or family or *anyone*."

Ronnie nodded. "O' course, Sam. I won't be puttin' out anything less you say we're ready."

"I'll talk to you tomorrow then."

I really hoped he could keep his mouth shut. Or would he attempt to pay forward a political favor and spill the beans to one of his friendly hacks?

———

It was almost time to close up shop for the night when I took off to find Ted Hanshe.

He lived in a large and fairly new redbrick home on Old Niles Ferry Road on the south end of Maryville. I pulled my Ford into the driveway and parked in front of the attached garage. To my right, a separate four bay garage sat on the property line and housed, I assumed, his plumber's vehicles and equipment. I knocked on the door, and he answered, wearing the same work uniform I had seen on him before; but now he was in stocking feet.

"Hey, Chief, how's it goin'? A little excitement today, huh?"

"Yeah, Teddy. I think we did a good one today."

"Come in, come on in. Don't stand outside."

I entered a neat home furnished in contemporary Early American-style furniture

"Sit down." He pointed to a sofa covered in a print fabric against a long wall in the living room. "Sit down. My wife's makin' dinner. Ya wanna eat?"

I smiled but shook my head. "No thanks. I just need to talk about today if you've got a minute."

"Yeah, sure, anything. Ya want a beer?"

"Are you having one?"

"Hey, you kiddin'? It doesn't take much ta talk me inta havin' a beer. Be right back."

Two minutes later, he walked back into the living room, carrying a tray with two bottles of Sam Adams lager and two glasses, with his wife on his heels.

"Chief, I want ya ta meet my wife, Margaret, but everybody calls her Maggie. Babe, this is Chief Jenkins. He's from New York."

I stood and shook the hand she offered. "Hi, call me Sam. Nice to meet you."

"Nice to meet you, too." She smiled. "Excuse me. I've got to keep an eye on dinner. Sure you won't stay and have something?"

"No thanks. My wife's got dinner waiting for me. I won't keep Teddy long."

She waved that away. "Take your time. Drink your beer. No hurry."

When she left, we sat, me on the sofa and Ted across from me in a recliner.

I poured the twelve-ounce beer into a pint glass. "Thanks for your help today, Teddy. I'm sure Stanley explained what was going down."

"Yeah, somethin' else, isn't it?" Ted took a drink from the bottle.

"That's why I'm here, Teddy. We're going to be making another arrest of a prominent person—with luck tomorrow or soon after."

"Ya need my van again?"

After a sip of beer, I answered. "No thanks. I think the FBI will have that covered by a small army of agents this time. I just need to make sure that you get the message that everything that happened today has to remain totally confidential. I mean totally. There's a good chance that if word leaks out the next subject may take off on us."

"Hey, Chief, don't worry about me. I won't say nothin' ta nobody. I understand what ya need. When I was a kid, my old man used ta say that World War Two thing to us—Loose lips sink ships. No problem, I'm tight."

I took a long drink of beer and understood why someone, I can't remember who, called Sam Adams the best bottled beer in America.

"Thanks, Teddy, and just so you remember, I appreciate what you did for us today...and all the time you spend working as an auxiliary."

I took another long pull on my beer, emptying more than half the glass. Sam Adams *is* good beer.

"No sweat, Chief. I get a kick outta directin' traffic."

I smiled. "Now, will you do me a favor?"

"Sure, name it."

"Call me Sam. Only the bad guys are more formal."

He laughed. "Yeah, yeah. Sure thing, Sam. You got it."

I knocked down almost all the rest of my beer and placed the glass back on the tray sitting on the coffee table.

"Listen, Teddy, I'm keeping you from your dinner. And my wife will think I've run away from home. Say goodbye to Maggie for me, and thanks for the beer." I stood.

"You're welcome. And don't worry about me." Then he repeated, "I won't say nothin' ta nobody."

He stuck out a hand for me to shake. The only thing missing was for us to spit into our palms and swear oaths to each other.

We walked to the front door. "Hey, Ted, I was thinking of making one of our auxiliaries a sergeant. That crew needs a supervisor. Interested?"

"You wanna make me a sergeant?" He showed me a big smile. "Sure, I'm interested. I was a sergeant in the Army. I could handle that."

"Good. Since you guys are all volunteers and there's no money involved, I don't have to check with the mayor or council. I'll buy you the stripes if you can get Maggie to sew them on."

At 8:30 the next morning, I had just finished breakfast when I received back-to-back phone calls from John Gallagher and Stan Rose telling me that Cal Pitts was on the move, driving himself toward the Justice Center.

Not wanting to miss out on the action, I called Bettye to tell her I'd be late, but earning my salary out of the office.

I buried my unmarked Ford among the many vehicles in the visitor's lot of the Justice Center where I found Stanley's white Cadillac parked in a spot where he could watch the front of the building and much of the employee parking area in the rear. I tapped the front fender of the Caddy. Both Stan and an FBI agent I'd never met were awake. I slid into the back seat.

"Starsky and Hutch, I presume?"

"I look like either of those Hollywood cops to you?" Stan asked.

"Maybe a little like David Soul if he was black."

He grunted. "Meet Agent Mike Butler. He used to work up in your neck of the woods."

"Good to meet you, Mike." We shook hands.

"Yeah, howz it goin'?" He spoke with an unmistakable New York accent. "Stan's been tellin' me about you. Kept me up all night."

"Sorry to hear that. I slept like a log."

"Yeah, I'll bet."

"Mike says he was on the real job up there before getting involved with the FBI."

"Yeah? Where'd you work?"

"Garden City PD for six years. After I got my law degree, I went into the Bureau. My last assignment was with the Joint Terrorist Task Force out o' Manhattan."

"Good duty?"

"If ya like followin' Middle Eastern assholes all over creation."

"More scenic than tailing our district attorney."

"Yeah. The bastard's probably inside planning who he'll kill next."

"If Heidi Piper gets a judge to sign her warrants quickly, we'll prevent little Calvin from pursuing those dreams."

"Hell, I'm awake now. Wouldn't mind finishing this job by takin' this guy off."

"Good. And Stanley is almost twice as big as Pitts and acts cranky when he doesn't get his beauty rest. Maybe he'll scare the little guy to death and save the government the cost of a trial."

"I'd rather see him go to jail," Stan said, "and then get someone to drop a dime on a few selected members of the general population. Ex-DA like him would have a *long* life sentence."

"Or a very short one," I said. "Deviants tend to get shanked in the shower at an alarming rate."

"That, too."

"You hear from Gallagher and his partner much?"

"Couple times. They're parked over in the bank lot watching the other end of employee parking."

"I'll mosey over and see if I can catch them sleeping. Good to meet you, Mike."

I walked through the parked cars and away from the building to blend into the landscape. In case Calvin Pitts was looking out his window, I didn't want him to see me skulking around. At the First Tennessee Bank on the opposite end of the lot, I crossed their blacktop and hit the sidewalk that paralleled US 321 and headed back toward the Justice Center and the US Bank where John had parked his Saturn.

He and his new partner were awake and alert. I opened the back door and took a seat.

"Jesus, John, look at all the crap you've got back here."

"You know, Boss, if you gave me an unmarked police car to drive, you wouldn't have to sit back there with all my necessities."

"Keep dreaming, John." I looked at the young agent sitting in the front passenger's seat. "Hi, I'm Sam Jenkins. Sorry to say, the long suffering chief responsible for Detective Gallagher's conduct."

"Howdy. Nick Colquitt." He turned further to the rear and extended a hand."

"New to Knoxville?"

"Been in the office six months, but I grew up just up north a little in Rutledge. Spent my first six years with the Bureau in Memphis." He shook his head. "Like bein' stationed in Hell. Memphis is hot and sticky. Only savin' feature is they make good barbeque. But I did qualify for these surveillance details by workin' bank robberies out there. Spent plenty o' time tailin' the boogers who think they can make a quick buck."

I looked at my watch. 9:30.

"I expect to hear from Heidi Piper soon. When she gives us the signal that the warrants are signed, a crew from Knoxville should be heading this way. But I figure with us five and a little help from the DA's investigators, we can take Cal Pitts into custody and turn him over to Carl and his merry men when they get here. You two good to make a few more hours OT?"

"Sure thing," Nick said. "I'd love ta hang out for the grand finale."

"You know me, Boss," John said. "I'll stay for the duration. And I'm all ready to chase this little guy if necessary."

"How's that, John? I've never known you to be a runner."

"I got new shoes. See?" He picked up his left foot and twisted in the car seat to show me.

"Yeah, black sneakers," I said. "You look like a high school coach."

"Walking shoes, Boss. Look at these soles. Plenty of *gripshun*."

Colquitt stared at John with a quizzical expression.

"Good, John. A street cop without *gripshun* is like a day without sunshine."

"Right you arc, Boss."

I wanted to change the subject before Gallagher taught Colquitt another new word. Most people can only handle one a day, and Nick hadn't gotten much sleep. "Hey guys, while we're waiting, you want coffee? I'll walk over to Sonic and get you something."

"Okay, Boss," John said. "Since you're buyin', how about a regular and whatever breakfast special they've got?"

"Just a black with two sugars for me," Nick said.

I called Stanley's cell phone, asked the same question and took their orders.

"Okay, gents. Be right back."

I didn't get twenty feet from the car when my phone sounded off. I checked my watch again. 9:49.

"Sam," Carl Harmon said, "She's got the warrants, and we're on the way."

"Good. We'll move in and secure him."

I stepped back to John's car and signaled for him to roll down the window. "Breakfast must wait, fellers. We're goin' inside."

I called Stanley who drove to the back door. I jumped into the back of the Saturn, and John pulled out of the bank lot and drove on the shoulder of 321 until he could make a right and stop at the front doors of the Justice Center. We jogged inside and after a quick stop at the security desk, took the elevator to the third floor and the DA's office.

I showed my badge to Pitts' secretary. "We need to see your boss immediately."

She smiled, and I admired her honey blond hair streaked with platinum highlights.

"I'm sorry. He just left." She looked at her watch. "Not five minutes ago."

"You're kidding?"

She frowned and looked at me as if I might cause trouble. "I'm sorry, I'm not. Did you have an appointment?"

"Not that he knew about. Where did he go?"

"He only said he'd be out for a while. Can I help you with something?"

"God damn it."

She frowned again and moved back a few inches. "I beg your pardon?"

"I'm sorry. I shouldn't have said that. Which way did he go?"

"I'm not sure. He left by his back door and into the investigator's room."

"Thanks."

We did the same, and I found Clete Dunn at his desk. Two other investigators were also in the room.

"Clete, did Cal Pitts come through here?"

"Yeah. Couple minutes ago. He borrowed O.L.'s car."

"He what?" I shook my head. "Son-of-a-bitch!"

The other investigators looked at me.

I pointed at one of them. "You're O.L., right?"

"I am."

"Pitts borrowed your car?"

"Uh-huh."

"For what?"

"What's this about?"

"We have an arrest warrant for him—which I guess he just heard about. What kind of car did you give him?"

O.L. looked confused. "Gray Grand Cherokee."

"Hang on a minute."

I called Stan Rose. "Did you see a gray Cherokee leave the lot?"

"A gray SUV was pulling out as we got around back."

"Shit. That was Pitts. He's on the run. Stay there, and I'll call you back."

I looked at the three investigators. "Anyone know where he was headed?"

The man called O.L. and the other shook their heads.

Clete said, "We don't usually question the boss when he leaves, Sam."

"Was he carrying anything?"

"A briefcase," Clete said.

"Does he carry a gun?"

"He owns a Sig nine millimeter."

"Why me?"

I called Stan. "Get over to Pitts' house pronto. Look for that Grand Cherokee. And be careful, he may be armed. I'll put out an alarm."

"Can I assume you're not a happy police chief?"

"The master of understatement."

I looked at O.L." Call the dispatcher and give her your plate number. I want everyone on the road looking for that car. Whoever finds it should take the DA into custody."

"Lord have mercy."

As O.L. spoke to the dispatcher, I jotted down the plate number.

"Alright, guys, let's get out of here. We'll head to his house, too."

Clete Dunn asked, "What can we do?"

"Hit the road. Look for that Jeep. Pitts is the Riverside Strangler."

Clete isn't an emotional guy, but his jaw dropped. "Oh, sweet Jesus. Okay, we're on it."

CHAPTER TWENTY-TWO

W e ran out of the building, tossing our visitor's badges at the
deputy sitting behind the security desk.

As we hit the steps outside, I said, "We'll use my car, John. Last row,
half way to the bank."

We left the lot with my grill lights flashing and the siren blaring as I
made a left turn onto US 321 heading toward Pitts' home in Maryville.

I grabbed the microphone from the dashboard as I hit the gas and
gunned the engine. "Prospect-one, headquarters. Switch me over to
county dispatch. This is an emergency."

"Ten-four, Prospect-one," Bettye said, as calmly as if I had told her I
just dropped a paper clip. "Stand by."

A second later: "Go ahead, Prospect-one, your traffic."

"County dispatch, this is Prospect-one. Did you put out an alarm for
an oh-nine Jeep Cherokee?"

"Affirmative, Prospect-one."

"Good. Repeat that transmission every two minutes. If you get a
confirmed sighting, send all available units as backup." I paused to take a
breath. "And add that the subject may be armed."

"Uh, Prospect-one, I'll have to get permission to do that."

"Dispatch, this order comes with the authority of the homicide task force commander and the AUSA. Tell your duty officer and do it."

"Uh, Prospect-one, stand by."

Quickly, I said, "Negative on the standby, dispatch. Do it now. You do not want to be the one to be responsible for this going south."

There was a long pause. "Ten-four, Prospect-one." A second later she repeated the alarm with amendments."

I racked up the microphone when my cell phone rang. I pulled it from my jacket pocket and handed it to John.

"Answer that."

He did and listened for a long moment.

"Okay," John said into the phone. "We're on the way."

John snapped my phone shut and held it.

"That was Stanley. They're at Pitts' house. The Jeep is in the driveway."

"Good." I leaned on the siren, stomped down on the accelerator and passed an old man driving a twenty-year-old white Buick.

———

As we pulled up to Calvin Pitts' home, my cell phone once again rang. I spoke to an exasperated Carl Harmon.

"Sam, what the hell happened? Mike Butler advised me that Pitts is in the wind."

"Afraid so. Five of us are at his house now. We're going to attempt to enter."

"How did this happen? How did he get word?"

"Good question. I told my mayor about Leary's arrest and instructed him not to put out a press release or discuss it with anyone. I know nothing went out to the media, but whether he complied about the other, it's anyone's guess. I never named Pitts as the second subject."

"God damn it! If he spread the word, I'll nail his balls to a tree."

"I don't know if he did, but why don't you do that anyway? It might keep him from playing political Russian roulette in the future."

"You don't know how much this pisses me off."

"I do. But I'm also wondering if someone in the Federal court might have spilled the beans. Who knows? We'd have an easier time learning who kidnapped the Lindberg baby."

Carl let out a large volume of air. "I know. We're almost at the Justice Center. Call me as soon as you have him in custody."

"The borrowed Jeep is in the driveway. I'm optimistic."

———

Stan Rose was standing at the front right corner of the house. He told me that Mike Butler was covering the opposite rear spot. I sent Nick Colquitt to join Butler and took John Gallagher with me to beat on the front door.

The place was a large two-story, traditionally-styled home with an attached garage. It looked way too big for a couple, much less the unmarried long-time DA.

I rang the bell. Synthesized chimes sounded off inside the house. After ninety seconds with no reply, I pounded on the door hard enough to cause a seismic blip at the closest monitoring station.

"Jeez, Boss, any harder and you'll take the door down," John said.

"If this bastard doesn't open up, that's exactly what I'm going to do."

I pulled a pocketful of paperwork out of my jacket to find Calvin Pitts' home phone number. I called and let it ring until voice mail kicked in.

"You miserable bastard," I said and slammed my fist against the door another half dozen times.

"You wanna kick it in, Boss?" John asked.

"Yeah. We're getting nowhere. That's next. Hang on."

I called the county duty officer's line, and a Lieutenant McPhee answered. I identified myself and brought him up to speed on our attempt to execute the arrest and search warrants at Pitts' home.

"Lieutenant, you need to cancel the alarm for that gray Cherokee, but send me whoever you can spare—at least two people from patrol. We should divert traffic from the street until this is resolved. A couple detectives would help us covering the outside of the house when we go inside. And have a crime scene unit respond. One way or another we're going in, and I'll need a thorough search of the premises."

"I'll do what I can, Chief."

"How about a battering ram? Do you keep one in a supervisor's car?"

"I'll have the road sergeant respond. He's got one in his ve-hickle."

"Sounds good."

Five minutes later, a marked sheriff's patrol unit drove onto the block with blue lights flashing. He switched them off and coasted into a spot one house away from Pitts' home. An all black traffic unit and a patrol supervisor in a marked SUV were only moments behind. Those three men walked over. The sergeant was carrying a metal, two-man battering ram.

"We gonna need this?" he asked.

"Afraid so," I said. "Our subject won't answer the door or the phone. We've got arrest and search warrants."

"Sounds okay ta me. Did I hear right? You're after the DA?"

I nodded. "Correct."

"Well then, ya ready ta go?"

"Before we do this, let's get your guys to hit three houses on both sides and everyone across the street and order them to stay inside until we give them an all clear."

The sergeant, a man named Shane Hacker, looked at the two deputies. "You heard the man."

One ran right and the other left.

"One more minute," I said. "These are FBI warrants. I'll call the SAC and tell him what we're doing. He's either at the Justice Center or already on the way here."

Hacker shrugged. "This here's your rodeo."

I called and found Carl Harmon still at the Justice Center with several agents. We had eight men at the scene and possibly more detectives on the way to help execute the warrants. I couldn't see that additional personnel were needed. Carl agreed.

When the pair of uniformed deputies returned, I sent them to cover the back of the house. The sergeant and John Gallagher would remain outside in front and deploy any plainclothes detectives who arrived after we entered the house. The two FBI agents, Stanley and I would be the entry team.

Sergeant Shane Hacker stood about six-two or more with plenty of solid beef behind him. Stan Rose is six-four and has probably weighed two-thirty-five since he was in high school.

"Will you two big gentlemen break down the door?"

Stan nodded.

Hacker grinned. "Be a pleasure."

"Once it's open, how about you two spry young agents run upstairs and sweep the second floor? Stanley and I will handle downstairs. I don't see any basement windows, but if we come up with nothing in the house, we'll check the garage. Shane, you and the outside guys keep an eye on that."

He nodded.

"And, everybody keep thinking about his Sig 9mm."

More nods.

"Okay, guys, let's go inside."

One well placed shot with the heavy metal, three-foot long battering ram to the doorknob and the entire frame broke, the door swung inward and we entered, scattering left and right, taking available cover behind furniture. I shouted out a greeting.

"Calvin Pitts. Police and FBI. We have an arrest warrant. Walk to the front door with your hands in the air."

We waited a few seconds. Nothing.

"Last chance, Calvin. If we come through the house, do not be holding a weapon."

Four sets of eyes clicked back and forth around the rooms, at each other and after fifteen seconds, everyone knew we needed to search.

I told the agents, "Go ahead. We'll wait for you to hit the landing before we take off."

Up they went, pistols pointed to the front, slowly and cautiously.

When they disappeared, Stan and I began moving to the left through the living room, which offered no cover or concealment if we were to move efficiently. The home was extremely quiet. A quartz mantle clock ticked off the seconds. Each click reverberated in my head. Faint footsteps on the second floor tapped the hardwood, then became muffled on the carpeting or area rugs. As we passed into the kitchen, the refrigerator's compressor kicked in and added a noise. It startled me, and I turned in that direction, but didn't shoot the Kenmore appliance. Stan pointed at a pantry door. I trained my gun on the opening as he jerked open the door. Nothing but canned goods and other supplies. More nothing in the lavatory and laundry room. We checked a closet in the dining room. Coats. We passed through another open doorway into the master bedroom and checked two closets, a bathroom and under the bed. There was only one room left.

If he wasn't in there or upstairs, we'd converge on the garage, the door to which opened from the laundry room.

We intended to do the same door routine as before. I would cover, and Stan would open. Only the door was locked from inside.

Stan shook his head. Locked tight.

From the stairwell, we heard Mike Butler call out, "We're clear up here."

Footsteps on the stairs followed. We waited until Mike and Nick joined us.

"Everything down here is clean," I said. "This room is locked. Stand clear of the door in case he wants to do a Butch Cassidy with us."

Everyone moved a few feet from the wooden door.

"Calvin! Open the door and stand back. This is over. Let's finish our business the easy way."

We waited ten seconds.

"He's had his chance," I whispered. "No sense telling him what we're going to do next."

"Solid wood door," Stan said. "But just a doorknob lock. No dead bolt. One kick should open it."

The two agents nodded.

"Too bad we don't have Emergency Services guys with helmets and shields to go in first." I said.

"Yeah," Stan said. "We jes' country folk. Ain't got us no SWAT cops."

"Okay, you're the biggest, you kick. Mike, go low and to the right. I'll follow. Nick, low left. Stan, cover the room from the doorway. Got it?"

"If he's in there," Mike said, "he's gonna be hiding behind something. Figure he'll shoot as soon as the door breaks?"

"I guess," I said. "Unfortunately, we don't have any grenades. They make life so easy."

Mike chuckled

"If we take fire, everyone snap off a half dozen shots in the general direction. Only Rambo wouldn't take cover after that."

Stan nodded. Mike shrugged. Nick winked.

It was time to go.

"Kick a field goal, Stanley."

He reared back and snapped a well-placed kick into the doorknob. The doorstop splintered, and the light interior door swung violently to the left. Mike Butler dove into the room. I followed him, but stayed high, looking for some place to take cover. Nick Colquitt scurried to the left, while Stanley braced his Glock on the doorjamb, prepared to shoot.

Calvin Pitts, a small man, not much more than five-five and proportionally lightweight, with short light brown hair and a thin almost gaunt face was sitting behind a large dark wood desk. His head rested against the back of a horribly expensive-looking leather covered chair, his eyes tilted slightly upward, with not much of a describable expression on his face. A single 9mm hole in the right side of his temple showed the dark red blood that had oozed from the entry wound. The maroon stream had trickled past his ear, down over his jaw and neck and stained his off-white dress shirt before seeping behind the collar.

Mike and I walked closer. Pitts' right arm dangled over the arm of the chair. A Sig P228 lay on the floor next to him. There was no note lying on the desk.

Mike was closest and checked for a carotid pulse. His actions were superfluous.

"Nothing," he said.

"The evidence technicians should be here by now," I said. "Stan, give them a shout. I'll call for the medical examiner."

———

When I exited the house, I gave the outside troops a wave indicating all the good guys were safe. Then, I called Lieutenant McPhee, the duty officer, and requested a morgue wagon and ME. When I hit the front steps, I met Crime Scene Investigators Neal Brickman and his partner Cobb Rankin moving toward the brick walk.

"Hey, guys. Take a walk inside. Stan Rose and two Feds are keeping the body company. It's all yours. ME is notified."

"Gotcha covered, boss," Neal said.

My phone rang. Carl Harmon asked, "Sam, It's been twenty minutes. What the hell is going on?"

"Situation resolved. Subject is DOA."

"He's dead? You killed him?"

"No, Carl. He killed himself. Before we got here."

"Jesus Christ!"

"He probably got here ten minutes before us. Maybe he heard us pull in. I didn't hear a shot. Who knows?"

"And now we have to take Leary's word that Pitts was the Strangler. Son of a bitch." Carl couldn't have sounded more frustrated.

"I don't know what to tell you, Carl. Think of it this way. Leary will be an old man when he gets out. If he's still able to get it up at age sixty-eight and needs to kill someone to satisfy himself, a young cop or agent full of piss and vinegar will know he's a good suspect. But for now, I've still got an open homicide that might have been a copycat killing."

"I know. I know. If we can help you somehow—"

"Thanks. We've got a good suspect. John Gallagher has hammered him, but he wouldn't go for it. We'll try again."

"Okay. I wish you luck. And my offer stands. If you need *anything*, let me know."

CHAPTER TWENTY-THREE

I t took me almost an hour before I left Maryville. Eventually, Carl
Harmon showed up with Marty Saunders, the senior agent at the task
force, Ralph, Bonnie and a couple other nosey Feds. Carl spoke to the
county duty officer and requested another team of crime scene
investigators to make the job of searching Calvin Pitts' home a little more
efficient. In true FBI form, he approved the charge-back reimbursement
for the overtime needed to bring in a pair of off duty evidence
technicians. Just before I left, Heidi Piper showed up to look over
evidence recovered in the search.

The last thing I learned before hitting the road was that Carl
Harmon would call me with a time and date for a press conference
extravaganza. I could hardly wait.

I dropped into the chair next to Bettye's desk with all the grace of a
fifty-pound sack of onions kicked off the tailgate of a farm truck.
"No offence, darlin', but you look like hell."
I grunted.

"I'm glad you called," she said. "The mayor's been lookin' for you."

"Who cares?"

"Where's John and Stanley?"

"Stan says he'll be here at four. He's playing the tough guy. John took the day off to sleep. They stayed awake all night. John's getting a little long in the tooth for such shenanigans."

"Did he seem alright?"

"Yeah, he still likes this stuff. Once we surrounded the house, his adrenaline kicked in and kept him awake. When it wears off, he'll crash. But he looked okay when he left Maryville."

"You doin' okay?"

"I wish I had a second defendant to confirm Leary's big story, but other than that, sure. Just another day in Paradise."

She shook her head. "Have you had anything to eat since breakfast?"

"No, and I'm a couple hours overdue for lunch. How about you?"

"I brought a container of yogurt, and Terri had a soda with peanut butter and cheese crackers from the machine."

"Ah, to be young again. I used to love peanut butter and cheese crackers."

Terri had been sitting at John's desk, listening to our conversation. She smiled.

"Before my stomach growls and I get embarrassed, would you ladies like some proper lunch? I'm buying."

Terri shrugged. "I guess."

"Lord have mercy," Bettye said. "You are determined to make me fat."

"Not on your life. Pick something healthy."

"What did you have in mind?" Bettye asked.

"Anything your heart desires. You call, and I'll pick up or ask them to deliver."

"You had Chinese yesterday."

"If we lived in China, we'd eat Chinese food every day."

"So you'd like that?"

"I'm always up for Chinese. Ms. Donnellson, do you like Chinese food?"

"Love it."

"Done. You have a menu. Make your choices. I'll have—" I pondered over that tough decision. "Something light. How about chicken in garlic sauce?"

Bettye shook her head. "Sammy, order whatever you'd like, but if you get that, please don't breathe near me."

Terri snickered.

I snorted. "You're as bad as my wife. Okay, make it Hunan sauce."

"Just as bad," Bettye said. "I'll ask Mr. Lum to deliver."

"While we're waiting," I said, "I'll go upstairs and report to the lord of the manor." I peeled thirty dollars from the bills I carried in my pocket. "Here, give the delivery boy an appropriate tip."

———

I didn't tease Trudy Connor by calling Ronnie Shields names. She announced me with her usual ceremony, and I entered the mayor's inner sanctum.

"What time'd you start work t'day, Sam?" he asked.

"I got to the Justice Center around 8:30. After that, things got exciting."

"I heard things on the news."

"Yeah. The TV crews pulled in before I left. Those guys at the sheriff's office never keep anything under wraps."

"I s'pose not."

"Now it's over for the Riverside Strangler business, but we've still got the Toby Bowman murder open. Leary said it wasn't him and Pitts."

"You reckon a copycat?"

"I *reckon* it was the kid's homophobe father, but he won't go for squat at the moment. We'll go at him again."

"Uh-huh. It was a relief when that TV woman said Calvin took his own life. Fer a minute there, I thought it was you who killed him."

I guess I was tired and hungry enough for me to take offense to that remark. "Since Calvin Pitts left his office carrying a handgun, it was always possible that one of the men chasing him could have used deadly force, but Mr. Pitts saved us the aggravation."

"Shame. He was friends with a few people on the city council."

My attitude wasn't improving, and my ability to hide it lacked conviction. "What does that mean?"

"Jest what I said. This doesn't look good. The district attorney and the sheriff's chief deputy involved with prostitutes and such. What's gonna happen to Joe Don Hartung now?"

I sighed. "He's going to be embarrassed when someone asks how two killers could have worked in the same building with him and he didn't know it. That's an unfair question, but that's the sort of thing the media asks a public servant."

"I wish you, uh, we hadn't gotten involved."

I wanted to reach over the desk and throttle him. "Ronnie, I'm beginning to sense something here. Look, Leary and Pitts weren't just banging hookers on company time. They killed eight people we know about and others outside our jurisdiction. If my father did that, I'd have locked him up. Regardless of their political positions, these guys were scumbags. None of the other cops or agents involved or I have anything to be sorry about."

"Now don't go gettin' excited, Sam. I'm jest sayin' I know a few council members are gonna be disappointed with the outcome."

I took a long breath, not wanting to bite the mayor's head off. "You think they'd rather the murders go unsolved than tarnish the names of two local politicos? Maybe those council members should examine their priorities." I stood. "You'll have to excuse me. I haven't eaten anything all day, and I expect my lunch is downstairs waiting for me. After that, I'd like to pursue the Arlo Bowman lead. Shall I check with the city council to see if he's on anyone's Christmas card list before I sweat a confession out of him?"

"That wasn't necessary, Sam." The mayor looked down at a pad on his desk and began writing something. "Thanks for stopping in."

I was being officially dismissed and/or ignored.

———

When I walked into the office at 8:45 the next morning, Bettye and John were already at their desks. I wished them a good morning and went into my office to hang my jacket on the back of the door. With all that ceremony out of the way, I was ready to begin work.

"Hey, John," I said, "did you talk to any of the Knox County dicks about Arlo?"

"I called their office and did a records check."

"I mean talk to someone personally to see if they have anything off paper about the guy."

"I don't know anyone up there. The secretary in CID ran him through Central Records and checked their card file."

"I'll call someone. Stick around in case I need some extra info from you."

"Sure, Boss."

I called Windy Hatmaker's line, but learned he was out working a case. I tried his cell phone, but it went to voice mail. I hate technology.

Lacking anything better to do, I called Carl Harmon about the press conference he'd have to arrange.

"Sam, I'll make this easy on you," Carl said. "You were an important part of the investigation, so we'll need you there—at your convenience. But I know Heidi will want to discuss what can be released to the press before we start getting questions thrown at us."

"Of course. I can make time around my schedule, and I'll be there when you call in the vultures. I assume you'll do it at the Blount County Justice Center?"

"Yes, if not in the Task Force room, then in the sheriff's auditorium."

"Maybe Joe D will have pressing business out of town that day. A few pointed questions about his role might ruffle his feathers."

"No doubt. I'll give him plenty of time to arrange a plausible absence."

"Okay, let me know when you need me."

———

Ten minutes after I hung up on Carl Harmon, Detective Wendell 'Windy' Hatmaker called.

"I bet you think you're jest the cat's ass after clearin' all those homo-cides."

"I'm too modest to let it go to my head. But just in case, who do you think should play me if they make a movie?"

"Shoot. Some old washed-up actor."

"You're so kind."

"That's me. Now, what kin I do fer ya?"

"I've still got an open case on that young male pross from your area. Leary emphatically said he and Pitts were not involved with him. We're looking at the kid's old man, a mutt named Arlo Bowman. Know him?"

"Don't ring no bells. I'll check his driver's license pitcher ta see if the face is familiar. He been arrested fer somethin'?"

"Not that we know. Aside from a couple of traffic tickets, no police involvement on paper."

"Why do you like him for killin' his kid?"

"The boy was openly gay. Arlo says he hated that and all homosexuals in general."

"Ain't much. Where's this Ar-lo hang out? Maybe one of the uniforms knows him."

"My guy, John Gallagher, has gone to some sleazy gin mill in your area checking on the guy. Hang on a minute, and I'll get the name." I covered the mouthpiece of the telephone and yelled, "Hey, John, come here. I need you."

A few seconds later, John sat in my guest chair and slumped backwards.

"What's the name of the place where Arlo says he hangs out?"

"A real dump on North Broadway. Weird name, too. The Bull & Banjo. A low class sports bar."

"Windy, you there? You hear what John said?"

"Tell me again."

"The Bull & Banjo. A blue collar sports bar on North Broadway."

He laughed. "Blue collar sports bar?"

"I was being kind."

"Plenty o' blue collar types go there, and maybe the owners call it a sports bar—well, kinda depends on yer definition o' sports. We know it as a blue collar gay bar."

That answer was and wasn't a shock.

"If Arlo goes there and says he hates homosexuals, what's he looking for?"

"You tell me."

"Have you got any open gay bashing cases out of that place? Maybe tuning up gay men is Arlo's idea of sport."

"We always get a few likkered up good ol' boys who do some gay bashing, but we usually close 'em out pretty quick. Them ol' boys ain't exactly criminal masterminds. The victims usually pick 'em out of a book and then a lineup."

I sighed. "You've got to have an open case or two."

"I'll check. If'n we do, I'll stick your man Ar-lo's pitcher in an array and check with the vic."

"That might help us, and maybe you'll close out a case."

"Might could. I'll let ya know."

Windy hung up.

"John, let's go pick up Arlo the asshole."

———

Arlo Bowman sat in an armless chair in the squad room, and like so many of the miscreants we question, he amused himself by picking away at his cuticles. Their way to act unconcerned.

He was in his late-forties and of medium height and weight— rawboned, and his sinewy forearms and thick fingers told me that Arlo had worked hard most of his life. He wasn't a bad-looking guy, but no one would ever accuse Arlo of being handsome. He wore his light brown hair short in the classic Julius Caesar style. He hadn't shaved in a while, or he favored the modern look of a perpetual three-day growth.

I slapped my hand on the desktop less than a foot from Arlo's shoulder.

"Hey! Leave your hangnails alone, and pay attention. I asked you a question."

"And I already tol' the other guy," He used his chin to point at John Gallagher. "I don't know nuthin' 'bout who killed Toby. How many ways ya want me ta say it?"

"Put yourself in our shoes, Arlo. You're a self-professed homophobe. Your son was gay. You admitted that his death was no loss, especially for you. Your only alibi is that you were drinking in some dive in North Knoxville, but no one remembers you being there when Toby was killed."

Arlo made a face, trying to convey the message that he was getting impatient with our questioning.

"We checked with the TBI. You legally bought a .38 caliber Colt that's still on paper in your name. Your son was killed with a .38, but miraculously you tell us you can't find your gun—yet you never reported it lost or stolen. Why should we believe you?"

"'Cause I'm tellin' ya the gat-dag truth."

John stuck in his two cents. "Yeah, says you."

"Yeah, says me."

"John, what exactly does the firearms examiner say about the bullets they took from Toby's body?"

"Based on the grooves and twist, they came from a two-inch Detective Special. Know what kind of gun Arlo bought?"

"Let me guess, a two-inch Dick Special."

"Absolutely. And there's no doubt in the firearms examiner's mind."

Arlo's expression changed. He looked a little more concerned. "Wasn't my gun that killed the boy."

"Give us the gun, and we'll eliminate you as a suspect. No gun and we'll charge you with murder, and you can tell your fantasy in court."

John took a pair of handcuffs from his waistband and dangled them in front of Arlo.

"You cain't do that. I ain't guilty o' nuthin'."

"Who cares?" I said. "We need an arrest. Circumstantial evidence says you look good for the murder. We don't have to be right, just reasonable. Everything you've said so far has been a lie. Convince a jury you're not guilty. But just between you and me, nobody with a public defender ever wins. You got lots of cash for a real lawyer?"

"You know I ain't."

"Then save us all the aggravation of writing this up and going to court. Help yourself by cooperating, and we'll go easy on you. Explain why you argued with Toby. Maybe he started pushing you. You got uncontrollably angry, and he pushed once too often. You shot him in the heat of emotion. The DA can work with that. Why spend the rest of your life in jail if you don't have to?"

That got him thinking. "What kinda time are you talkin' about?"

"Maybe a max of fifteen years. If you keep lying, you'll be seventy years old before they would even consider you for parole. Or you can die in jail with all those six-and-a-half-foot tall weightlifters who turn into homosexuals in the showers. That sound appealing to you?"

"Whoa, whoa, whoa! I ain't lyin', and I ain't goin' ta jail for no fifteen years 'cause I didn't kill my son."

"Bullshit. No one says you were in that bar for more than ten minutes the day your kid died. Give us a name who'll back up your story. Show us your gun."

Arlo shook his head in frustration and continued the attack on his left thumb. "Man, you guys are sandbaggin' me here."

I shook my head and smiled. "If I wanted to sandbag you, moron, I'd let you walk out the back door and shoot you in the parking lot. Everyone would believe me when I claimed you tried to escape."

"Do whot?"

"Don't make me slap you, Arlo. I don't like you, but I'm not sandbagging you. You're as guilty as hell. You've got no alibi."

He hung his head a little lower than before. "I do."

"What? And don't say you were in that gin mill all night again."

His voice was very low. "I was with someone."

"Sure you were. You just can't remember her name."

He sighed deeply and looked up at me, then at John. "I jest couldn't tell ya."

"Couldn't, but now you can?"

"Looks like I got ta."

His lip quivered, and a tear ran down his right cheek. Always a good sign.

I sat forward and softened my tone. "Alright, I'm listening."

Tough guy Arlo was beginning to waiver. "Ya gotta gimme a minute. You got me all tore up."

Time for the Dutch uncle act. "Sure, take a breath. You want something to drink?"

He looked at me in disbelief. "If ya got a Mountain Dew, I'd appreciate it."

"Hang on, Arlo," John said. "I'll get one."

After John left the room, Arlo asked, "Ya really gonna arrest me, I don't give ya a name?"

I nodded. "You bet."

"Oh, Lord have mercy, man. I ain't never said nuthin' like this ta nobody b'fore."

"I've heard my shares of stories. Yours won't be unique."

He sniffed. "This is hard fer me ta say."

"What are you going to tell me? You bought yourself a prostitute and don't want to admit to a misdemeanor patronizing charge?"

"Not exactly."

John returned and set a cold can of Mountain Dew on the desk next to Arlo's forearm.

He looked at John. "Thanks."

"Don't mention it."

Arlo popped the top and tilted the can up to his lips for a long moment, damn near draining half the twelve ounces of soda.

He set the can back on the desk, covered his mouth and stifled a burp.

Before speaking, Arlo rubbed the stubble on his chin and shook his head. "Ya know how I been runnin' my mouth 'bout how I hated what Toby was—I mean him likin' men 'stead o' women?"

"We heard you say that."

"Well, I was bein' *hypocritically*."

"Were you now?"

Arlo hung his head. I looked at John, just knowing what we'd hear next.

"Uh-huh," Arlo said.

"Can you explain that for us?"

"Hard fer me ta say it."

"I know, but it's a start in getting this murder charge off your back."

Arlo sniffed and wiped his nose with a wrinkled handkerchief he took from the back pocket of his jeans. "I's with a man."

"You mean you have a *relationship* with a man."

He just stared at me.

"You had sex with a man?"

"Couldn't say so, 'cause...Well, ya know. And he's married."

I nodded. "We understand."

John said nothing; his face remained impassive.

"You gonna tell people 'bout this?" Arlo asked.

"Probably not, as long as the other man corroborates your story and we can establish that it's credible."

"What if he won't?"

I shrugged. "Then you're screwed."

"Huh?"

"We can't just take your word."

"Damn, that was hard fer me ta admit."

"I understand that."

"And it's true."

"What's the man's name?"

He hesitated. "Georgie Pooter."

"How do you know Georgie?"

"Went ta school t'gether. Known him fer years. Do some work fer him now and ag'in."

"How do we find him?"

"Owns a used car lot up ta Fountain City."

I nodded. "And where's your gun?"

"Gave it ta Georgie ta keep in his office. He gits lot o' cash sometimes."

"You think George will deny all this?"

Another sniff and he wiped more tears with the back of his hand. "If I kin talk some with him, he might back me up."

"We talk to him first. You can come with us. If he denies being with you, I'll let you speak with him."

"Aw shit."

"That's the best we've got. I'll tell him what he says will stay confidential. We're not looking to hurt him or you. We just need the truth.

"Okay."

———

John and I drove north of downtown Knoxville to Fountain City and let Arlo tag along in the back seat, unrestrained by handcuffs. It didn't take us long to find Pooter's Motors on Broadway or Maynardville Pike or whatever the hell the road is called north of the city.

George Pooter was a well-dressed, good-looking middle-aged man who sat behind a scarred-up oak desk in the small sales office building amidst forty or fifty late model motor vehicles.

He wasted more than twenty minutes of our time bobbing and weaving around an incident he reluctantly admitted to after we swore on our deceased parents' graves that no one would ever hear the details of his ongoing relationship with Arlo Bowman. I assured him that he and his old school chum were guilty of nothing. I wanted to add: But bad taste on his part. Arlo was a certified skell. But I didn't.

George Pooter surrendered Arlo's Colt Detective Special. On our way back to Prospect we'd drop it off at the TBI lab and have Bill Werner compare a round fired from that gun with the bullets recovered from Toby Bowman's body.

We dropped off Arlo where John had found him and began the remainder of our journey.

A block down the road, John asked, "Would you have locked him up if this Pooter guy hadn't backed up his story?"

"Didn't really have anything but suspicion. But Arlo didn't know that. If I arrested Arlo, Moira Menzies would have laughed me out of court. My relationship with her is shaky enough."

"Just checking, Boss."

"Arlo seems to be in the clear, but we'll check everything to be sure. After that, we're back to square one with Toby's murder. Any suggestions?"

John shrugged. "You win some, you lose some, and some go unsolved."

"You're a barrel of laughs."

CHAPTER TWENTY-FOUR

I could set my watch by Stan Rose. Every day, Tuesday through Saturday, he arrives at work at 3:30, just a little early for his four-to-twelve tour. By 3:35, Monday to Friday, he's usually sitting in one of my guest chairs listening to what I've got to say about the daily happenings in and around beautiful downtown Prospect.

I had just finished the monthly vehicle reports—late as usual—and wanted to give John Gallagher a copy and deliver the original to Earl Biggins, the city mechanic. That was at 3:45, and I still hadn't spoken to Stanley.

When I walked into the reception area, I found Stan and John bent over, leaning on Bettye's desk speaking in hushed tones. I cleared my throat just to let them know I was alive and well and caught them conspiring about something. That surprised them. Not that I was alive and well, but that I caught them concocting a plan. Each of them looked guilty as hell—like three kids caught shoplifting candy.

Bettye spoke first. "Sammy?"

"I am he. You guys look like you're up to no good."

Stan added a comment. "Uh?"

"Why do you say that, Boss?" John asked. "We're just, uh, talkin'."

I mocked him. "Who are you, uh, kidding, John? The expressions on your faces are priceless. You make the Watergate burglars look innocent."

"We do not!" Bettye said. "We're just havin' a conversation."

"Yeah? About what?"

"Uh."

"That's what Stan said. It must be quite forgettable."

Before anyone could respond, I used a time honored ploy—act passive aggressive—something Gallagher calls *child psychiatry*. "Jeez. I never thought you three would end up being a pack of liars. But who cares. I'll be at the garage."

John might never have fallen for that one, and I doubted Stan would. But Bettye loves me and hates it when I act mad.

"Sammy, wait."

I was almost half way to the back door. I walked back up front. "Yes?"

"Are you mad?"

I tilted my head and tried to look petulant. "Just dreadfully disappointed."

Stan rolled his eyes. Gallagher deadpanned it.

Bettye asked, "You're kidding, right?"

"I feel betrayed. But if you don't want to include me in your conversation, it's okay."

"Will you please stop?"

She looked at Stan and then John.

"Don't fall for it, Sarge," John said.

Stanley shrugged. "Tell him. If you don't, he's only going to try and make you feel bad."

She looked back at me. "We were talking about you."

"Planning a mutiny? I feel like Captain Bligh."

She slapped her desktop. "You are impossible. You're spoilin' a surprise."

"I hate surprises."

"Oh, Lord have mercy. We were talkin' about your anniversary. In four days, you'll be here five years."

I smiled. "Aha."

She frowned. "Yes, aha."

"Well then, you guys are my pals. And you, madam, are my sweetie."

"We wanted to take you to lunch, Boss," John said.

"The off-duty guys said they wanted to come, too," Stan added.

"Wow, an anniversary party. You guys are okay. The 21st is the date I started, and my contract runs through the 31st. I wonder if Ronnie will ask me to stay or give me the sack?"

———

The next morning, I met Carl Harmon and the task force members at the Justice Center a half hour before the press conference, scheduled to begin at 10:30. The day before, I spent almost an hour on the phone with Heidi Piper discussing a strategy for answering sticky questions posed by our archenemies, the media.

At 10:25, we all filed into the Sheriff's auditorium through the back door to find a full house. The four local TV networks were represented as were a couple of talk radio stations. The Knoxville News-Sentinel, the Maryville Times, two wire services and a few others I didn't recognize— smaller news agencies or just nosey gatecrashers.

Carl did most of the talking and fielded most of the questions, but Heidi and I answered a few specific to our roles in the successful clearances of the Riverside Strangler cases.

Carl took his time bringing the conference to an end, acting more like an attorney giving his closing statement than a street cop basking in his most recent victory over the forces of evil. I took that time to whisper in Ralph Oliveri's ear.

"Where's Schmecke, the bullshit artist?"

Bonnie Rowatt, standing to Ralph's left, looked at me. "Sssh."

I leaned forward and looked to my left to see what her problem was. She frowned at me, acting like we were three junior high school kids, and I made noise during an assembly.

"Ralph," I said. "Smack her."

"You kiddin'? She'll hit me back."

WAYNE ZURL

"Will you two be quiet?" she said. "Someone will hear you."

Trying to whisper again, I said, "If you would shut up, he could have answered, and that would be that. You're the one reciting the Gettysburg Address."

She made a face and ignored me. No one else seemed to care that I wasn't listening to Carl.

"Ralph!" I whispered. "Where's Schemecke?"

"Carl gave him the boot yesterday. Told him his services were no longer needed and to send a bill to the sheriff."

"I'll be damned. Good for Carl."

"Yep."

"Too bad, though. I wanted to kiss him goodbye."

Ralph snickered.

Standing behind me, the second assistant junior deputy chief deputy sheriff in charge of pens and paper clips, or something like that, cleared his throat. I assumed that he was taking Bonnie's side and wanted me to shut up. I smiled at him.

When the festivities ended, the reporters and cameramen filed out through the double front doors while we all turned, intending to disappear the same way we entered.

A half dozen of those assistant and deputy chief deputies had assembled in the back row to get their faces on camera. The sheriff, however, was conspicuously absent.

One face I hadn't anticipated seeing was Lieutenant Billy Joe Elam, retired Judge Minas Tipton's personal assistant. I assumed he was there to get the scoop and report back to his boss. I walked over to say hello.

"Billy Joe, how's it going?"

He stuck out a big hand for me to shake. Everything about Lieutenant Elam is big. He's a beefy six-two with a shaved head and neatly trimmed dark mustache. He looks like the southern version of Jesse Ventura. I've never seen Billy Joe not wearing a neatly pressed suit. That day it was a dark gray. He blended in nicely with the Feds.

"Chief, you doin' all right t'day?"

I motioned for him to join me away from the crowd of cops and agents.

"I should have known the judge would have taken an interest in getting the scoop on this."

"Yes, sir, he surely was. Asked me ta invite you over for lunch sometime soon. He knows you must have had lots to do with clearin' these cases."

"He flatters me. And I'd love to see the old boy again. Just how old is he now, anyway?"

"Ninety-three last March."

I shook my head. "He looks good though, doesn't he? Pretty soon I'll be looking older than him."

Billy treated me to one of his rare smiles. "He's doin' pretty good. I just wish I could get him ta lay off the bourbon a bit."

I chuckled. "Too late to change him now. At least he doesn't smoke cigars anymore."

Billy Joe nodded.

"I noticed that Joe Don didn't make the press conference. Was he suddenly called out of town?" I asked sarcastically.

"I'll let the judge tell you what he knows about that, but between you and me, I don't think the sheriff's gonna stick around here much longer."

"He's not going to finish out his term?"

"That's the way I hear it. Kinda embarrassed that his chief deputy was a killer—or killer's accomplice—or whatever. Guess he figgers on doin' some politickin' and lookin' for a job to run for before the primaries next year."

I nodded. "Better to leave on your terms than feel foolish by not getting endorsed to run for sheriff again."

"Mmm. I think that's somethin' the judge wants to talk to you about."

———

O n Friday afternoon, Ronnie Shields called me up to his office. I found him, as I often do, staring out the window toward the town square, with its brick walks, park benches, tulip poplar trees and a lawn as thick as any well-groomed fairway.

He turned slowly toward me. "Hello, Sam." He extended a hand toward his green leather guest chairs. "Have a seat."

No smile. Uh-oh. Is that any way to treat a local hero?

"I saw ya at the press conference. Very well done."

"Thanks."

"So, I guess that's it with the Riverside Strangler murders?"

"Just about. Toby Bowman is a separate issue. John and I are still working on that, but as far as those attributed to Pitts and Leary, yeah. Leary is going to jail. Pitts is dead, and the FBI is working with a few other PDs to clear cases in those jurisdictions."

He nodded while I spoke but didn't show an appropriate amount of enthusiasm for someone who just heard that his police chief was primarily responsible for clearing eight grisly murders.

"We didn't get maximum prison time for our bucks," I said, "but at least a bunch of families get some degree of closure—if that's possible—or worth anything."

"Uh-huh."

"Joe Don Hartung was conspicuously absent from the conference," I said. "No one mentioned him, but it didn't look good. Any idea what he's up to?"

Again, Ronnie spoke without emotion. "Rumors. Could be he's ready ta move on. Might could seek a seat in the State House or Senate. Openin's are comin' up next election."

"Then I guess it's time for him to start kissing a few asses."

"Sam, I know you don't like politicians, but I wish you wouldn't be so disrespectful *all* the time."

I shrugged and really didn't care what he wished. "Sorry to be so offensive, but I've had my share of politicians trying to stick it to me so often, I can't muster much enthusiasm for them or the system."

He nodded and looked upward—to the heavens, or maybe there was a spider on the ceiling.

"Is there something you needed, Ronnie?"

He looked at me, looked away and nodded. "Sam, there's jest no easy way ta say this." He took a moment to shake his head.

"My dog already died, so I'm guessing that's not it. Go ahead. Spit it out." I knew what was coming.

"Sam, your contract runs out end o' this month. The council has decided not to renew it."

I'd been sacked!

I won't lie, *that* surprised me. But I'd be damned if I'd let Ronnie Shields see me look disappointed. I laughed silently. "I'm not surprised. Over the last five years, my service here has made the piss-ant politicians in this city and the county very nervous."

"Sam, I—"

"Save it, Ronnie. Don't make yourself look hypocritical. I don't mind. I've got nothing to be ashamed of. Quite the opposite. I'm proud to have stuck it to so many dishonest shitheads who pretended to be public servants. So, I'll leave and let one of the two good people in line to take the job get their chance. Who are you going to promote, Bettye or Stan?"

"Uh—" He hesitated much too long. "Uh, the council, uh, has decided ta bring in a supervisor from another department. Uh, Donna Wrangle, a sergeant at Murr-vull PD, will be the new chief."

I could hear my eye lids click open. "Donna Wrangle? She's Joe Rex Wilcox's niece. My God, you people are incestuous."

"Now, Sam—"

"Now, Sam, my ass. Donna Wrangle used to be secretary to Maryville's mayor. Then she wanted to be a cop. Joe Rex must have called in a favor, and she was promoted to sergeant. For chrissakes, Ronnie, she's in charge of the school crossing guards. You think she's qualified to be police chief?"

With a pained look on his face, he said, "Sam—"

"Can it, Ronnie. You and those nitwits on the council couldn't have made a stupider choice. She'll be bad for your PD and for the morale of its personnel. There are only two people you should consider for the chief's job."

"Sorry, Sam, that's not gonna happen."

"You think so, huh? We'll see about that."

"Sam, there's nothing you can do about this. I jest wish—"

"Stop. I'm off the payroll as of August 1st, so I don't give a flying hoot what you wish, Mr. Mayor. I just need to know, are you sure you want to bypass two excellent people to hire a mediocre...person as your police chief?"

"That's what the council decided."

"And you just rolled over like a whipped puppy. Okay, the gloves are off. When I leave the room, I suggest you drop your pants and see if you've still got a pair."

I stood abruptly and left without a goodbye. As I slammed the oak raised panel door, I heard Ronnie say, "Sam, I—"

———

I walked through the open double doors to the PD, and Bettye looked up from her computer keyboard. She removed her glasses and dropped them onto the desktop.

She frowned and looked concerned. "What's wrong?"

"Why do you ask?"

John looked at me. "Your ears are red, Boss. That happens when you're pissed off." He switched his look to Bettye. "Sorry, Sarge."

"What happened up there, Sammy?"

I took a deep breath. "You know that lunch you were organizing for my fifth anniversary?"

The frown came back, and she nodded. "Yes."

"You'd better make it a going away party."

Bettye stood abruptly. "Explain that to me."

"What's up, Boss?" John asked.

I shrugged. "The mayor told me that the council does not want to renew my contract. As of August 1st, I'm unemployed."

"You got canned?" John asked.

"Yep."

"Did he give you a reason?" Bettye asked.

I gritted my teeth. "Ronnie doesn't have the ba...the nerve to answer a question directly. It's no mystery. I've annoyed too many politicians in five years. Too many friends of the council members must have complained. Now they're getting even."

"And who's gonna be the new chief?" Bettye asked.

"I suggested two people from within the department who could step in seamlessly. But they've already picked someone—Donna Wrangle, a sergeant from Maryville PD."

"The former secretary who wanted to become a cop?" Bettye did not sound happy. "She supervises school crossing guards, not police officers."

"She's connected, huh, Boss?"

"That's what it takes."

Bettye picked up a book sitting on her desk and slammed it down. "This is not why I came back to work." A tear ran down her left cheek. "I guess I'll just have to resign again, won't I?"

Two more tears joined the other. I stood there silently like the village idiot. John said nothing.

"You gentlemen have to excuse me." Bettye turned and stormed off in the direction of the rest room.

I stared at John. "That's a shame."

"You bet, Boss. Some surprise, huh?"

"Not totally. Every time I didn't look the other way when some politico or his kid got into hot water, I'd hear about it—either from Ronnie, second hand or someone would pass a snide remark. Obviously, all men are not created equal. And I guess being in the middle of the crowd who bagged the sheriff's pet chimpanzee for murder and instrumental when his rabbi the DA ate his gun were the straws that broke the camel's balls. The timing was right. My contract will expire, and they're under no obligation to renew it."

"Some shit, huh, Boss? What's this place gonna turn into?"

"If it goes like they plan, we can make a good guess. But I'm not going away with my tail between my legs."

"Gonna stick it to them again?"

"Gonna try. Bettye's pissed. She probably wouldn't take the chief's job now if they offered, but I'll ask. Stanley deserves it. Getting him made chief would be easiest for me. I'm sure I could pull that off. And I think Bettye will be happy with what I could get her into."

"And how about me, Boss? The mayor say if he was planning to fire me?"

"He didn't say, but I'd start thinking about that possibility. You and Stan would get along fine. I'll see what I can find out and what I can do to keep you two together."

CHAPTER TWENTY-FIVE

Bettye stepped back into the reception area. The eyeliner she wore earlier was now missing. It looked as if she had been crying, but returned freshened up, if no less annoyed.

She pushed her swivel chair into the desk with more force than necessary. "So what happens now?" Certainly no less annoyed.

I held up a finger indicating I wanted her to wait.

"John, would you listen for the phones and the radio?"

"Sure, Boss. I got it covered."

"Let's go to my office, Betts."

"You will not make me feel any better with some logical explanation, Sam Jenkins. You do not know how mad I am."

"I think I do. But, please, we need to talk. And I promise, no lectures or silly suggestions."

"Alright."

Moments later, we sat facing each other in the tan saddle leather guest chairs in front of my desk.

"Do not try and smooth me over by sayin' everything will be alright," she said.

"I planned on no such thing. I wanted to know if you'd help me stick it to the city of Prospect—and if you like what I suggest, you'll get a big raise in pay for as long as you're interested in working."

She straightened up and pressed against the back of the chair. "And what's that supposed to mean?"

"I might be able to engineer a way to save Prospect PD from the embarrassment of getting an unqualified chief and everyone here from serving a political machine."

She raised her left eyebrow and looked skeptical.

"You want me to be the chief? How will Stanley feel about that?"

"Don't get ahead of yourself. I believe I can manipulate the situation because of people I know. I'm relatively sure I can name the next chief through simple fear of what could happen if Ronnie and the Council won't play ball with me. But you and Stanley have to agree with what I want to do."

Bettye nodded. "I'm listening."

"I've got something in mind for you. One quick visit to someone will tell me if I can pull it off."

I didn't give her a chance to comment.

"Both you and Stan are qualified to run this department. No one in their right mind could honestly disagree with that. For this big scheme to work, I'd suggest that Stanley get the chief's job. Could you live with that?"

The eyebrow went down, replaced with a frown.

"I could work for Stanley. Sure."

The look on her face showed disappointment. I assumed she thought I'd be selling her out.

"I didn't ask if you could work *for* him. I wanted to know if you were okay with him getting the job and not you. My primary intent is to make you happy while pulling off something that will show these people they can't screw with me and leave this police department floundering."

"I don't understand. If he's the one you want, do I have a choice?"

I sighed. "It doesn't come down to that. I'm not planning on leaving you out in the cold. Remember what I said? Getting Stanley this spot would be easiest. Also remember what I said about getting you a raise?"

"Sam, you're talking in riddles."

I shook my head. "Okay. I'll make it easier to understand. I can make Stan chief here. It will be pretty simple. And I think I can get you appointed as the interim sheriff."

Her eyes popped open.

"Joe D plans on leaving his job soon to begin lobbying for a nomination in the State House. That would give you two years to occupy the appointed job before you had to decide if you wanted to run for reelection."

"Me the county sheriff? Lord have mercy. Are you crazy?"

I smiled. "I might be crazy, but you'd be perfect. Remember when I got offered the job?"

"Of course. You were only here about a week."

"Exactly. Not many people knew me back then. Now, after all the hullaballoo I've caused the politicians in this county, I doubt my benefactor could pull that one off. And I doubt I could talk myself into taking the job. But you'd. Be. Perfect. You're much more politically correct than me. You're never nasty or abrupt with people—except maybe me—but I guess it's too late to bitch about that. You're smart. You know how to be a cop. And you know how to lead other cops. Voila! Sheriff Bettye."

"No maybes. You are crazy. And you have more confidence in my abilities than I do."

"Nonsense. You can do that job. But if you get stuck for a good decision, I'd be hurt if you didn't call me and ask for an opinion."

"Could I appoint you an under-sheriff?"

"I doubt anyone would agree to that. But no one can keep you from picking up the phone—as often as you want."

"And how do you plan on doing all this?"

"Simple, actually. But it might take a while to explain. Want a coffee?"

"No, I do not. You can pour me a drink, thank you very much."

———

A fter explaining my cunning plan to Bettye, I made a quick call to Stan Rose. It only took me a few moments to bring him up to speed on the developing situation. Then I asked the $64,000 question.

"How'd you like to be the new chief?"

"You serious?"

"Does this sound like a comedy routine?"

"With you I never know, but, no, I guess not. And you want me?"

"I think I could make that happen, and I think you'd be perfect for the job."

"Should I ask how?"

"No. If you're captured, *they* can never make you talk."

"Can I ask who *they* are?"

"Don't be silly. You have no need to know."

"That doesn't sound very encouraging."

"Piece of cake, really."

"Yeah?" He couldn't have sounded more dubious.

"We'll see. You in or what?"

"If this doesn't work, will I still have a job?"

"After I make my calls, I'm confident that a couple of heavies will work their magic to your benefit. These locals might think they're hot stuff, but in the big scheme of things, they're small and rotten potatoes. Have faith."

"Easy for you to say, white man."

"Yes, it is. Whadda ya say?"

The line was silent for a long moment. "For the last five years, I've trusted you through some pretty scary shit. I guess once more can't hurt."

"That's the spirit."

"Okay, Bwana, I'm with ya."

———

fter getting Stan's compliance, I made another phone call—this time to Washington DC, and got lucky. The party I needed to speak with answered his own phone.

After that, I made a local call and arranged to meet the next day with someone quite important to my plan.

At 5 p.m., I drove home to break the news to my wife.

Kate handed me a gin and tonic the way I like it, with a large wedge of lime.

"You don't look especially happy," she said. "Anything go wrong today?"

"Today reminds me of an old joke."

"Oh, yes?"

"I'll paraphrase the punch-line for you. Everyone who will be employed as a police chief after August 1st take one step forward. Not so fast, Jenkins."

"Say that again."

"I got sacked. Ronnie told me the city council does not wish to renew my contract." I took another sip of gin and tonic.

"That's ridiculous. Who do they think could do a better job than you?"

"Getting best results or even good results doesn't seem to be of paramount importance to those humps. They want to appoint a woman from Maryville PD who supervises crossing guards. Efficiency and good police work has nothing to do with it. She's related to Joe Rex Wilcox and won't cause any political trouble."

"Those bastards."

"My thoughts exactly. But I'm not going to make this easy for them. If they want to play politics, I'm going to show them how dirty their tiny little world can get by bringing in a couple of big guns."

"I can't wait to hear this plan." Kate looked at her empty glass and rattled the remaining ice cubes. "You ready for a new drink?"

———

The next morning, at 9:30, I knocked on Judge Minas Tipton's front door. His housekeeper, Loretta, answered and led me into the living room. Each time I visit the judge, I consider it akin to walking into the Museum of Early Southern Decorative Arts in Winston-Salem. I love to look at the real Federal Period furniture he owns and study the original Early American artwork. Besides being a genuine political cutthroat, the retired jurist was endowed with exquisite taste in furnishings.

A couple minutes after my arrival, the old man greeted me, and we planted our respective backsides on either end of the sofa. Shortly thereafter, Loretta walked in carrying a tray of cups, saucers, a plate of homemade cookies and an antique silver coffee pot.

"Miss Loretta," I said, "how does the Judge stay so trim while you're making all these cookies? If I visit more often, I'll need bigger pants."

"Oh, Chief, you've got a long way ta go b'fore you get fat."

"Pay no attention, Loretta," the judge said. "This rascal can't pass up the opportunity to flirt with a good-lookin' woman."

I smiled. Caught in the act.

"Oh, Judge, you stop that now." She blushed a little and then left us alone.

After a few preliminary words, Judge Tipton and I got down to business.

"Damn fools," he spat out and made a face that indicated that he was disgusted with his political colleagues. "And that young fool Ronnie Shields went along with them?"

I nodded and sipped a little black coffee.

"I'd hate to see the people at Prospect PD get hamstrung by some new leader who doesn't have the best interest of the people and that city at heart." I sounded like a crusader wanting to attack the Holy Land, saving it for God and the entire Christian world.

"Ha,ha,ha,ha." He slapped his knee. "You cain't never get your head around the idea that these rogues jest don't care about doin' the right thing, can ya, Sam?"

I threw my hands up about shoulder high. "Doing the *right thing* just isn't that difficult, Your Honor. I worry, seriously, about the morale of a dozen really good cops."

He nodded his snow-white head of hair for a few moments. "I know that, Sam. I do know that. What do you think I can do to help ya?"

"I've got a handle on my PD situation. I think I can iron out this new police chief business and save those cops from working in a lousy situation. It's actually something else I'd like to talk about."

"Shoot. You never ask for anything personal. When you need a favor, it's always directly related to the job. And although you've never in all these years mentioned it, and probably never would, I still owe you one, Sam—a big one. Remember, son, I'm not gettin' any younger, so this may be the time to let me repay."

I nodded and sighed deeply. "This would be doing something for a really good person and the county would gain a big benefit."

The judge tilted his head and frowned. I set the hook and began reeling him in.

"I hear that Joe Don Hartung intends to leave his job to pursue other political avenues."

Tipton nodded. "It's been a long time comin'. Went to the sheriff's office with no experience and big aspirations, that boy. Now would be a good time ta skedaddle. Lord knows he could get embarrassed in the next election if someone brought up that Ryan Leary scandal."

"So, the sheriff's job will be open for the remaining two years of Joe D's term?"

"You know it will." He flashed a big smile. "I offered you that job once, son. Want it now?"

I shook my head. "I doubt the political machine in Blount County could ever warm up to me. No. I don't want to be sheriff, but I will strongly recommend someone who could do as good a job as me and be much less offensive."

"Ha, ha, ha, ha. Less offensive. I know you don't mind stickin' it to these local rascals—probably enjoy it no end, don't ya?"

I smiled and would never begin to deny it to the old coot. "Oh, hell,

I'm immaterial at the moment. But I think Sergeant Bettye Lambert would make one hell of a sheriff."

I went on to explain all of Bettye's professional attributes and why I thought she would be the best person for the job.

"And don't tell your political friends, but I offered to be something of an unpaid silent partner or technical advisor if she ever needed a second opinion about some nuts and bolts police work.

"She's one hell of a good cop, Judge, and those two years will let her determine if she wants to run in the next election. You get the opportunity to observe and evaluate your interim sheriff without spending a dime on a campaign. If you like what you see and endorse her, she might even run unopposed. Sounds like a good deal all around."

The judge placed a half-eaten cookie on a plate and took a moment to sip his coffee. "Sam, a recommendation from you means a lot. I know you wouldn't back someone with the potential of embarrassin' ya." He paused for a brief moment. "She'd have ta sit down with Foxy Fanwick and allow his investigator ta vet her. From what ya say, she won't have a problem, but Foxy would want to make sure those Democrats couldn't discredit the candidate he'd officially back."

"Foxy Fanwick is a real name?"

"Ha,ha,ha,ha. Party chairman, Sam, party chairman. Been around since, Lord, I don't know, since Teddy Roosevelt served his first term. Name's Foxworth Fanwick. I'll tell him you'll be coming with this Miss Bettye to meet him. Hell, son, Foxy isn't a bad sort. Ya may even like him."

I didn't want to speculate on who I'd like or not before Bettye had a lock on the sheriff's job. I smiled as if Foxy and I might get to be fast friends.

"Let me see what I can do," Tipton said. "If the county mayor doesn't see things my way, I'll tell 'im you've threatened ta bring fire and sword down on his county. Ha, ha, ha, ha."

"Maybe you give me too much credit, but a good scare often works wonders."

I left Judge Tipton's house and hadn't gotten two miles closer to Prospect when my cell phone sounded off.

"Sam, where are you?" Mayor Ronnie Shields asked.

In five years, he's never called my cell phone.

"I'm in Maryville. You need something? You sound terrible."

"Sam, how could you do this to me?"

"I beg your pardon."

"I need ta see ya. Why are y'all in Maryville?"

He was causing me to get a little hot under the collar.

"I'm on police business. Is there a problem with that?"

His breathing sounded labored. I thought perhaps he was having a heart attack and figured I'd be the best person to call for assistance. Not really.

"I've had two disturbin' phone calls that I think you know about. I don't mind tellin' ya, I'm not happy about this."

"I don't know what the hell you're talking about, Ronnie. And, Mr. Mayor, excuse me for being blunt, but I don't rightly care. In effect, you've fired me. I have two weeks left in my contract. By my own high standards, I will, during that time, provide the city of Prospect with the services for which you pay me. And I believe that I owe you civility. But excuse me again because I don't think we'll spend those two weeks like a pair of best buddies."

"Sam, I need—"

I cut him short. "I'll be back in Prospect in ten minutes. I'll come straight to your office. Don't go anywhere."

I hung up.

Trudy Connor stared at me as if I was one of the famous Dead Men Walking.

"Oh, Mr. Jenkins, I'm so sorry to hear about what's happenin'. I don't—"

"It's okay, Trudy. Not your fault. Things happen. I'm going in. Okay?"

"Yes, sir, go ahead."

It was the first time she didn't bother announcing me.

I closed Ronnie's office door a lot more forcefully than necessary. At the sound, he turned from looking out his window at the town square and stared at me.

"What is it?" I asked.

"Two phone calls," he said.

"You've already said that. What do they have to do with me?"

"One was from your friend, that colored man you used ta work with. The one who came here to interview Stanley Rose when he got promoted."

"Alonzo Crosby?"

"That's him. From that national group of black policemen."

"Alonzo is president of The Guardians. They represent all black police officers—men and women."

"Yes. Yes. The man about threatened me."

"Shall I assume you mean he wants you to do the right thing?"

"Right thing?"

"Yeah, the right thing! Appoint Stanley the new chief. The man I recommended before you and the idiots on the Council decided to hire some political hack who supervises school crossing guards."

"You called him?"

"Ronnie, I've known you for five years. We haven't always agreed on things, but I didn't think of you as a nincompoop—until now. Of course, I called him. Do you think I'd let you people screw every person working at PPD?"

"He, this person, said if we didn't appoint Stanley, he'd get his lawyers ta slap an injunction on us appointin' Donna Wrangle and take us ta court."

I poked my right index finger at the Mayor. "Good for him."

"Do you know how much that could cost the city?"

"Yeah. Lots. Are you going to fight this?"

He didn't answer immediately. I witnessed some heavy breathing and wondered if that heart attack wasn't too far off.

"I wasn't off the phone with this Alonzo person twenty minutes when that, that other one called—also threatenin' me."

"What other one?"

"That Crofton person. The reverend. The activist. The one who brought in all those protestors when Officer Puckett shot that colored boy."

I nodded like I didn't know a thing about this. "The Reverend Hal Crofton? Despicable person. What did he want?"

"You don't know?"

"We're not on speaking terms."

"Same as that Alonzo person. He said if we didn't appoint Stanley Rose as po-leece chief, he'd claim we was discriminatin' against him, Stanley that is, 'cause he's black."

He stopped talking and just kept looking at me.

"Yep, Stanley sure is black."

He sighed and dropped his shoulders in all one motion. "He threatened to bus in hundreds o' demonstrators. He claimed he'd camp out here for weeks."

I laughed silently. "That's what Crofton does. And he's good at it. So, all you have to do is choose Stan as the new chief, and Crofton won't bring his protestors to Prospect?"

"So he says. Should I trust him?"

"He's letting you off cheap. Usually he asks for a million or two as a donation to his *church* to keep his hounds at bay." I shrugged. "You're lucky."

"Do you know how much overtime I'd have ta pay if he sent in hundreds o' demonstrators?"

I smiled. "Of course, I know. Not to mention the charge-back you'd be on the hook for if you got assistance from the sheriff, the state troopers and the National Guard. That's a huge expense. If the governor learned that you could have headed off that catastrophe the easy way and didn't, you'd be politically up Shit Creek."

Ronnie dropped into his oversized swivel chair and sunk into the leather. "You're lovin' every minute o' this, ain't ya?"

I shook my head. "I think what you did was reprehensible. The city council leads you around by your nose, and you expect me to roll over and play dead when you try to destroy the morale of a dozen good cops. You should be ashamed of yourself."

"You can't do this, Sam," he gasped.

"I already have. What are you going to do to me, cancel my contract a second time? Give me a bad letter of reference? I don't care, Ronnie. Read my lips. I. Do. Not. Care."

His shoulders dropped even further, and his heavy breathing made him look like an eighty-year-old man who just ran a hundred yard dash flat out.

"So what am I supposed ta do?"

"Simple. Promote Stanley, and you'll look like a hero to the troops, the people of Prospect and the media. Or don't and watch out for the tons of shit Alonzo Crosby and Hal Crofton dump on your head. In the end, Mr. Mayor, all the political heroes will hold you accountable. If this thing turns to shit, you will hang while they say, 'I told you so.' Your call, Ronnie. No one else's. Think about where your ass will be when the smoke clears."

"You're not leaving us much choice, are ya, Sam? This is blackmail, ya know."

I smiled again. "Don't be silly. It's coercion 1st degree. And what are you going to do about it? Not comply? If Crofton brought in a battalion of protestors, Stanley could handle it. You think Donna Wrangle is up to the job? Try it your way. Every swingin' ass among your political cronies will leave you hanging out to dry. This thing will go into the cesspool with you along for the ride."

Ronnie closed his eyes and shook his head. "I don't deserve this, Sam."

I snorted. "Balls. You deserve worse. For five years, I thought you were almost a standup guy. Sure, you were influenced by these shithead politicians on occasion, but when push came to shove, you did the right thing—under duress maybe, but you did all right. After this—you deserve a good beating."

His eyes popped.

"Don't worry. I won't mess you up."

Automatically, his hand went up as if to protect his hair.

"Ronnie, I plan on leaving Prospect gracefully. Just figure you're not invited to my going away party."

I turned and walked out.

CHAPTER TWENTY-SIX

I stopped at Ms. Connor's desk and smiled. "Trudy, why don't you get your boss a glass of sweet tea or something? I think he may need a little energy supplement."

She blinked a few times, and her mouth moved a little—almost a smile, but pro that she is, she held back and just nodded.

I smiled again. "Have a good day."

———

"You aren't in any more trouble, are you?" Bettye asked.

While she was frowning at me, I grabbed her side chair, spun it around and sat with my forearms resting on the back. John Gallagher looked at me, grinning like a Gestapo interrogator who just met his new victim.

"And why, Ms. Desk Sergeant, would I be in trouble?"

"Because you've only got a short time left here. You have nothing to lose. And I assume, based on my intimate knowledge of your personality, you couldn't resist bein' a wise guy and sayin' somethin' extra offensive."

I blinked rapidly and tried to look shocked at her statement. "I'm...

I'm...I'm aghast at what you think I'm capable of. If I had feelings, they'd be hurt."

"Oh, stop the act."

"Yeah, Boss, the Sarge figured out what you'd be like with a short-timer's attitude. The way I see it, she nailed you."

"Thank you, John. I can always count on you to stick up for me."

"Did you read the mayor the Riot Act?" Bettye asked.

I shrugged. "I told the mayor I thought he and the council members were reprehensible and that if he kept spreading his legs for all the political imbeciles in this county, someday he might find himself in the slammer. Plus a few other choice words. When I left, there was no doubt in his mind that I was ashamed of him."

John stifled a laugh. "So much for my grandmother's adage of 'If you can't say somethin' nice about someone, don't say nothin' at all'."

"Yeah, my mother had similar advice, but I told her I wasn't put on earth to be everyone's friend."

Bettye shook her head and clamped her lips together like she does when I frustrate her. "You are impossible, Sam Jenkins."

"You always say that."

"Can what you said get you in trouble?"

"With whom? I'm protected by the 1st Amendment. Besides, what could they do to me? I no longer work here."

"Sammy, I'd say, 'What am I going to do with you,' but there's no hope. I give up."

"Nonsense. You're just getting started. I've got news about your future. Come inside," I pointed at my office door, "and John will do the phone and radio routine."

"Take your time, Boss. I'll hold down the fort."

B ettye and I adjourned to my guest chairs.

"After a morning with my only political rabbi, Minas Tipton, I feel certain I'm looking at the next sheriff."

Her hazel eyes widened. A half smile said she wasn't sure she believed me but felt a spark of happiness anyway. She looked like a fifteen-year-old girl asked to the senior prom by an older guy.

"Me? You can't be serious."

"I am. When Judge T says, 'I'll see what I can do, I surely will,' you can figure the check has already started to clear."

"Well." Her smile got bigger. She looked lovely. Once again, I doubted that anyone could take a bad picture of Bettye Lambert.

"My last instruction from old Minas was that you'll have to meet a guy named Foxy Fanwick. Ever hear of him?"

"Sure. The party chairman."

"Every time I hear that, I think we're dealing with the Kremlin."

"Do I need to know anything before I see Foxy?"

"I doubt it, but when Tipton calls me with the appointment date, I'll ask how to play it. My guess—Foxy is going to ask for a brief sketch of your qualifications. But, based on the current Sheriff having been nothing but a semi-employed rich kid before he got elected, your background interview should be quite brief. His big concern will be if you've got any skeletons in your closet."

"Skeletons?"

"Potential embarrassment if the opposition party digs into your past."

She got a mischievous look on her face. "Shoot, darlin' if'n I've been able ta resist the likes o' you these last five years, you better believe I been a good girl *all* my forty-seven years."

"You mean those stories of you skinny dipping in the Little River weren't true?"

Another award-winning smile. "Wouldn't y'all like ta know?"

I chuckled. "If you do any campaigning, I suggest you use that Daisy Mae voice when you talk to the folks from up in the hills and down in the hollers. They'll jest love ya ta death."

Two days went by, and we heard nothing about Prospect PD's new police chief and nothing about Bettye's status. Uncertainty hung in the air like a cloud of smoke on a windless day.

At 10:30, John Gallagher walked into my office as if he owned it. And with nothing more than a, 'Hey, Boss,' poured himself a cup of coffee and sat in one of the chairs in front of my desk.

"So, what's goin' on," he asked. "Whaddaya hear?"

"Not a damn thing. And that bothers me. I wish those political goons would make up their minds and do something."

"You're always so impatient, Boss."

"Yeah, right, and you personify inner tranquility."

"That's me. Cool as a cucumber."

"You know something, my Irish friend, most people would leave loose ends for the next guy, but not me. Do you think we can clear the Toby Bowman murder in the next few days?"

John looked at me as if I suggested climbing Mount McKinley wearing shorts and flip-flops.

"How?"

"Good old-fashioned po-leece work."

"Boss, we've tried that. Doofy Arlo looked like our best hope, and that fizzled out. What's next?"

I sighed. "I pay you for good ideas, Detective Gallagher."

"Boss, you pay me to type and file papers. I work cases to keep from going nuts."

"Yeah, well—"

"When you were a squad dick, how many cases did you carry that went cold and unsolved?" he asked.

"Don't remind me."

"I've got no new ideas. This may be one of those we just can't clear by arrest."

I didn't want to admit defeat. "Maybe. But maybe a good lunch would help us think. You interested?"

"Sure. How about Howell's"

"You're one of his best customers."

"I know. They're cheap and good."

———

John and I got back to the office at five to one. Bettye needed to run a few errands, so John puttered around at his desk, and I answered the phones and dispatched a few calls to the sector cars.

At 1:40, a man in his early-forties walked into the lobby dressed in a current set of sage green Army camouflage fatigues and a maroon beret. A pair of unhappy-looking teenagers followed him in.

As he stood in front of the desk, I noticed that there were no name or US Army tapes over his pockets, no rank, no insignia on his shoulders or any flash or unit crest on the beret. He carried a wrinkled brown paper bag in his right hand.

I nodded. "Hi, can I help you?"

He must have looked at my open collared pale blue shirt and made a deduction. "Yes, sir. You a detective?"

"Not exactly. I'm the police chief. But I can help if you want to report a crime."

He nodded for a brief moment and looked terribly sad.

"Yes, sir, I guess we do. That is, my sons here need ta do that."

Not sure if he was implying that they were criminals or victims, I asked, "How old are your sons?"

If I thought the guy in cammies appeared sad, the pair of kids looked like they just watched some malevolent hooligan eviscerate their favorite pet.

He pointed to the taller boy. "Elijah here, he's seventeen. Jacob, this one," he poked a thumb at the shorter boy, "he's fifteen."

Elijah stood almost as tall as his father but lacked the weight and width of the older man. He had short dark hair and was attempting to grow a beard but couldn't quite pull it off. He wore a faded red T-shirt with a pocket logo I couldn't read and a pair of Real-Tree camouflage pants. The shorter boy had longer hair and wore a plain white T-shirt over washed-off blue jeans.

"What's your name, sir," I asked.

"Ethan. Ethan Blissard."

I began to write down the cast of characters. "Like the snow storm?"

"Sounds kindly like it, but ain't spelled the same. B-L-I-S-S-A-R-D."

"Uh-huh. Thanks. Are you in the army, Mr. Blissard?"

He looked down at his cammies as if he noticed them for the first time. "Uh, no, sir. I jest respect and appreciate what the people in the military's doin' fer us. And you po-leecemen, too. Thank ya fer ya service."

Ethan Blissard was beginning to throw me off balance.

"You're welcome. And thanks for the thought."

"Yes, sir."

"Were your boys victims of a crime?"

Ethan hung his head and shook it gently from side to side. The two kids dropped their chins to their chests and didn't look up.

Finally, Ethan said, "No sir. They done somethin'. Somethin' terrible."

"The boys are juveniles. Just how terrible was this thing?"

Blissard turned toward his sons and spoke. "Elijah, the man asked what ya done. Look at him while he's talkin' and tell 'im."

The older boy lifted his eyes, looked at me and swallowed hard. Tears showed on the younger boy's eyes when he looked up.

Ethan spoke again, in a voice that didn't sound harsh, but definitely came across as a parental command. "Go ahead, son. Tell the man what ya done."

In a voice barely above a whisper, the boy said, "We killed a man."

That grabbed John's attention—mine too. He stopped what he was doing and turned in his chair. I first envisioned a hit-and-run accident or some other unintentional act.

"You're sure about this?" I asked. "You know for a fact this person died?"

The boy looked as if he was having difficulty holding up his head—

like someone with a bad case of the flu. But he managed and continued to look me in the eye.

"Yes, sir, he was dead alright."

I turned my eyes to the father. "Mr. Blissard, you said, *they* did this. Did Jacob also kill someone?"

He nodded slowly. "Same person. And one o' their friends done it, too. Only he ain't here."

John spoke for the first time. "Your boys and a friend all killed one person?"

"Yes, sir."

I immediately thought of Agatha Christie's famous novel *Murder on the Orient Express.*

"Who's the third friend?" he asked.

"Boy name o' Mitchell Fannin."

"How old is Mitchell?" I asked.

"Jacob's age. Fifteen. Mebbe a little older. Could be sixteen. They's in the same grade in school."

After Ethan finished speaking, Bettye cleared her throat to let us know she had returned and was standing behind us.

I stood and faced her.

"Sarge, this is Mr. Blissard and his sons. John and I will be taking some information from them. We'll use the squad room. Will you handle the desk?"

"Yes, sir. Do you need me to do anything else?"

I nodded. "Yeah. Just a moment." I turned and spoke to Ethan Blissard. "Will you follow Detective Gallagher? He'll take you back to a private room. I'll be with you in a minute."

He nodded and offered me the paper bag.

"I expect ya'll be needin' this."

I unrolled the paper and looked inside at a blue steel revolver, an old Colt Detective Special. My guess of a hit and run just flew out the window.

"Is this loaded?" I asked.

"Yes, sir. Still got a couple live shells in it. I didn't want ta touch nuthin'."

"Is it your gun?"

"Yes, sir."

So much for keeping your weapons secure.

To Gallagher, I said, "John, I'll meet you down there in a minute."

He nodded and ushered the threesome down the hall.

"What's that about?" Bettye asked.

"Murder. Manslaughter, maybe. The kids and a friend killed someone."

"Who?"

I smiled. "Beats me, Blondie, but I'll find out."

She returned the smile. "I know you will, darlin'."

"With only a few days left, it looks like I'll go out with a bang."

"I'd expect nothing less."

"See why you're my favorite desk sergeant?"

She batted her eyelashes. "Who me?"

I let Humphrey Bogart issue my next statement. "I gotta put this roscoe in the evidence locker, sweetheart. Then me and the Irish gumshoe will be playin' shamus in the squad room for some time. While I'm gone, doll-face, call Stanley, and tell him ta get his keister in here pronto."

"Pronto? My, my. What will he be doing?"

"Making a few arrests for murder."

———

"Mr. Blissard," I said, "we don't plan on abusing your sons or violating their rights in any way, but I've got to ask, do you want a lawyer present before we listen to what they've got to say?"

"I expect they'll need one fer court but rot now they need ta tell ya what they done."

The boys sat in armless chairs facing me. I sat behind a battered gray steel desk. Ethan stood behind his sons, and John pulled up a chair facing the trio.

"In a case like this, Mr. Blissard, you're the one who would have to waive your sons' rights to legal representation. Would you sign the form for Detective Gallagher before we continue?"

"Yes, sir. They need ta git all o' this offa their chests. Ever since they done what they done, Elijah, he's been moody, actin' all sick-like. Jacob, he's about the same. The school's been tellin' his mother how he's havin' troubles they cain't explain. They need ta git this offa their consciences and git straight with the Lord, so they can git on with their lives."

Yeah, I thought, so they can get prepared for the jail time they're facing.

Ethan signed the document John handed him.

"Tell me one thing first, Mr. Blissard. Do you know who the boys shot?"

He nodded. "Not personally, but it's that *homasexural* boy y'all found in the creek."

It's not often that someone wanders into your police station and confesses to a crime. It's even less frequent that a civilian dressed head to toe in Army camo drags his sons in and makes them 'fess up to killing the victim of your open homicide—one which you have precious little hope of ever clearing.

"Okay," I said. "That young man's name was Toby Bowman. I'd like to speak with your sons now, one at a time. You need to be present with the one I'm talking to. I'd like to begin with Elijah. Jacob can sit in another room. That work for you?"

"Yes, sir. Yer the po-leeceman."

"John, take Jacob to the juvenile room. Give him a soda if he wants one."

"You got it, Boss."

John led young Jacob across the hall. The door closed, and the unmistakable click of the bolt being thrown to lock the door from the outside bounced off the walls in the narrow hallway.

John returned immediately. I assumed that Jacob wasn't in the mood for a Pepsi. John sat next to me. Ethan took the seat vacated by his younger son. He snatched the beret from his head as if he thought we'd be angry at him for not removing his headgear indoors. He folded it as neatly as would any soldier.

"Elijah, my name's Sam Jenkins. I'm the police chief here. This is Detective John Gallagher. We'll both be talking with you."

The kid nodded.

"You used the gun your father handed me to shoot the young man I identified as Toby Bowman. Is that correct?"

"Yes, sir."

"Where did you get the gun?"

"It's my Daddy's."

"I know. Where did you find it?"

"His closet."

"How did you know Toby Bowman?"

"Didn't."

"Excuse me?"

"Didn't know him. Jest found him on Charlie's List."

"Toby advertised himself on Charlie's List as a male prostitute. Were you looking to, uh...engage his services?"

"Do what?"

"Did you want to hire him to have sex?"

The kid looked shocked. "No, sir. We jest called him."

"Who are *we*?"

"Me and Jacob and Mitchell."

"What did you call him for?"

He hesitated. He looked at his father, looked at me, looked at John. And ended up looking back at Ethan.

"Tell 'im, son. Tell 'im like ya told me."

After another long moment, Elijah said, "Called 'im ta kill 'im, sir."

I've heard a few bizarre motives in my time, but this promised to be a doozie.

"If you didn't know him, why did you want to kill him?"

Elijah did the roving eye routine again and this time came back to me. "It's a long story, sir."

"We've got all the time you need, son."

He took a deep breath and let it out slowly. "Well, sir, we'd been talkin', me and Jacob and Mitch. And I guess it's me who said, 'Whaddaya think it's like ta kill a man?' The other two, they didn't know. But Mitch, he says, 'Ya wanna see what it's like?' So, I says, 'We might could.'"

Neither John nor I said anything. Ethan remained silent. Elijah paused for another moment to catch his breath before continuing.

"And then I said, 'Wonder what it feels like ta shoot a man, knowin' he's gonna die on ya.'"

I waited for twenty seconds as Elijah just sat there staring at me. "And what happened next?"

"Mitch said, 'Your daddy's got him a handgun. We could use it. Whaddaya think?' So I said, 'Yeah, my daddy's got him a gun. You really wanna do this?'"

The conversation went on for another twenty minutes. We established that each boy wondered what it would feel like to shoot and kill another human being. That was it—their sole motivation.

The boys' discussion led them to mention the Riverside Strangler cases and how, if they hooked up with an internet prostitute, the police might infer this was just one more from the serial killer. But none of the boys were up for killing a woman and figured that a male prostitute needed killing anyway.

Cold. Impersonal. Inhuman. But it was their plan, and they implemented it quickly and easily. Poor Toby Bowman had no idea what he was walking into.

"Who shot him first," John asked.

"I did then Mitch then Jacob."

"Was Toby alive after the first shot?" I asked.

"Don't know, but we each wanted to see what it felt like."

I nodded. "What did you do after firing the shots?"

"Drug 'im down ta the creek."

"Did you pick the creek as a meeting spot because it gave you a place to dump the body?"

"'Cause o' the other killin's were all by the water, and we figgered we could mebbe float him away."

"But he didn't float away."

"No, sir. Too shallow. We jest left him."

"What did you do with Toby's car?"

"Mitch drove it down ta Chilhowee Lake and drove it off inta one of them real deep spots near the road. Me and Jacob followed and picked 'im up."

Thanks to these kids and Ryan Leary, the lakes in and around Blount County will have more scrap metal in them than the jungles of Vietnam.

"Did you feel bad after you shot him?"

He didn't answer immediately. It looked as if he had to think about an answer. "I guess."

I took a deep breath myself. "Okay, son. Now I'd like you to write all this out for us. In your own words, but Detective Gallagher will help if you need it. Your dad and I will sit with Jacob."

"Yes, sir, that'll be fine."

Elijah switched places with his brother. I spent a long time with Jacob establishing essentially the same facts we had previously learned. That done, I started him writing.

───────

After reading the statements from our two juvenile killers and obtaining the address of their accomplice, Mitchell Fannin, I felt a five-star tension headache careening around inside my skull. With statements in hand, I walked up front looking for a half-dozen Advil and my share of comfort from Bettye.

Stan Rose intercepted me before I could cash in on either of the aforementioned necessities.

"What's up?" he asked.

I shrugged without moving my head too much and making myself feel even worse. "You won't believe this, but a guy masquerading as an Army paratrooper waltzed in with his two kids in tow and made them confess to the Toby Bowman murder."

Stan's eyes popped. "Say what?"

"You heard me, big guy. In my waning days as leader of this pack, we get the big one. And, my large friend, you're going to put your name on the arrest reports and get the credit. Then, if our dipshit of a mayor still harbors any thoughts of appointing that senior school crossing guard as chief, at least the Knoxville Press Corps can, with good conscience if they have one, ask why you didn't get the job."

"Yeah?"

"Yeah."

"Have you heard from Alonzo recently?" Stan asked.

"No," I said. "And that ticks me off no end. No one is telling me anything, and you know how lack of timely information makes me feel."

"I hear ya."

"I see you're a man of few words this morning. No problem. Go back to the squad room, and let John brief you. Then process these two juveniles. Before you finish, we should have a third one in custody, and you can start all over again. For now, I'll call the DA's office to see if they want to prosecute these children as adults."

"How old are these *children?*"

"Seventeen and fifteen are in the back room. The third accomplice is fifteen or sixteen."

"Three kids killed the male pross?"

"You've got it."

"Any good reason?"

"They wanted to see how it felt."

"Jeez."

"Exactly."

"And you're giving this to me? If they called you back to testify, you could make a small fortune in per diem wages."

"It would only put me in a higher tax bracket. Besides, you're my buddy and the guy I want to see as the next chief at PPD."

"Wow, thanks."

"You're welcome. Now start typing."

"As you wish, bwana."

———

"Hello, Moira," I said. "I've meant to call you before, but a few things have happened in rapid succession. Anyway, congratulations. I understand you'll be the interim DA until the next election."

"Thank you. I only wish there were other circumstances contributing to my promotion."

"Give any thought to running for election when the time comes?"

She snickered a little. "I guess I'm more popular than you with the local politicians, but I've never thought I could draw enough horsepower to get nominated for anything."

I thought about planting another suggestion in Minas Tipton's head. "You never know. Maybe some unlikely person will endorse you."

"Yeah, maybe I've got a fairy godfather out there."

"Stranger things have happened. What I do know is that I'm going to invite you to Prospect PD to make an important first decision as the new DA. You up for a road trip?"

"What is this all about?" She sounded skeptical.

"You're always so suspicious. I'm going to give you three people's heads on a platter. How about Toby Bowman's killers? Interested?"

"Good Lord. That's the Internet prostitute Leary wouldn't go for."

"The same. Three juveniles. I don't want to influence your decision before you meet these kids, but they're between fifteen and seventeen, and you may consider trying them as adults."

"I might, huh? Go ahead, and influence me. Tell the story."

I did.

"God, that was cold. Are these hardcore bad boys?"

"Outwardly, the two brothers just look like your garden variety of East Tennessee teenagers. I haven't met the third party yet. The youngest one is almost falling apart in the squad room. The seventeen-year-old told his story with a straight face, but his old man says he's been mentally screwed up ever since the murder."

"Sounds like a perfect case to refer to a shrink. What's the father like?"

I explained his appearance. "At first glance, he's a strange article, but it took a lot of character and a bushel load of scruples to drag his kids in here to confess to a senseless murder."

"I can't wait to meet him."

Sometimes I can't tell if Moira is trying to be more sarcastic than me.

"Stan Rose is writing up the first pair. By the time you get here, we should have the Fannin kid waiting for you."

"Why is Stanley doing the paper on this? They confessed to you?"

"Long story. I'll explain when you get here."

"Okay, I'll bring Shelby with me," she said. "I can't wait to hear your story."

CHAPTER TWENTY-SEVEN

M oira Menzies and ADA Shelby Johnson showed up just after POs Junior Huskey and Vern Hobbs walked in with Mitchell Fannin in cuffs.

Initially, Mitchell denied any complicity in the murder and claimed that the Blissard boys were crazy. When his mother, Sarah Fannin, showed up and I rehashed the allegations, Sarah pleaded with her son to tell the truth. After a few moments spent with me prying my way into the kid's brain and my implied threats of what could happen to him if he persisted in stonewalling us, Mitch finally gave it up and elaborated on his part in the crime.

I promised that if he cooperated I'd speak to the District Attorney on his behalf. To make the kid and his mother feel like they had accomplished something, I brought in our acting DA and her chief assistant to take his statement.

As Shelby worked with the boy, Moira and I walked up front. She told me she had no objections to trying all three as adults and letting their attorneys bring out any mitigating circumstances—if they could find any —for a judge to consider at sentencing. We both liked the idea of letting a court-appointed psychologist spend some quality time with the boys to see what made them tick.

All this took us several hours. Shelby Johnson worked with Stanley to get the arrest paperwork picture perfect, while Moira and I started working on a fresh pot of coffee in my office.

"Going to tell me why you kissed off this one to Stan Rose now? You aren't feeling sorry for these juveniles, are you?"

I waved a hand in the air dismissively. "Hardly. I just want Stan to start off his days as police chief with a bang."

She gave her wavy blonde hair a theatrical shake and showed me a pair of very wide baby blues.

"Say that again?" she said. "Stanley is the police chief?"

"He'd better be, or Prospect will witness the most spectacular civil rights protest since Selma."

Her eyes got even a little wider. "Whoa, whoa, whoa. You're losing me. Where are you going? Did you quit for some ungodly reason?"

"I didn't quit. I was wondering if I'd accept a new contract in August when the mayor and city council took the decision away from me. I've gotten the sack."

"You what?"

"They no longer want my services."

"Lord have mercy. Sam, I know you and I haven't always seen eye-to-eye—let me rephrase—you've driven me up a wall more times than I can count, but I've always thought—and said—you're the best street cop and administrator this county has ever seen. What is their problem?"

"Just best in the county? Not the whole state?"

"Don't start with me. I'm being nice."

I shrugged and got serious. "I guess I targeted too many crooked politicians. They couldn't fire me without cause, so they're happy not to renew my contract. They don't have to explain that to anyone. Actually, there's more, but you probably don't want to know."

She frowned and gave a serious case of the evil eye. "I'm going to be the new DA, stupid. Of course, I want to know."

I explained who the council earmarked for the chief's job, how I involved the Guardians to protect Stan's rights and might have mentioned how I lobbied to get Bettye the job as interim sheriff.

Moira smiled and shook her head. "You've got to be kidding. Mister, you're something else. Who would figure you as not only a civil rights advocate, but champion of women's rights? N.O.W. might choose you as man of the year."

"That would be nice. I hope they invite me to lunch."

"I'll bet you would. Listen, I like your ideas. If there is any way I can help this along, just let me know."

"Thanks, I will. For now, as soon as we're finished with these three young miscreants, I'm going upstairs and hammering home the last nail in Ronnie Shield's coffin."

———

With copies of the supplementary arrest reports in hand, I mounted the staircase in the marble lined lobby of the Municipal Building, heading toward Ronnie Shields' office.

Trudy Connor greeted me more warmly than she had in the previous five years. I suppose I was cashing in on the suffering hero syndrome.

I waved the reports in the air with a moderate amount of flourish. "I'll give Ronnie these soon enough, but I'll tell you first that we've arrested three boys for the murder of Toby Bowman. It's the last outstanding major case on the books here."

"Well, they—" she said, with me again wondering who *they* were.

"Since I'm leaving, Stan Rose will handle our end of the prosecution."

She nodded and gave me a hint of a smile. "I suspect ya want ta see the mayor now?"

"I do."

She winked and picked up the phone. "Mr. Jenkins is here ta see ya."

Trudy hung up the phone so quickly it gave Ronnie no chance to comment. Her way of exercising upward discipline. Who'da figgered?

As usual, I found Ronnie sitting in his oversized swivel chair. He said nothing as I approached his desk.

"I have two important things," I said, "and then I'll leave you alone."

Still no response.

"I'd like to know what you and the council have decided to do about the chief's job."

He opened his mouth to answer, but I continued.

"And secondly, I want you to know how Stan Rose has cleared the Toby Bowman murder by making three arrests."

"Do what?"

I wanted to smack him for that. I sighed. "Stanley, the guy you didn't think worthy of getting the chief's job, cleared that outstanding homicide. No one on earth would call that anything but excellent police work." He didn't need to know the circumstances.

He nodded. "Yes, I'm sure. You would know."

"That's right, I do know. I plan on putting out a press release unless you would rather do that."

"Uh, no, I guess you should send it."

"Right. Now about the chief's job?"

"We had a meetin' about that."

"And?"

"Joe Rex is gonna git back ta me."

I felt on the verge of losing it. "For Godssake! You are the goddamn mayor."

He pulled his head back as if trying to avoid a straight-on punch.

"Do you want your city to turn into something people remember like the Watts Riots?"

When I didn't swing at him, his entire body sighed. "Sam, why are ya doin' this ta me?"

"Because I want you to do the right thing. Okay, you have every right to fire me, but you do not have the right to destroy your own police department. Be a man or suffer the consequences."

"Lord have mercy, I don't deserve this."

"Then avoid any distress and simply promote Stanley. To hell with Donna Wrangle. Can she cause you major trouble?"

"No, but Joe Rex is the—"

"Screw Joe Rex. Stanley is the best man for the job. No one can refute that. Don't promote him and morale in that department will go down the crapper. My God, man. It's so simple."

"You want me to defy the council?"

"Not the whole council. Joe Rex is pulling the strings, and no one else has the balls to say he's wrong. I want you to be the courageous one who stands up and says to hell with him. Stan is now a local hero. Get your ass in gear and put out a press release. You send it. Not me. Announce the arrests and his merit promotion. Then call Joe Rex, and tell him you've made a managerial decision, something the people elected you to do—a decision you have the right to make. Hear me, Ronnie. Stop dragging your ass."

"I've never defied the council before."

"Take this advice to the bank. If Hal Crofton busses in hundreds of protestors calling you a racist and, as often happens, things get out of hand and people start looting the stores and set fire to who knows what, those council members will blame it all on you and throw you to the wolves. They will not take an ounce of responsibility. They'll say Ronnie B. Shields is the chief executive of this city, and his decision turned Prospect into an inferno."

Ronnie's breathing looked so labored I expected to see him keel over with a stroke or cardiac arrest. He remained mute but began nodding.

Finally, he spoke. "I believe you're right, Sam. I believe they would hold me responsible."

"Mr. Mayor, you do the right thing, and I'll back you 110%. If anyone tries to second guess you, I have enough friends in the media who'll listen to me."

"I'm gonna git major flak from Joe Rex."

"And if you bypass Stanley, I'll call Lon Crosby who'll call Hal Crofton who'll start the busses rolling."

He frowned. "You'd do that, wouldn't ya?"

I nodded. "Ronnie, I like Prospect. I've spent the last five years keeping the people safe. But I'm not going to lose this one. You bet your ass I'll make that call."

"So all I've got to do is what you call the *right thing?*"

"It's the easiest way."

More exaggerated nodding. "Okay, will ya at least write the press release for my signature?"

"Of course." I looked at my watch. "It's late. Can I tell Trudy to stick around after five?"

"Yes, we'll both be here."

"Thank you. Now I'm proud of you, Ronnie. You'll look back on this and be proud of yourself."

He shuddered. "I hope so."

"You will." I placed the arrest reports on his desk. "I'll be back shortly with that press release."

———

At ten minutes to five, I walked back into the PD. Bettye and John looked up. Their expressions asked the unspoken question. I couldn't keep a straight face for long.

"Hot damn! Two down, and one to go. And I've still got a few days left."

"You usually don't show this much emotion, Boss," John said. "What happened?"

I felt elation and knew it showed. "Stanley is in. The mayor rolled over and wants me to write a press release about the arrests and Stan's promotion. Ronnie wants to do the right thing."

"Did you threaten him again?" Bettye asked.

I smiled and pointed at my chest. "Who me?"

"You're a damn terrorist, Sam Jenkins," she said.

"But a nice one."

"Good job, Boss."

I bowed sheepishly. "Thank you, John."

Bettye pressed me. "The mayor really wants to do this?"

"*Wants* may be too strong a word. I'd say he sees no viable alternative. He doesn't want to see someone make a movie called *Prospect is Burning.*"

"You're lucky you don't end up in jail."

"Has anyone ever told you you're beautiful when you're being pessimistic?"

"Oh, put a lid on it."

At the stroke of five, the phone rang. Bettye answered.

"Yes, Lieutenant, he's right here. Hold on, please."

She covered the mouthpiece with one hand. "Billy Joe Elam for you. Want it inside?"

I shook my head. "Here is good."

She handed me the phone.

"Billy, what's up?"

"The judge is not feelin' too good and wanted me ta give ya a message."

"Anything serious?"

"Don't think so. Little indigestion be my guess."

"Okay, shoot."

"He got you and Miss Lambert an appointment with Mr. Fanwick tomorrow at 9:30. Do ya know where his office is?"

"Party headquarters?"

"Yes, sir."

"I'll find it. Thank you, Billy. And please thank the judge for me. I hope he feels better."

———

B ettye and I left Prospect PD at nine a.m. the next morning. In fifteen minutes, we pulled up in front of Republican Party Headquarters in an industrial area, near the intersection of US 129 and the Pellissippi Parkway in Alcoa—just a long chip shot from the Pine Lakes Golf Club.

I wore a tan blazer, brown slacks and a pale yellow button-down shirt with a weathered tartan tie. Bettye looked attractive and professional in a lightweight navy blue suit.

Foxy Fanwick could have been anywhere between seventy and the north side of eighty. He might have been twenty pounds overweight, but his big smile and genuinely happy face made him look healthy and almost honest.

He spent ten or fifteen minutes talking with us about the sheriff's job. Then, with as much grace as Attila the Hun's chief of staff, Foxy asked me to vacate the premises so he could speak privately with Bettye.

I never like to leave a friend of the female persuasion alone in the company of a suspected sleaze ball. It's been a long time since Sergeant Lambert attended defensive tactics classes at the police academy, but I knew she was packing a Chief's Special .38 in her handbag. If Foxy tried to get cute and lure her onto his casting couch, she could at least shoot him between the legs and curb his lustful desires. Maybe the old coot only wanted to give Bettye a chance to bow out gracefully if the closet skeletons he was looking for had black eyes. But I'm suspicious by nature and over protective of the women in my life.

I twiddled my thumbs and listened to country and western Muzak in the outer office. *The Party* didn't even provide any outdated magazines. Twenty minutes later, Foxy's door opened. He ushered Bettye out—both were smiling.

"Miss Bettye," he said, all syrupy, "It's been one real pleasure meetin' you. I believe I can say Blount County has never seen such a beautiful Sheriff. I'll be in touch, and y'all be careful out there."

Three down. All I need now is to pick a good entrée for my going-away luncheon. It all seemed too easy.

———

That afternoon I wandered back upstairs to speak with Ronnie Shields. I found him pondering the fate of the city of Prospect and the Free World as he watched a pair of manic squirrels circumnavigating the trunk of a big tulip poplar in the town square. He turned as I approached the edge of his behemoth of a desk.

"Sam." He didn't look any happier than when I left him yesterday.

I nodded. "Ronnie. People from the media have been calling, asking why there's going to be a change of command at the PD. I answered all the calls with a quick, 'I'm old and tired and want to retire again, and I'm just as pleased as punch to be able to pass the torch to Stan Rose. They might believe it—or not—but it's official. I told you I wouldn't throw you to the jackals, and I didn't."

He did that exaggerated nodding thing again. Ronnie looked ten years older than when I left him less than twenty-fours earlier. I assumed Joe Rex Wilcox or some other political werewolf jumped in his...gave him a hard time after he announced that Stan Rose would be the new chief at Prospect PD.

"Thank you, Sam. I don't mind tellin' ya that I've gotten some major fallout from what I done."

I thought that deserved a grammatically correct response. "From whom?"

"Joe Rex is not happy."

"Ronnie, I think it's time to stomp on Joe Rex and establish yourself as king of the hill."

"Do what?"

I really could just smack him when he does that. "Joe Rex is acting like a bully. And bullies only flourish and terrorize you if you let them. Call him back, or I will. Tell him if he screws with you, I—Sam Jenkins—will come down on him like a ton of bricks. If he doubts I can do that, suggest that he and I play chicken and see what happens. I'm on a roll here, Ronnie, and sticking it to Joe Rex would be just icing on my cake."

"Should I ask you to explain that?"

"No. But you can tell him I plan on withdrawing every nickel I've got from his stinking bank. Tell him I want a check waiting for me so I can take it to 1st Tennessee."

Ronnie's lip twitched, but I didn't buy it as a smile.

"Sam, I've always considered you a friend and a person everyone in this city could trust. I don't know what I need right now, but please tell me I've done the right thing."

Shocker. I now felt terribly sorry for the mayor and didn't want to minimize his apprehensions.

"I told you yesterday," I said, "I was proud of you. I'll say it again. And more than that, I'll make sure Stanley and everyone else downstairs knows what you've done. I'll personally speak to every cop in Prospect and tell them that they owe you, and they should make sure they've got your back. The cops will do that for me. You know it."

"Yes, sir, I do. And thank ya...I hope ya harbor no hard feelins towards me."

I offered my most sincere smile. "We're good, Ronnie. Now and if you ever need anything. Understand?"

He nodded. "Thank ya, Sam."

"You're welcome. Now, can I suggest something?"

"O' course."

"Have Trudy organize a small change of command ceremony. I need to pass the colors to Stanley. We don't have a departmental banner to hand over, so I'll give him my badge. That work for you?"

He nodded, like a 'Bobblehead' sitting in the back window of an old car. "Yes, sir, it shore does. And now can I ask a small favor?"

"Ask away."

"Can I come ta your goin' away party?"

It shouldn't have, but that touched me. "Of course you can. And bring Trudy. I'll make sure the boys behave themselves."

CHAPTER TWENTY-EIGHT

Bettye stood in my office doorway while I dropped the personal items I'd accumulated in my desk over the last five years into a cardboard box.

She often does the same thing: Rest one arm on the doorjamb, cock her hip to the side and set her other hand there. I've been grateful all these years that she's a faithful wife, and I have the willpower and ethics of Clark Kent. Bettye Lambert is one good-looking woman.

"Foxy called me last night," she said.

"Uh-oh, secret messages sent to your private line?"

She smiled at my foolishness. "He says everything is all set. Joe Don Hartung plans on announcin' his retirement this week. They'd like me there to start the transition in three weeks, then make it official in two more."

"Good for you. I guess it's time to give Ronnie notice."

"I guess. Poor man's gettin' hit with everything at one time."

"Serves him right."

"Don't be mean."

"Nuts. He's lucky I don't cut his heart out."

"I'd rather you didn't speak like that."

I can spot a serious woman a mile away. "Okay. Sorry."

She smiled.

"When are you going to tell him?"

"Soon as I type up a letter of resignation."

"Better touch base with the pension system first."

"Good idea."

"Call them today. Make sure everything gets squared away. You don't want to lose any time because of a clerical screw up."

"Sure don't," she said.

"Gonna miss this place?"

She made a face. "I had a little practice already."

I shouldn't have, but, fool that I am, I did. "Gonna miss me?"

Her eyes clouded and closed for a moment. Then she turned and walked away.

———

"You can start hauling in your stuff whenever you want," I told Stan Rose. "I'm cleaned up and almost outta here."

"Got plenty of time for that."

I shrugged. "Drive me home tonight, and you can have the car. I feel like driving the Healey for the rest of the month."

"You sure?"

"Yeah. Just leave the chief's spot for me. I don't want some nitwit putting dings on that car if I park in general pop."

He smiled. "No sweat."

"I guess Sheryl and the kids are coming to see Big Daddy get his new badge?"

"Yeah, wouldn't miss it."

"I think we've covered all the little stuff. You already knew everything else. Should be a quick and quiet transition."

"Yeah. Hey, you gonna visit occasionally?"

"If the mayor allows me back in the building."

"I might need some help or advice."

"You'll do fine. But if you want a second opinion, just whistle."

"Thanks. Not gonna be the same without you."

"After a week people will be saying, 'Sam who?'"

"Probably not."

"And don't forget, beneath all his foolishness, John is a good guy to bounce ideas off."

He nodded. "We'll need to fill the vacancies quick as possible. John will be busy handling the background investigations on the new cops."

"Tell you what," I said. "If those investigations get complicated, give me a call, and I'll help out—on the arm. I don't want to see John stressed out and Prospect PD be under strength for too long."

"Okay. Thanks again."

"Yep. Know what I'm gonna do now?"

"No."

"Neither do I, but you're going to do the chief's work."

———

O ur passing the torch ceremony lasted less than thirty minutes. The TV stations and newspapers sent crews to cover the event, but everything was so straightforward that they did little more than listen to Ronnie Shields and take their videos and photos.

I refused to wear a uniform, but Stan showed up wearing his new chief's outfit. At the appropriate time, with all East Tennessee watching, I handed his wife my old badge. She pinned it on Stanley's tunic, gave him a big kiss on the lips then turned and kissed me on the cheek. I shook Stanley's hand, and that was it.

Five years earlier, something similar took place when Sheryl Rose pinned on her husband's new sergeant's badge. Now, she was almost forty, the time I consider the best years of a woman's life. She was an attractive girl with a great smile. I've always thought she looked like a young Oprah Winfrey during one of her thin periods.

The two kids, Martin and Coretta, had been small when Stan pinned on his stripes. Now, as their dad became police chief, they were on the threshold of young adulthood.

And I was again retired. I felt old.

———

Foxy Fanwick had announced Joe Don Hartung's retirement and Bettye's imminent appointment as interim sheriff a few days earlier, so the reporters had plenty to talk about with her and Stanley. It was only cameraman John Leckmanski and that tall and attractive blonde from WNXX who spoke to me. I was old news.

John Gallagher and I wandered back into the PD lobby while Joey Gillespie and Terri Donnellson looked after the department.

John dropped into his chair, and I sat in the one next to his desk.

"You think they'll let me stay, Boss?"

"Why would they do otherwise? You and Stan get along fine."

"I know, but what about the mayor?"

"Where could he get someone else to do your job for what he pays you?"

"I know, and that's why I'm thinking."

"About what?"

"I was talking to Lonnie Ray. He says private investigators make good money nowadays, and most of their work can be done by computer. He says he'd help me out if I got a PI's license and set up shop."

"He gonna charge you seventy-five bucks an hour?"

"Gets charged back to the client. He does it for other PIs."

I shrugged. "You certainly know how to find a missing person. Following a cheating spouse can't be too hard."

"I know. Wanna go into business together?"

"Me?"

"Yeah. You and me."

"I'd have to come to work every day?"

"Maybe not. Maybe just if I catch a big case."

"Hmm. You mean like an occasional partner?"

"Sure. That would work."

"Like you'd run the business and if I came in and picked up a piece of the pie, I'd get paid?"

"Yeah. We'd have good credibility with your name on the business."

Bettye walked up and stood next to us. "What are you two cookin' up?"

I told her John's plan.

"Private detectives?"

"Investigators," I said, just to be contrary.

"Whaddaya think, Sarge," John asked.

"I don't know what to say, except maybe the new sheriff might need to hire you gumshoes for something."

"Sure," I said. "Sounds good—Jenkins and Gallagher, consultants to Blount County's highest ranking law enforcement official."

Bettye smiled.

"Uh, Boss," John said, "I'd be working more hours. I was thinking about calling us Gallagher and Jenkins."

I looked at him as if he had two heads. "Don't be silly, John. You've got to think sound. People will remember Jenkins and Gallagher because it sounds good. Anyone would forget Gallagher and Jenkins. Sound is everything. We've got to make that good initial impression."

"Yeah?"

"Sure. Do you think anyone would have read the Maltese Falcon if the two dicks in that book called their business Archer and Spade? Of course not."

"I never thought about that."

"Trust me, John."

Bettye laughed. "Are you two gentlemen ready to head out toward our big luncheon?"

"I'm ready, Sarge, but after lunch, I'm gonna take half a vacation day, if that's okay with you."

"Of course, John."

"I'm ready," I said.

"Good," she said. "I plan on having a glass or two of wine, so, Mr. Sam Jenkins, private eye, how'd you like to drive me to the Villa Napoli in that sexy sports car of yours?"

"Love to. Should I put the top down?"

"Darlin', do I look like I want my hair blown all over creation?"

"No, ma'am. You're the sheriff."

THE END

THANK YOU FOR READING

Did you enjoy this book?

Tell the world and leave a review at the site from which this book was purchased.

DID YOU KNOW THAT LEAVING A REVIEW...

- Helps other readers find books they may enjoy.
- Gives you a chance to let your voice be heard.
- Gives authors recognition for their hard work.
- Doesn't have to be long. A sentence or two about why you liked the book will do.

If you enjoyed *A Bleak Prospect* and would like a free copy of the award winning *A New Prospect*, simply go to http://waynezurl.authorreach.com

Don't miss out on your next favorite book!

Join the Melange Books mailing list

Perks include:

- First peeks at upcoming releases.
- Exclusive giveaways.
- News of book sales and freebies right in your inbox.
- And more!

ABOUT THE AUTHOR

Wayne Zurl grew up on Long Island and retired after twenty years with the Suffolk County Police Department, one of the largest municipal law enforcement agencies in New York and the nation. For thirteen of those years he served as a section commander, supervising investigators. He is a graduate of SUNY, Empire State College and served on active duty in the US Army during the Vietnam War and later in the reserves. Zurl left New York to live in the foothills of the Great Smoky Mountains of Tennessee with his wife, Barbara.

Zurl has won Eric Hoffer and Indie Book Awards, and was named a finalist for a Montaigne Medal and First Horizon Book Award. He has written seven novels and more than twenty novelettes in the Sam Jenkins mystery series.

www.waynezurlbooks.net

ALSO BY WAYNE ZURL

A New Prospect

A Leprechaun's Lament

Heroes and Lovers

Pigeon River Blues

A Touch of Morning Calm

A Can of Worms

Honor Among Thieves

From New York to the Smokies: A Collection of Sam Jenkins Mysteries

Murder in Knoxville and Other Sam Jenkins Mysteries

The Great Smoky Mountain Bank Job and Other Sam Jenkins Mysteries

Graceland on Wheels and More Sam Jenkins Mysteries

A Bleak Prospect

www.ingramcontent.com/pod-product-compliance
Lightning Source LLC
Chambersburg PA
CBHW031109030726
47496CB00002BA/462